6.00

DESTINY

Also by Tim Parks

Fiction
Tongues of Flame
Loving Roger
Home Thoughts
Family Planning
Goodness
Juggling the Stars
Shear
Mimi's Ghost
Europa

Nonfiction
Italian Neighbors
An Italian Education
Adultery and Other Diversions

DESTINY

Tim Parks

Arcade Publishing • New York

6002495

FIRST NORTH AMERICAN EDITION 2000

First published in Great Britain by Secker & Warburg 1999

This is a work of fiction. Names, places, characters, and incidents are either products of the author's imagination or are used fictitiously.

ISBN 1-55970-517-5
Library of Congress Catalog Card Number 00-130423
Library of Congress Cataloging-in-Publication information is available.

Published in the United States by Arcade Publishing, Inc., New York
Distributed by Time Warner Trade Publishing

Visit our Web site at www.arcadepub.com

10 9 8 7 6 5 4 3 2 1

BP

PRINTED IN THE UNITED STATES OF AMERICA

DESTINY

I

Some three months after returning to England, and having at last completed – with the galling exception of the Andreotti interview – that collection of material that, once assembled in a book, must serve to transform a respectable career into a monument – something so comprehensive and final, this was my plan, as to be utterly irrefutable – I received, while standing as chance would have it at the reception desk of the Rembrandt Hotel, Knightsbridge, a place emblematic, if you will, both of my success in one field and my failure in another, the phone-call that informed me of my son's suicide. 'I am sorry,' the Italian voice said. 'I am very sorry.' Then replacing the receiver and before anything like grief or remorse could cloud the rapid working of my mind, I realised, with the most disturbing clarity, that this was the end for my wife and myself. The end of our life together, I mean. There is no reason, I told myself, shocked by the rapidity and clarity with which I had arrived at this realisation, entirely bypassing those emotions one might expect on first impact with bereavement, no reason at all for you and your wife to go on living together now that your son is dead. And particularly not now that your son has committed suicide. So that gazing blankly across the deep carpet and polished wood of that unnecessarily sumptuous lobby, as again now, tickets in hand, I am blankly gazing across a strike-bound Heathrow departures lounge, it was, it is, as if this were the only real news that phone-call had brought me: not my son's death at all, for he died long ago, but the peremptory announcement of my imminent separation from my wife. Suddenly I could think of nothing else.

Not only was air-traffic-control working to rule – over France, over Italy – but the underground was out too. My wife was completely numbed. I hurried her to South Ken tube, knowing it was quicker than the taxi. I felt deeply sorry for my wife, yet was already aware of a growing fear of her eventual reaction. Which would surely be punitive. People were milling around the barriers and every two or three minutes the p.a. system repeated that a handicapped woman had chained herself to a train at St James's Park. We must get a cab, I said. Unusually, my wife allowed herself to be led like a child. Needless to say all the cabs were taken.

Yes, it was a stroke of luck, I reflect now, gazing across the departures lounge, one of those queer strokes of luck in the midst of catastrophe, though hardly a silver lining, that I should have been down in the lobby and actually speaking to the receptionist when that call came through. Otherwise it would have been directed to our room and my wife would have heard the news with the same brutality I did. Your son stabbed himself to death with a screwdriver, Mr Burton. How? she asked. It had taken me some fifteen minutes to get up to our room. An accident. The line was bad. He didn't explain. You could call again, she said. There was hardly much point. We should get moving. For a moment I was ready to hear her answer back: You always say there's not much point when I suggest something. But she was quite numbed. This news has broken the compulsive back-and-forth of our recriminations, I thought. And as she allowed herself to be led by the hand up the steps out of the tube station, the way once one led one's tiny children by the hand, savouring their trust and innocence, I again thought: It is quite over between us now, between my wife and myself. This news has blown the whistle on a stalemate that should have ended years ago. I felt excited. And remembered there was an airport bus that ran along the Brompton Road.

I had gone down to the lobby, I recall, still staring at the departures board where the word 'delayed' figures prominently, in order to renew our booking at the Rembrandt Hotel for the forthcoming week. There is a copy of the artist's self-portrait by the lifts. I paid a compliment to the receptionist, who must be a German girl I think, and decided to take the opportunity of enjoying the hotel's extravagant breakfast without reproach. Your wife objects, I thought, to the expense of the house you wish to buy, as likewise to the expense of these extravagant breakfasts, but she says nothing of the expense of living for months in a well-appointed hotel, nothing of the cost of maintaining a well-appointed house we do not live in. Scooping up fried eggs fried bread fried tomatoes sausages and bacon, I thought: Your wife objects to these extravagant breakfasts because they push up your weight and thus are bad for your health. This is true. But other things that are equally bad for your health – as for example the uncertainty generated by your wife's constant changes of mind, her inexplicable rancour, her obsessive attachment to your unhappy son Marco, things that undeniably lie at the root of your various nervous disorders – do not concern her in the least. Your health, your heart, do not concern your wife in the least, I told myself, deciding it would be too much to add a

3

kipper, except insofar as they offer an alibi for her objecting to what she anyway wishes to object to for her own private and perverse reasons. Though I love kippers. Which one never finds in Italy. The chief of these being her growing and entirely unreasonable concern with money. Why is my wife so concerned with money? I wondered. Why won't she sell the house? Except that then this thought, deciding yet again that I must not have a kipper, this perception, that is, though hardly new, of the way my wife's objections to whatever I did were always falsely attributed to the best of motivations, and above all my health, my heart, or even more crucially Marco's health, if one could rightly speak of such a thing, reminded me of a note I had scribbled down the previous day on the flyleaf of my potted version of Montesquieu's *Esprit des Lois*: To the extent, I had scribbled, to which government is not for the public good, it is legitimate for me to disobey it, though it is rarely *for that reason* that I disobey it. One's tax evasion, for example. And perceiving a connection between these two lines of thought, this search, I mean, which seems at once innate and obsessive, for the comfortable camouflage of legitimate motivation, I had immediately felt happy, in form. I had laughed. Your mind is extremely agile this merry morning, I told myself, smiling at the generous spread of the Rembrandt Hotel breakfast buffet. I suddenly felt immensely well-disposed to the whole world, my wife included. One small kipper can do no harm, I decided.

And how wise the management had been to put down such a deep carpet in the breakfast room! I spread out my newspaper – one of my three newspapers – propping it up carefully on ashtray and cruet, and read about Tony Blair's decision to banish calculators from primary schools. Nothing is more pleasurable, or more tricky to set up, than reading and eating at the same time, satisfying both body and mind at the

4

same time. And nothing could better distinguish the English mentality from the Italian, I had thought, only minutes away – but how could I know this? – from hearing about my son's suicide, than this extraordinary enthusiasm, indeed euphoria, over a new prime minister. Picking up a piece of fried bread to dunk in the tomatoes, I remembered Rousseau and how he would steal wine from his employer's kitchen and search out cakes from remote bakeries so that he could then eat and drink while he read. On his bed. As tricky as 69 sometimes, I reflected, when the pepper pot toppled. *Troppa carne sul fuoco.* I signalled for more coffee. No, nothing could be more indicative of the health, the ingenuousness, and a certain coarseness too, in the Anglo-Saxon mentality, I reflected, blissfully unaware that my life was only minutes away from the most radical of changes, than this wild excitement over the replacement of a government they had after all voted for themselves on three previous occasions with another government they would no doubt make haste to replace as soon as they had had enough. Number-crunchers, no thanks, was one sub-heading. The carpet made a wonderfully muffled hush of things. I broke a fresh bread-roll to clean my plate. Unthinkable in Italy. This belief not so much in change, but in the right kind of change. In progress, no less. But how could I work this into the book? How does one turn such a vast amount of disparate material into a monument? I was very excited by the prospect of writing a book, something I had never done before, and above all a monumental book, one that would say once and for all and quite irrefutably how things stand. It would require system. On the other hand, how could I even start if my wife refused to settle on any of the houses we looked at? Refused to make up her mind. How can one write a monumental book in the cramped and temporary circumstances of even the best hotel room?

There was a very large photograph of a smiling Tony Blair with his young children. The English, I thought, and I had decided I would treat myself to a cigarette if I could get hold of one, have this extraordinary ability to start from scratch, to believe they are starting from scratch. For years and years, I thought, spooning marmalade onto a second roll, the English vote Conservative, they breathe and believe conservative, they teach the world the meaning of the word conservative, they espouse the doctrinaire notions of monetarism and privatisation and invent marvellous expressions like 'rolling back the boundaries of the state', until all at once they realise they've had enough, all at once there they are wriggling on the edge of their seats, fidgeting and frantic for the two or three years they must wait before they get the chance to vote Labour. Then, oh the excitement when the first thing their new prime minister does is to banish calculators from primary schools! Tony does his sums! says the caption beneath smiling faces. Andreotti also had a large family, I reflect, but was rarely photographed with wife and children. It is admirable, I thought in the admirably carpeted hush of the Rembrandt Hotel breakfast room where even the scraping of knives on fine china is reduced to a distant tinkle, this ability of the English to rise from the ashes, to believe one can rise from the ashes. And how can it not go hand in hand with their extraordinarily high divorce rate? For the point of my book was to show the oneness of private and public life, to establish once and for all the dynamic of the relationship between a people and its government, its destiny. I did the right thing, I suddenly thought, returning to England. After all, I am English myself. Ever after all these years away, these decades, I am still English. If you had remained in England you would surely have divorced your wife ages ago, I told myself complacently in the Hotel Rembrandt breakfast room. If you had remained in England you would surely have made major and salutary changes. Salutary for my wife as much as myself. And above all for Marco. On the other hand, when you ask an Italian waiter for a cigarette, he will give you one and this saves you from buying a pack and smoking them all at once and feeling ill. That is service. A single cigarette. A circumscribed transgression. Whereas the stiff, white-jacketed fellow at the Rembrandt seemed not so much offended as bewildered. Clearly he imagined I was American. In Italy they take me for a German, I thought, in England for an American. And you are set to write a book about national character.

I laughed. My wife is weeping into her handkerchief as she sits beside me on one of a row of ten plastic seats bolted together for convenience sake in the departures lounge of Terminal One. It is important that people sit in rows in a large public concourse, otherwise can you imagine the confusion? She is crying quietly into her hands and handkerchief, but in a way, I'm aware, that rejects rather than invites consolation. While only two hours ago, I reflect, or perhaps less, you were laughing heartily in the breakfast hush of the Rembrandt Hotel. To yourself of course. One laughs mostly to oneself. And what you were laughing about was not so much the destiny that has had you everywhere mistaken for something you are not, German here, American there, and then the irony of such a person's embarking on a monumental book, a book whose ambition is to pin down, once and for all, precisely what people are, or rather what *peoples* are, no, but the exhilaration at your perception of that irony. Quick as lightning this morning, I had thought, there in the breakfast room. Why does my mind cling to thoughts now entirely inappropriate, I wonder, here in the departures lounge? Why won't my wife accept my consolation? A breakfast hush seems to encourage thought, I thought in the breakfast room, imagining the day when Tony Blair would be photographed on resigning office and some other prime minister would startle and enchant the British public perhaps by reintroducing school milk or banning the use of roller-blades in public parks. I would gladly console her if she would let me. Tony leads from the front, another caption said. Yes, you're in form, I had thought. And this pleasure, I can't help, however inappropriately, remembering now, as my wife rocks slowly back and forth in her grief, her exclusive grief, this wonder – the kipper, as I knew it would, beginning to repeat on me – at your own mental processes, was, is, part of a general feeling that has been developing for some time, from my fiftieth birthday on perhaps, yes, or my long convalescence after the bypass operation, the feeling that I am approaching the height of my powers, that I am, in some sense, coming into myself, my true and most profound inheritance, fruit of decades of experience and self-nurturing. Why else would I have resigned my various posts and embarked on such an ambitious project? Personality is the greatest happiness, said Goethe. The liveliness of the mind. The active mind. I cannot think of Marco. I must strike while the iron is hot, I told myself in the breakfast room of the Rembrandt Hotel. I drained my coffee. I must start now. I must force my wife to see reason, settle on a house, sell the house in Rome. And shifting back my chair on the deep carpet of the breakfast room, I could see a spacious study perched over suburban gardens and all the books I had been collecting ranged in sober colours around the walls, and all the laboriously-written notes I had compiled organised in numbered box-files, and on the desktop a white sheet of paper and a simple fountain pen already blocking out the first simple sentence: National character does exist.

One week as of tomorrow night? the receptionist enquired. She picked up the phone to take a call, tucking the receiver between neck and chin. And although this division of attention is something I loathe, I was smiling at the German receptionist, doing my best to show her that while I had no intention of playing the fool I found her extremely attractive. It is not the rudeness I loathe, I thought, watching the receptionist tuck the phone into creamy skin, but the distraction, the lack of focus that plagues so much of our lives. My wife, for example, I was thinking, has always been willing to break off the most crucial conversations, or even love-making, to answer a phone-call, or speak to a neighbour at the door, or a priest or a doctor or a tradesman. Nobody, I suddenly thought, watching how the tucking gesture was forming the most endearing of double chins, could be more willing to break off love-making or wrangling than my wife. To turn away from me at crucial moments. Even for a Jehovah's Witness on one occasion. But that was in Rome. A *testimonio di Geova*. And immediately her voice is full of a politeness or a warmth or an unction that is absolutely false. Absolutely false, I thought, observing how the tone of the German girl's voice had altered on picking up the phone. We put on voices like hats, I thought, enjoying the chance to smile vaguely at that double chin. The call is for you, Mr Burton, she said. Would you like to take it here at the desk? Then, still smiling across at the German girl, enjoying her generous Teutonic fleshiness, in much the same innocent way as I had enjoyed the generously fleshy kipper which is now so predictably repeating on me, I heard a voice speaking Italian say: Your son has killed himself. I put the phone down in the sumptuous lobby of the Rembrandt Hotel where a copy of the artist's self-portrait hangs between the lifts. And with the awful clarity that always accompanies our perception of the worst, I realised that this was the end for my wife and myself. Our impossible alliance is over.

9

I I

It was galling that I had not yet been able to collect the Andreotti interview, since the place it must occupy in my book was that of a final demonstration, a proof even, of all that had gone before: the predictability, given a proper understanding of race character sex and circumstance, of all human behaviour. Yes, the Andreotti interview, I have often told myself, quite apart from forming the explanatory link between a not insignificant career in journalism and now this monumental account of national destiny – the latter at once a maturing and a repudiation of the former – must clinch the whole question of necessity, obvious and inevitable correlate of predictability: Andreotti would say *exactly* what was expected of him. Exactly what I had said he would say. Exactly how I had said he would say it. As would Blair, come to that, had I chosen to end on an interview with Blair. Or indeed my wife – most of all my wife – if only one could put one's wife in a monumental book. People are who they are, I thought. I have always thought. Most particularly your wife. So every study in character, and above all in national character – this is the thesis I have been working on for so long – is a study in prediction, in political calculation, and all failure to predict is a failure to understand character. Andreotti, of all people, I was certain, would not let me down in this respect. Who is at once more himself and more exquisitely, as the Italians put it, Italian, than Andreotti? Had Andreotti ever, I asked myself, in all the years I reported on these matters, which were many, too many, been anything less than his irretrievably ambiguous self? Entirely predictable. Character is necessity's momentum, it occurs to me. That would be one way of putting it. Knowing means knowing the future. Still, I was loath to start the book and predict its end – what Andreotti would say and how he would say it, down to the very last detail and inflexion – without having actually done the interview. Without cheating, to be honest. For some reason – and more than once these words have formed quite clearly in my mind – I feared the sin of hubris. Of presuming too much, presuming, that is, not just to have understood things after the event, as Oedipus, but before, as the oracle. Though isn't it to this in the end that all human knowledge aspires? Predicting elections, predicting earthquakes. I never doubted I was right, merely felt it might be wise to do the interview first. At a quarter to eleven, seated beside my wife in a concourse ever more crowded and chaotic, the trill of my mobile reminds me of this now trivial anxiety: the Andreotti interview. It must be my fixer.

On arrival at the airport I had gone to purchase the tickets, my wife being unable even at the best of times to speak any but the most rudimentary English. Your wife, I thought, and I was still completely unable, in the queue at the Heathrow ticket desk, to summon up anything resembling a proper sense of bereavement, my mind still running – I know this is unacceptable – on all its normal tracks, your wife made an extraordinary concession when she agreed, in her mid-fifties, to come to live in a country whose language she is not only unable to speak but has always, I am convinced, at some subliminal level, categorically refused to learn. An extraordinary concession for a woman as gregarious and sociable as your wife, a woman for whom conversation, in the three languages she does speak, means so much. No, for a woman, I thought – wondering if a bereavement I was still absolutely unable to feel entitled me to push to the front of a long queue at the British Airways ticket desk – who has always been the heart and soul of every party, every one of her many parties, not to mention an incorrigible flirt, to come to a country where she cannot engage in any but the most rudimentary conversation, the most banal of pleasantries, is an extraordinary concession. An extraordinary sacrifice, as she would say. A concession is always a sacrifice, for an Italian. Albeit wrung from her not just, or not even, by myself, but by the doctor, Dottor Vanoli, who so often insisted that our absence could only have a positive effect on Marco. What Marco needs, Dottor Vanoli would say, and despite all her flirting my wife could never get him to change his mind on this one, is not your assistance, but your absence. And not for the first time I was bound to reflect that far more than her concession in coming to England, to a place where she cannot speak and cannot flirt, or not easily, it was her concession in leaving Marco behind in Italy that mattered. Though only made *for* Marco of course. Predictably enough. I played no part in the decision. A sacrifice for her son. And only to try out the one solution that had not been tried out, the solution, what's more, she believed in least of all. Perhaps only to prove Dottor Vanoli wrong. But in any event, I thought, suddenly and unexpectedly finding myself face to face with a British Airways clerk whose name-tag ironically identified her as Italian, in any event and cavilling aside –

but how did I get to the front of the queue? – my wife has made some very considerable and creditable concessions. Did I push past the others? Last night at Courteney's, for example, she sat through a whole dinner party without engaging in any but the most rudimentary of exchanges, her customary flirtations limited absolutely to glances and smiles and generous gesturing. Did I lapse into a kind of trance? Though these are hardly areas where she is deficient. Nobody seems upset, I thought, glancing quickly over my shoulder. And even when a certain name came up, I told myself, but at the same time vaguely reminded now, as the girl's elegant fingers enquired something of her computer, of those mysteriously lost minutes earlier on in the morning, between the phone-call and the return to my room – even when a certain name came up, last night at Geoff Courteney's party, my talkative wife was limited to inquisitive glances and mild uncomprehending nods. That was a considerable sacrifice. And I wondered, what did I do or think in those fifteen minutes? Down in the Rembrandt lobby. Here in the ticket queue. Or even twenty. I hadn't looked at my watch. The girl clicked at the keyboard. And despite – to return to the matter of my wife's concessions – her repeated and obtuse blocking both of a house purchase in London and a house sale in Rome, the kind of significant shift of resources that would have consolidated, perhaps irreversibly, our intention to stay in England, there had even been some wistful talk these last few weeks, on her part and indeed on mine, of our somehow getting back together. Of our becoming real partners again. Even lovers. Perhaps we can get back together again, my wife had said wistfully last night. In Italian. After the argument in the cab. The London cab. And the word *heal* was used at some point, I remember – *heal our relationship*, she said. Was this what I was thinking about, in those lacunae? Sitting in the armchair beneath the portrait perhaps? I can hardly, she had laughed – we were climbing out of the cab on our return from Courteney's – annoy you by talking to an *English* Jehovah's Witness. Can I? It had been a bitter argument. We laughed together. *Flirting* with a Jehovah's Witness, I corrected. She was hugely amused. Yes, your wife has made huge and generous concessions, I suddenly thought. All at once, at the British Airways ticket desk, my eyes were streaming with tears. And now it is over between us.

Ms Iacone looked up. The flight to Turin is full, sir.

Then to stem this flood of emotion rising from an entirely unexpected direction and nothing to do with Marco at all, I switched to Italian. *Allora a Milano, il primo volo a Milano, per favore*, I said, wondering at my suddenly being entirely and unexpectedly overcome by emotions that had nothing at all to do with Marco. And at once I could see the girl take my switch in language as criticism of her competence and she sold me, tight-lipped, two first-class seats to Milan-Linate before telling me that all flights were delayed because air-traffic-control was working strictly to rule. Over France and over Italy. Serious delays, she said with evident satisfaction. Your wife's reaction will surely be punitive, I thought. Perhaps I *had* pushed to the front of the queue. She will not remember that it was Dottor Vanoli and not I who insisted on this experiment of our absence. Prolonged absence, he insisted. Not I. I had only been scrupulous in following the doctor's advice. Was this why I had told her it was an accident rather than suicide? Did that decision have something to do with those missing minutes? But it was like casting about for a forgotten dream.

Returning from the ticket desk, I found my wife on a row of seats in the concourse, bent forward in her grief, as on the bus she had simply sat bent forward in her suffering without ever a word the whole length of the journey from South Ken to Heathrow. Given that she consented to this experiment only with the keenest of misgivings, I thought, considering her bent and bowed body as I approached, how could her reaction be anything but punitive? What form will it take? Air-traffic is working to rule, I said. There are delays. She had brought out a photograph of Marco she keeps in her handbag and was weeping over it, quite silently. Perhaps silence, I thought. No one is capable of such punitive silences as your talkative wife. We'll have to fly to Milan, I said. She was rocking slowly back and forth on her seat. Of such extended periods of miserable and uncooperative mutism. Elective mutism, is the technical term. In between weeks of chatter. I tried to put an arm around her, but a small shrugging of the shoulders told me my consolation was not welcome. Your wife, I repeated an old reflection, while at the same time earnestly wishing I could focus my mind elsewhere, and above all on Marco, my son Marco, has always displayed her grief, whatever its cause, in such a way as to make it clear that there is absolutely nothing you can do to console her. And this has always been a source of immense uneasiness for you. Not only can you not feel grief the way she does, cannot even focus on the object of grief, your mind like the strangled chicken still clucking about in its usual dirt, but you are not permitted to console her in the extravagant grief that she feels. You are considered too vile to offer consolation. Or in any event unworthy. And it occurs to me, as the phone now begins to trill in my pocket – it must be my fixer – and the kipper to repeat, so predictably, in my oesophagus, that there is a terrible simultaneity about marriage. Our marriage. However long ago something happened, it occurs to me, hearing the phone trill in my pocket, in my mind, it is always the same thing. Isn't it? In marriage. Always the same dynamic. The shouting match in a London cab, or stubborn silence in a bar in Trastevere.

No wonder you have so many nervous disorders. It will be the fixer, I tell myself, starting nervously at the sound of the phone in my pocket. The nocturnal urination and scratchy oesophagus. Of course it's partly to do with heavy drinking and heavy eating, with generous breakfasts in thickly carpeted hotels and nights soaking spirits while waiting for interminably delayed press conferences. But only partly. Only a very small part. And even as the telephone trills in my pocket, I see myself sitting beside my wife in another airport many years ago – twenty-five? thirty? – quite unable, then as now, to comfort her after another doctor had said she would never be able to have a child. You will never be able to have a child, Signora Burton, this doctor said, kindly, solemnly. I forget his name, but not his kind, solemn manner. Many years ago. Our story is long and complicated, it occurs to me, very long and very complicated, should anyone ever wish to tell it, yet seen another way everything is simultaneous, fixed as the revolving planets. How can that be? And pulling the mobile from my pocket, I announce to my wife: Perhaps it's Paola, and switch the thing off. I am feeling queasy is the truth and, frankly, in need of a lavatory. It must be Paola, I repeat to my wife, then am immediately aware that any decision now to get up and go off to the lavatory can only be interpreted as an attempt to go and phone Paola on my own. As if I had only switched the thing off to deceive. Perhaps I should have answered, I insist, eager to understand if my wife intends to punish me with silence. She may have more news. Or she may not even know. Definitely provoking now, I remark: After all Paola deserves to know. Doesn't she? Suddenly necessity obliges me to head off to the lavatory.

The fixer said Andreotti would not see me personally, but had finally agreed to answer my questions in writing by return of fax. That was no good, I said, automatically businesslike.

The fixer laughed. There was a way round it, he said. Or half a way. Since Andreotti thought the interview was for a major national newspaper, indeed would never have consented to it otherwise, he, the fixer, had told him they would need a photo session. As a special concession he will let you sit in on it. You can talk to him then. I can't pay for a photographer as well, I protested, and despite this setback was somehow finding the mental space to reflect that the fixer, in Rome, couldn't imagine how I was now sitting with shivering flanks spread over a parlous lavatory bowl in the Heathrow Terminal One departures lounge. Odd, I thought, the contrast in such circumstances between the extreme vulnerability of your trouserless trunk and the peremptory confidence of your voice, your manner, speaking now in a foreign language. Though this visit was proving a false alarm. I shivered. There are all sorts of hospital tests I feel I should do. Just bring a friend with a camera, the fixer was saying. Anybody. Even a girlfriend. The man laughed. How's he to know? Just make sure it's an expensive looking camera. We've arranged it for Wednesday. You're to fax him the questions today or tomorrow. No more than ten. But he won't give you a proper interview. Then there seemed no point, having gone this far with the discussion, in telling this clever man, this clever Italian, who was only doing his job, fixing an interview, that my son had committed suicide at some time during the night in a community for chronic schizophrenics east of Turin and that as a result these arrangements were completely out of the question. From outside the cubicle came a subdued shuffling. I'll be in Italy this evening, I said. And sitting on a Heathrow lavatory, speaking to Rome on my mobile, perhaps to another lavatory, who knows, off the via Nazionale, or even Corso Venezia, my voice apparently calm and relaxed, or at least no more tense than it usually is, I committed myself to writing

the ten questions today or tomorrow and going to Andreotti's
office on the Wednesday afternoon. Four o'clock. Piazza Santa
Maria in Lucina. The fixer was giving directions. Andreotti, I
told myself, at the same time remarking how unimaginable
it was that I should ever say the words, *my son has committed
suicide*, is hardly the kind of person you try to negotiate an
appointment with. Is he? I knew that much about him. You
go when *he* says, I told myself, but perfectly aware that this
was quite unthinkable. It was unthinkable that I should go to
an interview on the Wednesday. Perhaps the very day of my
son's funeral. Remember to address him as *presidente* the fixer
was saying. Once a president always a president, he laughed.
Even in gaol he'll insist they call him president.

Then pushing out of the loo, I saw Gregory. I saw Gregory's
face. For a moment I didn't know I was seeing Gregory, only
a face at once familiar and disturbing, a great black-and-white
photograph, a yard high, someone one sees on television
perhaps, though here it was in the airport bookshop. In
the window. On display. And although I was now painfully
aware, after that telephone conversation I mean, of having
come to the airport solely and exclusively in response to my
son's suicide, and not for work or pleasure, and aware too of
a pressing need to return to my wife's side as soon as possible,
knowing as I do the kind of things she is capable of when
she gets in her emotional states, so that I am frequently both
scared *of* my wife and scared *for* her, and although again, on
pushing out of the unnecessarily heavy lavatory swing door, I
was already feeling foolish if not furious with myself for having
accepted the fixer's totally unacceptable arrangements for this
major interview, and accepted them, what's more, without a
word of protest, being as I was in a daze, in a state where twice
already today I had found myself without any consciousness
of the immediately preceding minutes, something over ten

in both cases, I nevertheless went straight into the airport bookshop to get a closer look at this face which I had now recognised as not, or not only, someone one sees on television, but as Gregory Marks. Gregory Marks. Modern life creates these incessant distractions, I was thinking, distractedly, even as I hurried into the bookshop to look at that huge face with its buttery nose and avuncular smile: the phone that rings while you are chatting to a hotel receptionist, the message that bursts into your life from a thousand miles away, the Jehovah's Witness who tries to convince your wife of the imminent end of the world over the house-phone, interrupting one of the rare, extremely rare, occasions when you attempt to make love to each other. And she saying: I know what I'd do if they told me the end of the world was ten minutes away. And laughing raucously. Her raucous side. And asking the idiot to come up. By all means come up and chat about the end of the world, she laughed. In Italian. How amazed I was the first time I came across the Jehovah's Witnesses in Italy. *I testimoni di Geova*. I had somehow imagined only the English and Americans could be so stupid. Or so stupid in *that* way. Such distractions are shameful, I thought, walking impulsively into the bookshop to glower at Gregory's face suspended above a counter described as Best Summer Reading. Yet, in my defence, it was clear there was no way we could be on a plane, and thus on our way to Marco, for at least another hour or two. What was I guilty of? What did it matter if I went into a bookshop in the meantime to stare at an acquaintance's face? There had been absolutely no movement on the departures screens so far as I could see. Who was I offending? WAIT IN HALL, the board said. DELAYED. And what can one actually *do* when someone has died, I demanded of myself, and must have said it out loud, though already absolutely furious for having got into this muddle with Andreotti. What can one actually do? I said the words out loud. How is the mind to be filled? When a son commits suicide? *Italian Traits* the book was called. A young man looked away when I caught him looking. *Italian Traits*. I picked it up. And immediately I wondered. Has he beaten me to it? Gregory? Of all people. My book on national character. And why didn't Courteney say anything when his name came up last night?

Then I was in a queue again and then for the third time this morning face to face with a young foreign woman, from Eastern Europe perhaps, perhaps from Russia. She smiled at me, taking Gregory's rather expensive, I felt, book from my hands. Across chocolate bars and chewing gums. Together with my Barclaycard. There are so many pretty women, I thought, efficiently and sensibly serving the public across one sort of counter or another, distributing these smiles. Pretty young women are really the most wonderful thing the human race has to offer, I thought, returning to an age-old reflection, a default setting almost, while remembering in particular the German girl's wonderfully fleshy neck as she tucked that terrible phone-call into her chin at the reception desk of the Rembrandt Hotel. What man, I found myself thinking, entirely inappropriately, though quite predictably, or woman for that matter, with any service to sell, would not want to have a pretty young woman behind the counter to sell it? Drawing customers like a magnet. Foreign women in particular. Young foreign women. They are the best. But these were old reflections. And what man has not at some point in his life, however vaguely, I wondered, measured his age by the changing nature of his response to such pretty women thus deployed? For the phenomenon of the pretty young woman remains the same, my mind chattered away to itself as I signed my name on the credit-card slip – that is obvious – from year to year, while you are ageing and changing,

changing and ageing all the time. To the point where you have had a multiple-bypass operation and shouldn't really eat kippers any more, let alone smoke cigarettes. Anything else, sir? she asked. Perhaps even sex is dangerous now. No, for years, I thought, picking up Gregory Marks's expensive new book that nobody had mentioned at Geoff Courteney's party, though everybody must have known about it, Geoff in particular, and known what's more that the bookshops were full of it, for years one is shy in the presence of such women as this, this beautiful East European girl. Or Russian. In one's adolescence and early twenties. One approaches them timorously, then hurries away, cherishing a moment's oblique contact, a glint of the eye, a suspicion of perfume. Then for years one is wary of them, aware that approaches might be made, but wary of the consequences, since your life has a positive centre of gravity now, a marriage. You fear what might happen to your psyche, your wife, your bank balance, if you allow your libido to be dispersed in every chance encounter. The eyes fence. The voice is subdued. Impulses at loggerheads, trading insults. Then all at once the next phase begins, the one you always knew about while pretending not to. All at once you are approaching them boldly, you let slip a remark that might be a wink, you engage them knowingly in knowing conversation, in Madrid, in Copenhagen, and on the most memorable occasion there was a terrace bar looking out over the Bay of Naples and everything that followed. That's another phone-call one might make. At any moment one might make that call. Yes, for years this goes on, I reflect. Until at last one learns, perhaps after some final embarrassment, or no, perhaps merely because suddenly weary of it all, suddenly not interested, or only intermittently so, at last one learns the present formula, the complimentary smile, the deprecating I've-been-there complicity, as with the

German girl in the Rembrandt: Some time ago, that smile acknowledges, I might have made a pass at you, perhaps, and perhaps you would have flirted with me, but not now, no longer. Though my wife continues to flirt at fifty-five, exactly as she did at thirty.

Will there be anything else, sir? Suddenly, in the queue at the Terminal One bookshop, I realised that the cashier was wondering why I hadn't moved. I wasn't moving. There were people behind me with newspapers and toffee bars to buy and I was riveted to the spot. Are you all right, sir? She isn't foreign at all, I thought, not if the accent is anything to go by. Why had I imagined she was Russian? I who know the Russian physiognomy so well. And moving away I told myself: Your wife flirted with you and flirted with Gregory Marks and flirted with Jehovah's Witnesses and flirted, most of all, with your son. Your only son. As all these girls flirt. In their pretty ways, I thought. These pretty girls. Your only flesh and blood. Whereas Marco, so far as I know, never had a woman at all. I stopped in the busy entrance to the Terminal One Departures Lounge bookshop. Rather injudiciously. Marco, I repeated, never had a woman at all. People were pushing past. And never will have. I was in the way. This simple reflection overwhelmed me. Are you all right, mate? You think you are thinking about one thing, I thought, completely overwhelmed, but stumbling on again now, refusing assistance, the concourse coming and going as if through faulty reception across the stormiest of airwaves, when really you are thinking about another, about something quite different altogether. One thinks one is distracted – I had recovered my balance now – even castigates oneself for this distraction, when actually the opposite is the case. You're not distracted at all. And suddenly I knew that behind the morning's missing minutes lay the urgent and intolerable question: *What did we do to him? What did we do?* Our marriage is over, I thought. There are terrible emotions ahead, terrible tides of emotion. It was a vague thought, coming and going, foreground and back. Hurrying once more to the lavatory, I pulled out my mobile, flicked through the memories and allowed the machine to call Paola.

Paola was out. There was Giorgio's voice on the answer-phone. I have always liked Giorgio, I thought, I have always found Giorgio reassuring. And hearing out his simple message on the answer-phone explaining that he and Paola were out and inviting me to leave my name and number, I realised, despite the crackle and fuzz more or less inevitable when you call abroad on your mobile from an airport, that this was a quality of voice. Giorgio's tone of voice is reassuring, I thought, the exact opposite of your wife's, or your own for that matter, and at the same time, back in the same cubicle, I realised there was no paper. So in a way it was a blessing I hadn't performed the first time. We'll be on the first available flight to Milan, I said. Though now I would have to change cubicles if I wanted to get on with it. I stood up, tugging at my trousers, then realised I hadn't closed the call. I still had a line open to Italy, to Novara. Unsure whether the end-of-message beep had gone or not I added, Your poor mother is in something of a state. Time to bury the hatchet perhaps. I paused. Did I have anything else to say? I closed the call.

Settling in the adjacent cubicle, I thought, You are afraid of your wife, yet you seek to protect her. The neon was flickering. I pulled Gregory's book from its bag and considered the Tuscan landscape on the cover. As if she were more fragile than yourself. There were peasants hoeing between vines. You leave this conciliatory message on your daughter's phone, I thought, hoping that this might lead to some rapprochement

23

that would ease the suffering your wife never allows you to be part of, and now you are hurrying to be through with your stool to return to her side in the departures lounge, you who have been warned by more than one specialist that haste with your stool is a luxury a man with a heart condition can ill afford. The back flap, I saw, reminded readers that Gregory's was a familiar face because he had been a BBC correspondent for so many years. You seek to protect your wife, perhaps, I told myself, vaguely amused at having once wanted that job so much for myself, because you are afraid that her reaction to pain will be at your expense. I looked at my watch and found I had been away from her for more than an hour. I was genuinely concerned. Where had the time gone? My wife was in a state, I thought, a serious state, and I had abandoned her in a crowded Terminal One departures lounge for upwards of an hour making fruitless visits to the lavatory and fruitless, if not calamitous, telephone calls. How could I write the questions for Andreotti today? Of all days! Then fruitlessly purchasing Gregory's book. This was ungenerous. Unless her reaction is directed against your attempt to protect her, against this constant tension between us. You are impelled, I thought, to go to the lavatory, as if about to explode, and then produce nothing at all. I must hurry back, I told myself. To my wife. But then, still sitting on the lavatory, turning Gregory's book over and over in my hands, I experienced a moment of complete detachment, not unlike those I had enjoyed at the hospital immediately after anaesthetics were administered. Your son died last night, I reflected, died at his own hand after a long illness which seemed to have killed his real self some years ago. I felt immensely detached. Your dear son has died, I repeated, and now, to go and see his body for the last time, to pay the respect due to the dead and then to bury the poor boy decently, or cremate him, as must be done, in order to perform the necessary ceremonials that is, you are condemned to a period of inaction. Here in the airport, then the plane, then the train. A period of inbetweenness. During which time all kinds of thoughts will come into your head. No doubt. Thoughts you are hardly responsible for, I told myself. We can hardly be responsible for the thoughts that just float into our heads, I thought, registering the first words of the blurb: Perhaps never in all the history of travel writing . . . The neon flickered. Then from that utmost detachment and equanimity, perhaps twenty seconds of it, perhaps thirty, the serene withdrawal of a Buddha, I was plunged directly into the most urgent and compelling of anxieties. When somebody dies young – suddenly the words surfaced and froze on the rapid currents of my mind – when somebody dies young, it is somebody's fault. You know that, I told myself. It was as though flickering neon had frozen its image on the liquid surface of the retina. Always. Especially when somebody kills himself young. I had passed from detachment to despair with the caprice of a faulty contact in a parlous public space. A Heathrow lavatory no less. I was in tears. There are huge tides of emotion to be faced, I told myself. The sooner the better perhaps. It is over between yourself and your wife. What can she be thinking? I wondered, giving up on my stool, my impossible stool, while at the same time reading the first line of Gregory's preface: The most marvellous thing about the Italians, my ancient rival had written, is their unerring unpredictability. I burst out laughing. He had actually brought those two words together: unerring unpredictability. The neon flickered. I've been away too long, I thought. Gregory was never a serious threat. I must get back to her. But on returning to the departures lounge, my wife was gone.

I I I

When, some ten years ago, I began the extensive reading that
was to lead, though I was only dimly aware of such a prospect
at the time, to my repudiation of journalism, my decision to
embark instead on a work I hoped would be monumental
in both scope and scandal, it was the connections that most
excited me, the correspondences, or, as I saw them defined
in one awesome and arcane work on the Vedic texts, the
bandhu. Across centuries, even millennia, one would catch
two writers saying exactly the same thing. This excited me
immensely. Not so much their having said and thought the
exact same thing, though that was exciting enough in itself,
but the fact that I, so many years later and perhaps in a language
neither had used, had grasped this connection. Or rather, my
mind had grasped it. For in the making of connections it is
hard to know what part any 'I' might play. A door swings
open between two stale rooms, current flows across a faulty
contact, you sense a sudden rushing together and recognition
comes unbidden, the intending personality left far behind.
The *bandhu* survive the individual personality, that awesomely
arcane work on the Vedic texts explained: the 'I' may die,

but the connections the mind has made and the web they form are unaffected. Sitting on a Monarch Airways charter in a holding pattern over Genoa, after the wild scene at the departures gate, the prolonged silence on the flight, vaguely recalling something both Schopenhauer said and Leopardi, a connection I set down in a notebook somewhere, one of the many notebooks now stored in the Rembrandt Hotel lumber room, and Plato too I think, though in a different way, it occurs to me that it must have been about the time that I gave up on other sources of fulfilment — on work, that is, and women — and began instead to seek my pleasure inside my head — it must have been about that time that my son's head went to pieces.

For some ten minutes I wandered about the row of seats where my wife had been. I checked that it was the right row of seats. I wished I had not stayed away so long. I would have sat down and waited for my wife on the same seats, since all my experience and education tells me that when two people have lost contact, each of them will take their last meeting place as a point of reference, returning there regularly between repeated reconnoitres — I would have sat down, had not the seats been occupied by a young couple, anxiously checking the departures screen between warm embraces of the determined-to-have-a-happy-holiday variety: then on each side of them a group of Moslem women in high spirits. Qualities, Schopenhauer remarked, and he meant qualities of character, constitute a continuum: a good quality merges into a bad without any perceptible interruption to mark the passage from positive to negative: patience slithers into procrastination; impetuosity matures into decisiveness; tenderness tends to suffocation. You fell in love with your wife for her vivacity, her vehemence, I tell myself, my face turned to a smeared window over storm clouds. Her energy.

I have told myself this a thousand times. Only to find it was vulgarity. Or worse, at the departures gate, hysteria. Within the overall range of any given quality, love sees only the positive half, Schopenhauer commented, perhaps regretted. My hands are still shaking. But later discovers the continuum complete.

Unable to find my wife, unable to sit down, I circled the row of bolted seats beneath great slabs of blanched neon in the thickening throng of the departures lounge, my eyes casting this way and that but always returning to the now entirely static messages on the departures screen. How many times have we lost each other like this, I asked myself, in a whole variety of public places and foreign towns, or even simply supermarkets, because your wife has suddenly chosen to do something completely unannounced? Something we hadn't discussed. Or had even ruled out. Something there was absolutely no cause to do. Then blamed you for not having intuited it. Times I have waited for her outside metro stations, in cafés, in the waiting rooms of clinics and hospitals. A toddler bumped into me and ran off crying. There were suitcases all over the floor. The check-in desks had ceased to check in. And while still wishing I hadn't stayed away so long − that was a mistake − and wishing in particular that I hadn't telephoned the fixer, nor wasted what must have been, though I couldn't see how, a good half-hour circling the Best Summer Reading counter in the Terminal One bookshop, I nevertheless began to feel irritated with my wife for having once again, and so predictably, done something to make this worst of all mornings even worse than it need be. Was it my wife Gregory was thinking of when he wrote, 'unerring unpredictability'? In which case what he should have written, surely, was predictably erring.

I circled the row of chairs, and again collided with the

toddler. Feeling irritated, I found, was somehow better and worse than feeling desperate. And circling the airport here, over Genoa, where thunderstorms and torrential rain have apparently reduced visibility on the ground to zero, the plane bucking fitfully in constant turbulence, I'm reminded of another difficult landing, another holding pattern, over Moscow, so many years ago. Holding pattern is an excellent description of your life these last ten years, it occurs to me. Your marriage. And it likewise occurs that this thought is another *bandhu*, another connection. How the mind takes pleasure in its grip on defeat! Circling forever round an impossible landing. Running out of fuel. And how well, I thought, there in the departures lounge, going round and round the happy young couple and the giggling Malaysian women, how well irritation defends one from panic. Where was my wife? At this of all moments. Suddenly I was furious. Where was she? Fury is an antidote for panic, I excused myself. Except we were happy, then, I reflect. On the flight from Leningrad to Moscow, in stormy weather, with Paola on our knees. Learning to call her Paola. Teaching her to call herself Paola. Teaching ourselves to call her ours. What a vigorous, decisive, impulsive woman your wife is! Such were the thoughts I was thinking on that flight. Positive thoughts. An Italian woman, I told myself. What qualities she has! Positive qualities. The Antonov bucked violently in storm clouds over Moscow. I'm so proud of you, I told her. My wife clutched Paola to her breast, weeping for joy and laughing at my Aeroflot jokes. Laughing raucously. We were determined to be happy. Unable to produce a child, I told myself the story of my wife, unable to adopt a child in the mad bureaucracy that reigns in Italy, this marvellous Italian woman moves heaven and earth to find a daughter from another country. What could I do but support her in that quest? It was a daughter she wanted. What could I do but follow her lead? An undernourished waif from Leningrad, purchased in the times money mattered a great deal more and she cared about it a great deal less. A prostitute's carelessness it seemed. Half Kazakh, half Ukrainian, the bribed official supposed. But did it matter? The plane banked steeply. The engine noise deepened. Don't worry, I saw 'em taking on plenty of coal, I told her. She laughed. We were so determined to be happy. As likewise the young couple gathering up their whining toddler in the departures lounge. Each national character has its special qualities Leopardi says in his essay on the Italians. And the vices that go with them.

After the wild scene at the departures gate my wife stares mutely at the seatback in front of her. She will not talk. Her body is rigid. She will not respond. Whereas it is all I can do to stop myself screaming every thought out loud. How is it, I demanded out loud, still circling the row of plastic seats among suitcases and backpacks and adolescents now sprawling on the floor beneath the neon, how is it that while finding so many things predictable you never manage to predict anything? Didn't predict your wife's disappearance, didn't predict your son's despair? And how am I to write those questions, I wondered, in such a way that Andreotti will answer every one of them exactly as I want him to? Today of all days. In the next twelve hours. The happy couple were suddenly arguing over something to do with the toddler's behaviour. He'd had his hands on the floor and now in his mouth. Somebody should have intervened. I stopped circling to watch them. The woman clucking with a handkerchief. The man resentful. It was the beginning of their happy holiday, their flight was delayed and now they were quarrelling. Over a matter of infant hygiene. People are constantly imagining themselves as living this or that happy life, I reflect, remembering the young couple in the departures lounge on the row of bolted seats where I waited for my wife, remembering ourselves on the Aeroflot circling Moscow, constantly planning South-Sea holidays, rowboat picnics, Tuscan farmhouses, loving pets, cheerful children. Above all cheerful children. Only to find that they are sterile, or there is an air strike, or their partner deserts them. Or more commonly, themselves. They find they had not reckoned on themselves, their own internal frictions and irritations. There is no place in our dreams for the burden of being ourselves, I thought in the Terminal One Departures Lounge. You do not think, I thought, seeing pictures of people pleasure-making on the beach, perhaps in an advertisement for rum or Martini – the airport was full of them – that for all the beauty of their surroundings and indeed themselves these fortunate people are nevertheless obliged to think, obliged to be conscious. Can this beautiful young model be *thinking*? you ask yourself, leafing now through the in-flight magazine. One hopes not. You set out to seduce a beautiful young woman only to find that she is thinking, she is unhappy. She is thinking you don't really love her. It is making her unhappy. That is a phone-call I might make if I do go to Rome, I thought. Our lives run parallel to our dreams, I thought. But never quite connect. Our holidays are parodies of prospected bliss. No, it is appalling, I suddenly thought, my eye ranging over the huge throng of people in the airport concourse, to have to recognise that everybody at all times is obliged to have at least some trash or other going through his head. Or hers. If only the repetition of a song. How my wife loved to sing songs when she was in a good mood. Over and over the same song. Like a mantra. And how I have loved her for that. For the thought of a mind happily reposed in the words of an old song. However trite. How she sang over and over to the tiny, undernourished child as the plane banked this way and that over Moscow, waiting for snowploughs to clear a runway. *Ninna nanna, ninna nanna, la bambina è della mamma.* She had found someone to mother, someone to save. Found a child for her ancient family. But when she sang to Marco last he put his hands over his ears and shrieked. Thinking can be the greatest of pleasures, I reflect, staring out at storm clouds, separated from storm clouds only by the perspex of this window. As for me in these years of reading, of researching what I trust will be a monumental book. And the greatest of horrors. As for Marco in his inexplicable despair. Or somehow both at the same time. Both a pleasure and a horror. As now. Parallel lines meet at infinity, I recall. Or perhaps the mortuary of some Piedmontese hospital.

We should have flown Monarch, the young man was saying. I was standing embarrassingly close to them. Almost on top of them. Had I suffered another lapse? We should have gone to Genoa, he said. Immediately, I realised where she was. My wife, I knew, would move heaven and earth to get to Marco. As she has moved heaven and earth to do so many things. Moving heaven and earth is what your wife does best, I thought and at the same time felt sure I had not suffered another lapse. It was only twelve forty-five. My eye followed the young man's to the only flashing entry on the screen. A flight that should have left at seven a.m. When heaven and earth will budge, that is. I pushed the length of the hall. The chaos round the check-in desks was complete. But now I was concerned I might be wrong. For our suitcase was already with BA. What would my wife do in such circumstances? Exactly the same, I was immediately aware without actually thinking it, exactly the same as she did when she found she couldn't have a child, exactly the same as when Gregory served his ultimatum. Refuse to be thwarted. My wife is never thwarted. She moves heaven and earth. That was why it was such an enormous concession for her to come to England. Though only part of her determination not to be thwarted in another area of her life. Not to give in with Marco. I found the Monarch check-in desk but no one was there. At the adjacent Britannia, two girls in uniform shrugged their shoulders. You can hardly praise your wife, it occurs to me now, looking out through bright sunshine across leaden clouds, for one manifestation and then condemn her for another of what is in the end exactly the same quality. Plato says something of the kind about different forms of government. Her determination to seduce people, to seduce events even. Her refusal to be thwarted. The way she dresses is emblematic of that, I reflect. You haven't seen a woman in a bright red coat? I asked, at the Britannia check-in desk. Fiftyish. Blonde. Upset. I have always loved and been embarrassed by the way my wife dresses. Floppy green hat? As likewise by the way she makes herself up. And sitting now beside her silent presence, infuriatingly locked into this slow holding pattern over the city of Genoa, a city I have not visited since some ferry disaster years ago, I'm suddenly afraid that she really does believe there is something to hurry for. Something to be done. Otherwise why this urgency? This fixity. The steady gaze, the stony intensity. Why? Whom or what is she planning to seduce? And I decide: I must phone Dottor Vanoli as soon as we land.

Foreign woman? they asked, smiled. Kept speaking in a foreign language? Couldn't understand a word. Kept waving her arms about. My wife had obviously caused them some amusement. Various languages, they said. They were smiling. But not English. I burned my boats and hurried over to passport control. No point until your flight's called, sir. Then showing my boarding card I realised I had both tickets. How

33

could she have got past without a boarding card? Yet I feared she was capable of this and more. I have mountains of shopping to do, I said. Rather be on that side than this, if you see what I mean? I even laughed. I could see no point in asking after an Italian woman in a red coat bereft of a boarding card since I already felt sure she had got through. My wife can move mountains. And of course she knew I would follow. She knew and did not even reflect on the anxiety I would have to go through before acting on my intuition. I always follow. No wonder you have a heart condition, I thought. But at least the need for action seemed to have solved the problem of my stool. I felt as brisk and decisive as a new prime minister. She had a head start. I must hurry.

I have not brought out Gregory's book during the flight, because I do not want my wife to see it. I do not want my wife to know it exists and above all do not want her to see I bought it. Unless she already knows. It wouldn't be appropriate to buy the book of a man you have always envied while on the way to the clinic where your son committed suicide. The better to gloat over the man's vacuousness and resent his success. In Italy I always have the wonderful feeling that anything might happen: thus the second vacuous sentence of Gregory Marks's vacuous book, read and immediately despised in the Terminal One lavatory while my wife perhaps was already prowling for whichever flight would be the first to go. How could my wife, who is anything but unintelligent, not see through such a man? And how is it, I suddenly find myself wondering, that you have to really live with someone, and do it for years and years, decades even, before you can truly feel alone? In your head everything connects, I reflect, everything flows together, while beside you is the person from whom all secrets must be kept and whose own you have never fathomed. As you never really fathomed the Italians perhaps. Despite spending all your adult life in Italy. Or even Andreotti. After thirty years of political journalism you never really fathomed Andreotti. Will he answer my questions as I expect? I have never, it suddenly occurs to me with great force, felt so alone as when beside my wife. That is the truth. Nor so much myself, so human, so aware of the greatest moral issues and the smallest matters of propriety. I understood at once, for example, how inappropriate it would be for me to accept the meal the stewardess was eager to give us somewhere over France. Over Paris even. However hungry I have now begun to feel. However much and perversely I have always enjoyed airline food. On my own I would have accepted that airline meal, but beside my wife I did not. Or the offer of a drink. A gin and tonic. A whisky. Are we to eat nothing then, I ask myself, until poor Marco is buried? To drink nothing? Or until we ourselves are separated perhaps? It can't be long now. Perhaps not a single morsel is to pass your lips until you have separated from your wife who notoriously associates eating with not caring enough, not suffering enough. Never mind drinking. The airline magazine has an article on Tuscany, but there is no ad for Gregory's book. For weeks now, I reflect, I am condemned to looking for ads for Gregory's book. That is the kind of person I am. Until sweeping aside all such idle speculation, the morning's one great thought comes crashing down once again: Marco's death, a voice announces, is how this holding pattern ends. There is no earthly reason why my wife and I should stay together now our son is dead. Has she realised that?

Je dois partir! She was at the gate shouting at two men, benignly uniformed. Pleading. *Mon fils est malade. Gravement malade. Er ist krank. Verstehen sie nicht*?

There is something raffish and theatrical about my wife even at the calmest of moments. Something loud. I heard her voice the length of the corridor. The scarlet coat was royal against the drab colouring of airport interiors. *Il peut mourir, même aujourd' hui.* The green hat has a feather. And there was a gypsyish touch now about the way she clung to a uniformed arm. As though begging. *Est-ceque vous comprenez, messieurs?* Three languages perfectly, but not a word of English. Her voice echoed in the empty hall. The last of the charter crowd were disappearing through swing doors opposite. She was smiling through her tears. Don't you have children, *messieurs?* She was pleading with them. Seducing them. In French. In German. In Italian. I must get on this plane. Here is his photograph. Look at him. She clutched at the man. It was brilliantly melodramatic. Before he dies, she was pleading. She was lying. That is how she moves heaven and earth, I reflect, cruising the storm clouds over Genoa, travelling empty miles of pointless space seen through a slab of perspex, with nothing at all to do but reflect. Round and round. That is how she does it. Pleading and lying. Though she never pleads with me. She is theatrical and she is lying, I thought, hearing her voice the length of the corridor, quickening my pace, out of breath. And at the same time she is entirely sincere, entirely convinced. Heaven and earth always move for my wife when she makes love. Or so she says. So it seems. With that extravagantly theatrical way she has of making love. Which is so wonderful. When not distracted by Jehovah's Witnesses. As heaven and earth moved for her when Marco was born. She is so loud. And with a start I see polished red nails digging deep into my wrist. The blood welled. The last shrieking push. She had proved them all wrong. I was so happy for her that day.

I'm so sorry, I said politely. We have first-class tickets on BA. Perhaps . . . My wife swung on me. Age is accentuating the hook in her nose. The two men were mild-mannered, practised in the art of affability. Likewise the set of her lips. There's no need for you to come, she told me. She spoke rapidly in Italian. As always there was a cloud of perfume. You follow on the regular flight with the suitcase. Tell them he's had a car accident. He's in *rianimazione*. She'd had time to put on her make-up this morning while I was foolishly eating that kipper. The perfume is always flowery. Now tears had reduced her to a sorry state. I felt sorry for her. Her cheeks were streaked with tears. Her thick hair was down. But still irritated. Perhaps we could exchange them for this flight, I finished limply. We're not worried about the difference in price. My wife had managed to grasp a hand in both of hers and was caressing it. The official pulled gently free. She is such a fine-looking woman, I thought, with that nose and chin. Such a handsome, aristocratic woman. Our life together is over. She has blue blood. Quite over. National airlines had agreements for accepting each other's tickets, the official said. The two men were embarrassed, eager to explain. But not charters. My wife had grabbed the hand again. And I knew she would never give up now. She will have to be taken away kicking and screaming now, I thought. And this is her genius. How high she raises the stakes. How many times, I ask myself here in this Monarch Airways charter as the stewardess inches along the aisle serving orange juice right and left, how many times have I found myself in situations like this, where in an unfailing double-act, never discussed but endlessly repeated, Mr and Mrs Burton extract some extraordinary concession from some official or other? Paola's adoption; Marco's acquittal. We can pay again, I said, pulling out my wallet before their shaking heads. They felt sorry for her. Sorry for me for having to deal with her, with someone who raised the stakes so high. And this was what she wanted. What I wanted too, I suppose. There have been times we have collapsed in laughter after a performance like this. When it was just a question of begging a last ticket for a première. Getting into an embassy party. I don't care how much it costs, I went on. One gets caught up in the theatre of it. *Dio Cristo*, show some emotion, my wife was urging. Tell them he's in *rianimazione*, she insisted, tell them this is our last chance to see our son. It is a situation of the utmost urgency, I said and I spoke as one who is sadly stilted, too well versed in life's little proprieties to let himself go. But suffering for it. Beside a wife who is quite the opposite. A volcano. The formula is infallible. Who would not put such a couple out of their misery? And remembering our faces now as we played our parts, I'm bound to admit that there was a deep complicity between myself and my wife in that wild scene at the airport departures gate, a deep and disturbing complicity. How can there be such a complicity between two people who are never more alone than when they are together? There's a conundrum. Until you reminded her that Marco was dead. Dead. She would not forgive you for that. She would not talk to you after that.

They had no facilities for accepting payment at the departures gate, the official said. Then there were strict regulations restricting last-minute ticket purchases. That was what made a charter a charter. It was the younger man who spoke while my wife was still gripping the older fellow's arm across the gate, searching for his eyes. Perhaps where there are humanitarian considerations, I was saying politely. *E' malato*, she insisted loudly. She was weeping, photograph in hand. *Moribondo, non capite?* The genius of my wife is to be at once perfectly sincere and perfectly false, I thought. Sincere in her suffering, false in her manipulation. And ludicrously I am reminded that this is something I meant to bring out in the Andreotti interview. This brilliantly ambiguous mindframe which believes what it acts and acts what is convenient. Is that an Italian thing then? Was there something in Machiavelli? Until finally it does believe its lie. Does she believe Marco is dying, not dead? Can be saved perhaps? You must have facilities for credit-card payments on board, I said. For the duty-free. Tell them you don't need to come, she turned to me. Tell them we only need one seat. And when she turns to me, her voice always switches from the pleading to the imperative. She has never pleaded with me. She pleaded with Paola, pleaded with Marco, pleaded with Gregory, pleaded with a whole host of doctors and officials. But never with me. *Un posto basta*, she was saying. *Solo un posto*. She held up a finger, a lacquered nail. One, she said. Amazingly speaking English. A word of English. Un–derr–stand? One place. After all, there are seats, aren't there? I suddenly cut in more forcefully. It's crazy not filling them if someone wants to go.

The older official was just picking up the phone on his desk when my mobile again trilled in my pocket. I reached down to turn it off. Give it to me, my wife demanded. At the same time two elderly passengers came rattling down the corridor with a trolley full of duty-frees, twenty minutes late for a flight six hours delayed. We had given up, the woman laughed, speaking Italian, her husband fumbling with boarding cards. My wife began to moan. She had the phone jammed to her ear. The face is nobler now the nose has come out, craggier. An expression of pure will. He's dying, she announced. God knows who it was phoning. I don't give this number to everybody. A question of hours, she screamed. The elderly Italian couple were alarmed. My wife handed back the mobile. Our son had an accident, she told this audience who spoke her language, this couple who until a moment before had obviously been finding their long morning at the airport an entirely jolly experience. The man had been drinking.

They were loaded with duty-frees, booze, and cigarettes and chocolate. The veins in his face were glowing. Some elderly couples do seem to be happy, I reflect, remembering their glowing faces at the departures gate. Some people do seem to enjoy life. More the old than the young, I suspect. There are problems with our getting on the flight, I explained soberly. I was both embarrassed and inured. And envious too. Of the sheer effrontery of it. My wife's manipulative powers. And excited. Something to do with its being a charter, I said. My wife started to sob. She had her forehead on the older official's wrist and wept, at once entirely authentic and brilliantly coercive. Pressing a green button, the display told me it was Paola had phoned. Paola. But you 'ave the seats, no? the Italian was asking the younger of the officials in a comically poor accent. He was busy with their boarding cards, a hint of exasperation about his rapid movements. His colleague had turned away to speak in a low voice on his phone. Is ridiculous! The new arrival was tipsy. His voice slightly slurred. You English are ridiculous. You 'ave not to obey regulations when a person is in need. What happened? his wife was enquiring softly of mine. My wife sobbed. Turning to her husband the woman said: We should not get on the flight if they don't let these poor people on. What on earth had Paola heard? I wondered. Over the phone. Did she know anything as yet? Was she just answering my call? And what had I said exactly in my message? Then for a split second I caught my wife's eye. A glint. Her meaning flashed through tears and smudged make-up. My hands were shaking. She is amazing, I thought. This is ridiculous, the man was saying, refusing to take his boarding card and move. You can have our seats. He turned to me. And now he took the boarding cards and made to give them to us. We will give these un'appy people our seats, he said in English. Does she realise our marriage is over, or not? I'm sorry, the younger official was objecting, that's impossible, but now his colleague put the phone down and was telling us we could go. He'd squared it with someone. Some authority. Hurry along now or we'll miss our slot. You'll be sorted out on the plane, he said. *Ottimo*, the elderly Italian was saying, forgetting we were supposedly hurrying along to our dying son. This must be totally against the regulations, I thought. What if there was a bomb in our bag on the BA flight? And quite inappropriately I experienced a moment's exhilaration. Done it. We had done it!

Then as soon as she realised I was walking beside her, my wife said, What for? There is no need for you to come too. What about the suitcase? she said. She stopped in the tunnel sloping down to the plane. Go back and wait for the other flight. The officials had gone. The elderly couple were boarding ahead of us, making heavy weather with the duty-frees. Soon we too will be elderly, I thought, but not a couple. Somehow such thoughts were making the morning bearable. But delaying something too. There is no need for you to come, she said. We were standing in the gangway delaying a flight of perhaps two hundred people. Go back. I could see the steward staring from the door, eager to close, eager to go. Suddenly I was furious. What need is there for *you* to go, I demanded. For a rare moment we looked straight into each other's eyes. A very rare moment. My wife stared defiantly. The usually pinned hair had fallen across her forehead. Marco is dead, I said and said it out loud. I shouted it. He's dead. There is nothing we can achieve by hurrying. Understand? There is nothing we can do. And at that moment I realised the boy had been forgotten. It came to me in a flash. Marco has been forgotten, I thought, as my wife turned away and hurried into the plane, refusing to speak. Instead of our son, I thought, there is only the drama of our getting to our son. I was completely unsurprised by this revelation. It seemed obvious. As previously, I reflect now, there was the drama of our finding a treatment for our son, and before that the drama of our educating our son, and before that the drama of our producing our son. Hello, a stewardess said brightly, handing me the *Evening Standard*. Without taking my seat, I went straight to the back, to the loo, pointlessly as it turned out. Does she imagine, I wondered, spreading the *Standard* on my knees, that because they were wrong about her not being able to have a child they can be wrong about this too? Marco born against the odds. Marco resurrected against all odds. The drama of our resurrecting our son. Is that what comes next? Our bringing him back from the dead. You will never have a child, the doctor told her. Your son has killed himself, Mr Burton. Government Off to Flying Start, the *Standard* claimed. Another photo of Blair en famille. Is this why she has not pressed me, after the initial knee-jerk question in the Rembrandt, as to how he died? She doesn't want to hear perhaps that he is not in one piece, doesn't want to hear of a corpse that might not, miraculously, sit up on his mortuary slab. My son. Major's Miracle Manqué, a smaller column was headed. It's extraordinary, I thought, that she hasn't pressed me on any of the details. Extraordinary how concentrated she seems. Does she imagine she can seduce him back to life? Heaven and earth moved yet again. Myself and my wife to play the same spiel before the Almighty as we did before the airport officials? Before judge and jury when Marco was acquitted.

Then against all the rules, sitting pointlessly on the loo, the *Standard* spread open on my knees, I switched the mobile back on and called Paola. She was crying. *Piccola*, I said. The signal was coming and going. The plane began to taxi. We'll be arriving in Genoa, I told her. Then had to call back. A

42

couple of hours' time. Your mother doesn't know it was suicide. She's not my mother, Paola said. Feeling in my pocket on my way back to my seat, I realised I had forgotten my pills.

I V

Where did it all begin? That was certainly one of the questions I had planned to put to Andreotti. And what I meant was: this business of a seven-times prime minister being accused of mafia crimes. Where had it all begun? A question it would cost me very little to jot down now in the back of this car, perhaps even type out, should I get the opportunity, when we arrive at our destination, without any offence to anybody. And the answer I am sure Andreotti will give me, in the very unlikely event that I should go through with this interview, or rather the non-answer, will be as follows: At my age – and this with a deprecating hunch of hunched shoulders, that smile of his between the sly and the offended, something that will be sadly missing if the interview is to be conducted by fax – at my age and after half a century of service to my country – for he is as sure to mention service to his country as my wife, if ever you asked her where certain things began (her inexplicable rancour, for example, or this business I never really understood with Gregory) would be sure to speak of decades of dedication to her husband – at my age I have the right, I think, Andreotti will say, to believe myself invulnerable to such libellous

44

accusations. Or words to that effect, words, in any event that will amount in substance and spirit – for this is the point of the question – to the very words Francesco Crispi answered a hundred years ago when accused, as Italian Prime Minister, of the exact same thing: massive corruption in the purchase of power. At my age, Crispi answered Parliament, deploying that blend of piety and effrontery I now recognise so well, and after fifty-three years of service to my country, etc. etc. And he actually used the word invulnerable. I have the right to believe I am invulnerable. For to every question I asked, I hoped to show that Andreotti was answering not only in the way he, Andreotti, *would* answer, the way I had predicted in previous chapters he would answer, but in exactly the same way that other leading Italian figures of every period of history had already answered in circumstances in every way analogous. At my age . . . invulnerable. Thus at a deeper level the answer to the question, where did it all begin, would be there precisely in the evasion and petulance of the response, or rather in its similarity to other evasive and petulant responses by other discredited leaders. The answer to where did it all begin is always there. It began in a certain mindframe. In ourselves and at every moment. It is always beginning. Here and now. For if there is, indisputably, in any person's behaviour a horizon of predictability, as the mathematicians say, beyond which chaos presides, so that you can never know exactly which of a dozen hats your wife will put on when she goes out, nor whether she will choose to apply her red lipstick, or her pink, or her orange, still there is – or even her mauve – as Montesquieu put it, an *esprit generale*, you can know the kind of behaviour to expect, the kind of hat she will put on, the kind of thing a disgraced Italian leader will say and do. As, even if you can never predict the exact interval of time between the fall of one raindrop and the next on any given point, even when the stuff is, as now, positively deluging onto the top of this car in heavy traffic, still you do know that it rains more in Preston than Palermo. Yes, and that, whatever colour she might choose, your wife always and invariably wears bright lipstick when she goes out. Gloss lipstick. How could she flirt otherwise? How could she seduce people? The Italian leader either dies in power, I tell myself, sitting in this car in heavy rain – Cavour, De Gasperi – or dies in disgrace – Crispi, Andreotti (no doubt), and others too. And this due to a certain play of forces that is as irretrievably Italian as the play of forces that brought Blair to power is irretrievably British. Irretrievably. I must make it clear that I use that word advisedly. Every Italian man, Dottor Vanoli once said to me – and one of my problems with Vanoli was that I could never decide how seriously to take him with his overly dapper beard and neatly cropped hair, his ever-amused eyes – Every Italian man is either made or broken by his mother. He laughed. Sometimes I thought he might just be bouncing ideas off me, to see how I would react. The way shrinks will. The child's developing ability, Vanoli explained – though he was not a shrink – or chronic disability, to escape his mother's intrusions. Clichés even. He must have been aware that this was a cliché: Italian men and their mothers. Though Andreotti, of course, I remember, had grown up with his widowed mother and remained very attached to her. And he, Vanoli, talked to me at length about the way each nation, and within each nation each age, had its own particular mental illnesses. He quoted Freud and various pathologies unheard of today. Well-to-do Viennese women of the 1890s. But I knew all this of course. I was far from ignorant. I'm sure you do, he said and he said that a certain and very particular kind of schizophrenia among males in their early twenties was one of Italy's current specialities.

46

He smiled. These were the early days before I was sufficiently familiar with Vanoli's method of proceeding. I had wanted to discuss some new hormone treatment they were developing in the USA. I had searched high and low, used every possible contact to find the very best psychiatrist Italy had to offer. Someone who would be up to date with all the latest research. With my wife moving heaven and earth to find out what was wrong, what else could I do? And it was a pleasure to be able to show my wife that in certain areas I had a distinct edge. I had access to research facilities she knew nothing of. I'll find you the best doctor in the land, I told my wife. Not to worry. And no expense spared. Since neither of us, I remind myself, slumped here now in this car in heavy traffic, in heavy rain, neither of us has ever spared any expense in Marco's regard. So much so that that conversation held in Vanoli's stylish office on the Lungotevere must have been costing me in the region of five thousand lire a minute. Why else would I have started evading tax? Have you heard of this new treatment? I demanded. I showed him an article. Vanoli smiled his charming smile. Much depended, though, he remarked, apropos of mothers, and clearly this was the barb he had been working towards, on the example given by the father. In handling his wife, that is. And by other members of the family, he said. It was the sort of remark one would have expected from a shrink, but not a psychiatrist supposedly up to date on the latest hormone treatments. But I wasn't familiar with Vanoli's methods at the time. We can hardly be considered a typical Italian family, I countered. It was a doctor I wanted, not a quack. I had made that clear when we first spoke. And still feel that way. Otherwise I'd have gone for family therapy or something of that variety. Some palliative or placebo. It's from *Scientific American*, I told him. He nodded, he had read it. I was English, I said, our adopted daughter Ukrainian. He nodded. There followed one of his long silences. I've been reading a lot about race myself, I said. I smiled. I mean, I agree that while genetically there is very little to choose, given the present state of the art, between a Ukrainian, an Englishman and an Italian, still there are evident differences in group behaviour patterns, in politics for example, or the family, that seem to perpetuate themselves over . . . He smiled. He asked: As you see it then, Signor Burton, where did it all begin? I said I was planning to write a book about it, starting with Machiavelli in Italy, Hobbes in England. Though of course one might go further back. Much further. There was so much reading still to be done. He showed interest, advised me to look at a study by an Italian geneticist living in the States. I forget the name now. Sforza perhaps. But there was something irritating about the way he was so amused. Until a week later I called him from a hotel in Palermo. There had been a big mafia murder, rumours that Andreotti was involved. Gregory was on the same floor. It wasn't unusual. We had had a long and frank discussion together about my wife and about Marco. Gregory is not so bad when you can get him on his own. And about marriage. I almost felt sorry for him. It began, I told Vanoli on the phone from my hotel room in Palermo that morning, when Marco started refusing to speak to his mother in Italian. Maybe three years ago. He would only speak to her in English. Which of course she couldn't understand. It was very strange. Why do you laugh when you tell me that, he asked? Then he said: That was just an early symptom, Signor Burton. What I wanted you to help me understand was, where did it all begin?

Stepping off the plane, the rain was torrential, the sea lashing at the rocks beyond the runway. Between gangway and bus we were soaked. I held my wife's hand on the steps in case she slipped, then spread my jacket over her head as we hurried across the tarmac. There was something reassuring about making these old gestures, though it must be said that my wife's robust health is proverbial. Can you remember a time, I asked myself, even as I spread my jacket over her head, over her green felt hat rather, when your wife was ill? The answer has to be no. My son likewise for that matter. I cannot remember a time when my son Marco was ill. Physically ill. My wife and my son share the same robustness of health, I thought. Physical health. *Torello mio*, she would call him. *Torello mio*. Paola was jealous as any older sibling would be. *Torello mio*. She tickled his baby fat legs. Only more so. You would never have adopted me, Paola said plainly – she was six years old – if you had had him first. And this was true, however much I denied it. You would never have done it, she said. Don't worry, *piccola*, I told her, I will look after you. Paola was a plain child. And not gifted either. Frequently ill. What can you expect, my wife murmured, with who the parents were. Not to mention those first two years' not eating, not sleeping, no affection. For two years Marco didn't sleep. It never affected *his* health. I too was frequently ill. My wife kept him in our bed. She gave up her work. She had had her child against all the odds. I was on the lower of the two bunk beds, beneath Paola. But they were happy years, I explained to Vanoli. Before we moved into the old house, the house of ghosts. I never thought of it as beginning there, I said. Then realised my wife was tugging at me to get off the bus.

And while I was caught at the passport desk she hurried ahead, presumably to find a taxi. Though nothing had been said about how we were to proceed. A taxi to where? The station? Or, paying a fortune, directly to Turin? To show how much money we were willing to spend on our son. Even when our son was dead. Even when we had been arguing so much about money lately, and in particular last night in that other taxi on the way home from Courteney's, discussing the purchase of a house in London, the sale of a house in Rome. She will return to live in that house now, I thought, on the via Livorno, she will return to live in her family home, the so-called house of ghosts, while I will find myself a small flat to rent in London. She will never consent to the sale of that house now, I thought, the house of ghosts, with all the memories it holds of Marco. However unpleasant.

Having at first addressed me in German, the official at the passport desk now gazed and gazed at my British passport and checked the name off against data on his computer screen. Would it show I was under investigation for tax evasion? I suddenly asked myself. I hadn't thought of this. Could they seize the house we owned? My wife's family house. I hadn't been back to Italy since that trouble began. Would I be arrested perhaps? And why do people insist on assuming I am German? Then I even wondered, watching the official's eyes moving back and forth from passport to computer screen, if I mightn't be pleased to be arrested for tax evasion. Pleased to have our house seized. At this of all moments. Anything to derail the catastrophic confrontation that must surely come between my wife and myself. No sooner than our son was decently buried. At least we could bury him now. I had never liked the house of ghosts, I thought. But business voices behind me were muttering it was just a way of getting back at the English for not joining the Schengen Accord. How predictably English, I thought, not to join the Schengen Accord, and on receiving my passport under the glass was immediately hurrying after my wife.

Then, as frosted doors slid apart and I stepped through into the modest concourse of this small provincial airport, it was suddenly as if I had stepped back into myself. Something shifted in my head, in my psyche, and I was back with myself. My most lucid self. As I had been in the breakfast room of the Rembrandt Hotel. As I am most days most of the time. And in particular when I am reading, when I am making connections. My wife is unbalanced, I told myself. She has disappeared again. My son had become a schizophrenic not because of anything I, or even his mother, had done, but because his mother herself, as I always suspected, or at least after I began to understand Italian a little better, was, as I said, unbalanced. Perhaps attractively so, but nevertheless unbalanced. And her mother before her. Ten per cent of schizophrenics commit suicide, I told myself. That is a known statistic. Stepping through sliding doors into a recognisably Italian interior, into the country where I had spent my entire adult life, I suddenly felt extremely lucid and in charge. Marco's great-grandfather on his mother's side committed suicide. Marco's aunt, my sister-in-law, was the strangest of recluses. There were dangerous genes at work, I thought. Italy's minor aristocracy was notoriously in-bred. Any guilt I was feeling, or seeking to feel, had more to do with my Christian upbringing and the kind of guilt-hungry society we live in than with anything I had actually done. What had I done? Or even failed to do? Was there anything, I suddenly and peremptorily demanded of myself, that I had not done? Any stone I had left unturned? There was not. No, the fact – and I always insisted on this line with Vanoli – the fact that a child's clinical condition may prompt him to interfere in bizarre fashion with the conflict in progress between his parents, suddenly choosing to please the father, rather than, as previously, indeed ever since he was born, the mother, and in particular by suddenly refusing to speak to the mother in anything but the father's tongue, a tongue she herself did not speak, did not want to speak, or again by suddenly seeking a transgressive intimacy with the father involving all kinds of odd sexual innuendo at the expense of the mother – that kind of interference does not mean that the child's disturbances were prompted by that conflict. No. All medical research suggests the contrary. All medical research suggests that what we are talking about here are enzyme and hormone imbalances. Which was why I had come to a psychiatrist rather than a psychotherapist. Was it not? Do you really think, I demanded of Vanoli, intensely aware of the ludicrous fees I was being charged for this conversation, that one person can drive another person mad? I would have gone to a therapist if I thought that, I said. A quack. And at the door I said, if my wife hasn't driven me mad, then such things are demonstrably impossible. Case closed. Dottor Vanoli laughed. Why do you come and see me on your own? he asked. Why don't you come with your wife? Because she drives me mad, I said. And he laughed all the louder. We'll continue with the Thorazine, he said, that will calm him down. Vanoli was on my side in the end. The Thorazine will do the trick, he said.

Yes, I suddenly felt extremely sure of myself, adventuring across the tiled floor of the airport foyer in Genoa. Not so much despite my wife's fresh disappearance, but because of it. She was unbalanced. No danger of lapses now, I thought, looking this way and that to see where she could have got to. The taxis presumably. If it was anything other than a question of genetics, I reminded myself, of inherited mental disorder, it would have been Paola went mad not Marco. Paola had had far more to cope with. That much is obvious. Poor child. Though I should phone Vanoli at once, I thought. Where was my wife? Then instead of rushing out to the taxis, as I had planned, or supposed I had, to catch up with my wife, I suddenly found myself standing by the till at the small airport café. *Cappuccino e brioche, per favore.* Two carabinieri stood in front of me. I hate the Italian business of having to pay at the till and then order at the counter. Even after all these years, I hate it. But I needed to eat. I didn't give a damn if my wife saw me. I needed sustenance. It was almost four. Five Italian time. Nothing of what had happened had been my fault. I hadn't eaten since breakfast. Hadn't shat either. And pulling out my mobile to call Vanoli I was simultaneously aware, in my new-found lucidity, that if this was the end of my relationship with my wife, then it was also the end of my relationship with Italy. Yes. I finally got my receipt and then had to fight to find a place at the bar between carabinieri and various airport officials. One always seems to be elbowing for space in Italy, I thought. Between officials and bureaucrats often enough. Italy irritates me, I thought, flicking through the memories for Vanoli's number. Though I'm very efficient here. That's an odd thing. Most efficient when most irritated. Most lucid when most beset. No, the kind of image of Italy – I finally got the barman to pay me some attention – that Gregory Marks subscribes to in order to please the crowd, is immensely irritating to me now. How can one pay taxes that are so outrageously high? Like those comedies where they pretend a madman is funny. Or an unhappy marriage. Not to mention the way they spend the taxes you do pay. In Italy I always have the wonderful feeling that anything can happen. And usually it does. Please! How could I ever have seen the man as serious competition? No, when something really happens to you, I thought, like having a schizophrenic in the family, or marrying someone like my wife, someone from an in-bred family of minor and poverty-stricken aristocracy, or even just living in Italy, just dealing with a Byzantine and fickle bureaucracy, it somehow excludes you from enjoying any popular representation of the experience. Any agreeable caricature. If they confiscated the house, where would my wife go to live?

Pronto? Vanoli's secretary came on the line, just as the brioche arrived, and the cappuccino, and my wife. Simultaneously. I asked for Vanoli, said it was urgent, bit into the brioche and all at once my wife was beside me, tugging at my sleeve, gesticulating. Giorgio's here! she said. Remarkably, I kept calm. I didn't feel I had been caught out at all. With my brioche. Let me say a word to Vanoli, I told her. I'm calling Vanoli. Drink this. I gave her the cappuccino. Remarkably, she picked it up and drank it without objection. As if we were two ordinary people, in an ordinary situation, being sensibly pleasant to each other. Nor did she object, it occurs to me now, to my having called Paola from London. She drained the coffee and used a napkin to dab at her lipstick. She always wears bright lipstick. Surely she must have made that connection. That I had called from London. Giorgio would have said as much. How else could he have known to be there? But before Vanoli could come on the line the battery went. The phone was dead. My wife and I walked rapidly across the small concourse, passed through another set of sliding doors, and bundled into our son-in-law's car before the police could move him on.

In normal weather, Giorgio said, a couple of hours. My son-in-law is well fed, bespectacled. We sat at a traffic light with the rain drumming torrentially on the roof. How is Paola? I asked. There would be landslides, he said. Perhaps he hadn't heard. I was in the back. The rain was loud. There were always landslides. He spoke evenly and sensibly. Not surprising when you thought how carelessly this city was built. On these hills. He spoke about surface areas of cement and drainage problems. Amazingly I could see my wife's head nodding, as if in normal conversation. We are on our way to see Marco's body, I told myself. Which would mean deaths, he was saying, and scandal and protest and judicial enquiry and absolutely nothing done until the same story repeated itself next spring. My wife was nodding. The thick hair has come unpinned. The hat has gone. That is the kind of Italy Gregory presents as endlessly funny, I thought, watching the cars ford a badly drained junction. Remorselessly quaint. There was a mudslide blocking the Torino–Savona, Giorgio said. As every spring. My son-in-law speaks as he drives, calmly and sensibly. It's a voice I have always found reassuring. A relationship I always felt was positive. A wise choice on Paola's part. If unadventurous. But then look what happened to my adventurous marriage, I told her. If you knew how adventurous we thought our marriage was, I remember laughing to Paola, to my daughter. That sudden meeting of two nations. Two cultures. Hounslow lower-middle and Roman aristocracy (so-called). Oh, if you knew, I laughed! From an Acton terrace to the house of ghosts! So-called. Via Livorno. You could do a great deal worse than marry Giorgio, I told her. We were so young when we married, I told her. But Paola too was very young. I will buy you an apartment, I promised. I did. Flood alert along the Arno, Giorgio was saying. Calmly. He sighed. Nothing changes, he was saying. Say nothing to your mother, I told her. And it occurs to me that I could easily jot down the question Where did it all begin? on my notebook in the back. Why not? Together perhaps with the question about change. Giorgio had reminded me of my question about change. Though this will have to be carefully framed to get the response I want. How would you reply – the typically cautious beginning – to those who claim that despite all the instability – usual cliché – little ever changes in Italy and that – him now expecting the barb – your long period in office – here it comes –

served more to keep things as they were than to improve them? But it's a fake barb. It's a bait. Perhaps you should have taken the train, Giorgio was saying. I could still take you to the station if you want. His voice is monotonously reassuring. Not unlike the rain. Though I heard there were problems there too, he droned. He sighed, looking to my wife for guidance. One of the rail unions, he explained, but not all three. He hadn't caught the last news. I could even mention the trains, I reflect. Though of course it is out of the question that I actually do this interview. At some point I shall have to phone and cancel. Signor Presidente, you didn't even manage to solve the problem of the trains! Perhaps to elicit his old quip: There are two kinds of madman in Italy: those who believe they are Jesus Christ and those who believe they can make the trains run on time. Andreotti is a man who endlessly recycles old quips. As my wife endlessly recycles her mother's bon-mots, the bon-mots of a minor aristocracy fallen upon hard times. Her father killed in his prime. Marco never believed he was either. Marco never believed he was Jesus Christ or that he could make the trains run on time. And Marco was certainly mad. Giorgio shook his head, tapping on the wheel. The cross-traffic was still coming solidly through as our light turned to green. The junction froze. But what I really wanted to get Andreotti to say, what I was sure I could get him to say, if only I could frame the question the right way, was something along the lines of Mussolini's I am the most disobeyed man in history, or Garibaldi's The only way to get Italians to agree with each other is by armed force. The pretence, that is, typically Italian, typically Andreotti, that power, in Italy, is not really power because nobody will obey you. How can anyone change anything in a place where nobody obeys? Granted, he will say, I was Prime Minister, but a prime minister is only a figurehead. I was only the mediator between a number of ministers, Andreotti will say, a number of quarrelling parties. How could I solve the problem of the trains? The kind of sop foreign journalists always swallow because it plays to their portrayal of Italian anarchy, of a country, as Gregory will no doubt have described it, where people cross on red lights even when they see the traffic is blocked up on the other side. Before going on to insist – Andreotti this is – that in many ways Italy *has* changed and proudly listing all the legislation his government introduced. Deprecation and effrontery were the characteristics I was eager to bring out. Apparently paradoxical. My thesis is that there is always a paradox at the heart of character. Some contradiction that ties the knot, holds two conflicting halves together. Marco never obeys me, my wife insisted. My wife who in so many ways was so powerful. You do something, she ordered. It's horrible. *Do* something. Knowing that I on the contrary always obeyed. A sort of stable schizophrenia you could call it, an enigma at the core. Only the incomprehensible is worth understanding. That must be the burden of my book. Defining that area. The horizon of predictability. Pushing it back a little. No, pushing it back a lot. And I said I would do something, gladly, if only she hadn't made it so impossible by giving the boy every single thing he wanted these last eighteen years. You spoiled him horribly, I told her. No wonder he behaves so weirdly. I made a wonderful man of him, she was weeping, and now this is so horrible. She wept. Neither of us could believe how suddenly and horribly our son had changed. She never admitted he hit her. Our world changed utterly. Everything has changed. She slipped on wet tiles and fell against the bidet, she said. For a couple of weeks her cheeks were powdered white under dark eye-shadow and she wore the broadest-brimmed hats she had. When we went to court, I explained to Vanoli, but this was on another occasion, she actually asked me if I would confess to having thrown a knife at her.

How's Paola? I asked. Quite loudly this time I thought. Albeit from the back. And I thought, your wife can hardly object to your asking your son-in-law how your daughter is, his wife. But this time there was only silence from up front. The windscreen wiper whined on its fast setting. The car inched. Giorgio said something about roadworks they were always beginning and never ending. They were always beginning roadworks and never ending them. He really is a dull fellow. A contraflow above Alexandria, he said. There is safety in dullness, I reflect. And I remember thinking that exact same thought when Paola married him and I bought them the apartment. Dullness rarely overlaps with imbalance, I told myself. We were fireworks when we met. Your mother and I. Dullness is supremely reassuring, I thought. I liked Giorgio. And I was proud of having managed that: having bought an apartment for my daughter. Don't say anything to your mother. How's Paola? I asked again. Nothing. I watched the traffic. Until, as the afternoon suddenly darkened outside around scribbles of wet neon, the blurred invitations of furniture warehouses and shopping centres, I finally noticed, between the front seats, that my wife had laid her hand on his. On the gear stick. I finally realised she was crying. Your wife is crying. He had moved over to her a little. She lay her head on his shoulder, her son-in-law's shoulder. Your wife is crying, I told myself, she is seeking comfort on the shoulder of your stalwart, bespectacled son-in-law. I felt at once immensely pained, immensely sorry for my poor wife, my shattered wife, and at the same time deeply hurt that she was not seeking comfort from myself. This is the state of our relationship then, I suddenly realised. Despite all the fine words, despite all the talk of starting again, of healing our marriage, your wife cannot seek comfort from her husband. From the moment, from the very instant I gave her the news of Marco's death – though I never said the word suicide – a terrible coldness has descended upon us. A terrible, unbridgeable distance. Despite all our recent talk we cannot talk. Despite our attempt, only last night after the party at Courteney's, to make love together. To make love! After the argument in the cab. I can hardly chat with an English Jehovah's Witness, she laughed. I was happy. There was even a pleasant togetherness when we didn't manage it. But you foresaw this, I told myself. When *I* didn't manage it that is. My heart perhaps. You knew it was over the moment you put the phone down on that terrible call. Your son has killed himself, Mr Burton. Why else would you have lost fifteen minutes returning to your room? What were you thinking about in those fifteen minutes? Your wife, I am suddenly reflecting, shrieks and tears her hair in front of a couple of airport officials, but says not a word to you. She has not said a single word to you about your son's death. She seeks your son-in-law's hand as he drives, she weeps and lays a head on his shoulder as he drives along a busy road. A dull boy. In appalling weather conditions. But did not seek so much as a crumb of comfort from yourself for all the length of the flight, all the time you were sitting there with nothing to do but nurse your misery. Why? Why has this happened to us? Why do her expressions of emotion always exclude you? Can't you prescribe something for my wife as well, I asked Vanoli, while you're about it? I had been describing her behaviour with the police, her contradiction of all the evidence Paola had given. Her hysteria. Her refusal now to talk to her adopted daughter. Can't you prescribe something for my wife? Vanoli smiled. Something that will help her to understand English? he asked. And he asked, How come

Marco speaks such perfect English? Because we sent him to an English school, I said.

Then suddenly it occurs to me that I must do the Andreotti interview after all. The lucidity so unexpectedly recovered in the airport lounge comes to my aid. It is a mistake, I tell myself, suddenly and very peremptorily, to interrupt work that is at last gaining momentum. After many years of preparation. True your son has killed himself – that is a most terrible thing – true your marriage has been a failure – that, at your age, is a most frightening admission. But this is now decidedly spilled milk. No, this is milk that was spilled years ago, I tell myself. Marco died years ago, I reflect. You know that. That is the truth, the very truth. That is why you are not grieving. Milk that curdles and smells and moulds and will not go away. There is nothing you can do about this, I tell myself, watching my wife keep her hand on Giorgio's despite the fact that he is now changing gear with a certain regularity as we approach the tollbooth for the autostrada. It is one thing, I tell myself, with quite frenetic lucidity, weeping over milk that was spilled yesterday. And you have wept. You have. But quite another to weep over milk that was spilled years ago. At least Marco was now dead in a way he could be buried. Decades ago perhaps. Where did it begin? Vanoli insisted. When? Not when you have it in you now to make a major contribution. To bring together the chaos theory and our understanding of character, of destiny. To pin down once and for all and quite irrefutably all the different horizons of predictability for different groups and for different individuals within different groups, or relative to different roles and relationships within the same group. What a monumental contribution that would be! Basing your study on an analysis of national character. An extraordinary achievement. Despite the failure of your marriage. Despite your son's suicide. To define once and for all and quite irrefutably the problem of predictability in human behaviour. What can be known and what cannot. This would be extraordinary. The children of many famous people have committed suicide. Joyce. Hugo. The Italian vocation, for example, I am suddenly rehearsing very urgently – the Italian vocation for stalemate within conflicts apparently fluid will always characterise group dynamics in this country. Always. My wife always flaunted the relationship with Gregory, but was never clear as to its content. It never led to anything. And on the larger European canvas that Italian trait will always thwart the Anglo-Saxon thrust for clarity, always leave the English excluding themselves from arrangements they find ambiguous. Why do you mind so much about my seeing Gregory? she demanded – Schengen would be another example – she would be painting on her lipstick, trying on a hat. He's the only Englishman I know who speaks decent French. The contribution I can make is enormous, I reflect. But how much time do I have to do it? How much time? Usually an hour, Giorgio is wittering on, from here to my client in Asti. A man who has suffered a serious heart attack. A man who has undergone extensive bypass surgery. Then another twenty minutes along the *statale*. Would I ever get another chance to interview Andreotti? Who is himself perhaps at death's door. Pushing eighty. All downhill now, Giorgio is saying. My wife nodding. And now she says: It was so kind of you to come, Giorgio. So generous of you. Such a help. Suddenly I lean forward between the two seats. I am almost standing up in the Mercedes. I'm on my feet. And I yell: I left my pills in the suitcase! I haven't got my pills!

I haven't got my pills, I insist, speaking Italian obviously. Yelling Italian. I have often reflected on this switch of language whenever I move from thought to speech. My heart pills! I yell. The heparin. For Christ's sake! You're being ridiculous, I tell myself. I'm shaking. The heparin! I left it in the suitcase. And the charger for my mobile, it now occurs to me. In the suitcase. How am I going to charge my mobile? It has often occurred to me how ridiculous I make myself when I move from thought to speech. My marriage has been conducted in Italian, but I continue to think in English. I'm sorry, I tell Giorgio, sitting back. Something cuts against the grain. We're so upset, I explain. I just realised I haven't taken my pill. My medicine. It's for preventing blood clots, I explain to Giorgio. Heparin. I'm so sorry, my nerves are on edge. The old heart. I'll need a laxative too. This has all been so awful. It's so good of you to come. My wife makes no comment, tight-lipped. You'll be able to get some at the hospital, Giorgio says. My wife does not remark that it is not a hospital, but a closed community for chronic schizophrenics, most of whom are notoriously healthy. Physically. They won't have heparin there. Give me the tickets and I'll phone the airport about the suitcase, Giorgio offers. You can see he relishes these practical details, these little things he can do. My wife says absolutely nothing. Is she worried about my heart or not? And I'm back on my seat. I sink back. It was a mistake, I reflect, to imagine I had recovered my balance and composure. My lucidity. A big mistake. I would never have burst out like that if I had truly recovered my balance. My composure. Perhaps you are more upset than you give yourself credit for.

Giorgio drives on. My wife says nothing. In only an hour or so we are to see Marco's body. His physical body. Where will the marks of the screwdriver be? I watch the traffic. The headlights and rain. I wish I was driving. When you are driving, I suddenly reflect, exhausted by my ridiculous outburst, the mind is occupied in a narrow and sensible way. When you are driving the mind is an obvious ally in the straightforward business of survival. Gauging distances, gauging braking speeds. Whereas sitting on a plane or on the back seat of a car, it occurs to me, the body is trapped and disorientated. You are denied activity. The mind paces about like a predator. It talks to you incessantly. How incessant the words are, Marco told me once. One of his moments of clarity, they were the saddest. Words in English, words in Italian. But when you are driving, the mind joins forces with you. It rails and shouts at the other drivers. It caresses the car. It savours the elasticity of the wheel, the sensitivity of the pedals. It reads the lights, the speed, the temperature, the road. A world where everybody is always driving would be a happy world, I reflect. In the teeth of the environmentalists. A world of minds happily engaged, I reflect. In steering and accelerating and braking. Happily at home in their bodies. Happily railing at each other, without ever speaking. Separate and complicit. I never minded driving up to visit Marco, I remember, even when Vanoli insistently advised my wife to try a period without visits. I never minded the long hours at the wheel, her sombre presence beside me. When they locked him away in Turin. Even when I was ill, even when my chest was bursting with pain, I didn't mind driving. Perhaps my happiest moments with my wife, I reflect, have been when she tells me where to drive and I have driven her there. She told me to drive to our son. She never learned to drive. Though it would have been nice to take the opportunity to go over to Paola's. It was quite ridiculous to drive up from Rome to Turin without making the very small detour necessary to visit Paola in Novara. For two years we drove weekly from Rome to Turin without ever visiting Paola and Giorgio in Novara. Only half an hour away. And sitting in the back of Giorgio's Mercedes now speeding up the autostrada towards Turin, it occurs to me that my relationship with Paola, dear Paola, is the one personal relationship in my life that has always worked. This waif of a girl picked up in the Ukraine, as if in a market, or purchasing contraband cigarettes, this girl is the one and only person in all my life whose company has always brought me pleasure, and whom I have never let down. I must see her.

Leaning forward I ask, quite unmistakably this time, even menacingly: How is Paola? How's my girl? And knowing this will irritate my wife I ask, Is she going to meet us at the hospital?

Giorgio stares at the road. He says, Paola and I have split up.

V

Dottor Vanoli is planning to leave his wife for a young and beautiful woman. He says. I have been invited to his home to discuss the matter. It is less sumptuous than I imagined. If I wasn't shown in by Vanoli himself, I would say I was in Paola's flat. The layout of the rooms is the same. Even the kitchenette. It is drab, but in the circumstances I couldn't afford anything better. The wife is hovering behind him. We are so grateful you could come. She is fussing. My coat. My hat. Then I discover the girl on the sofa. The mistress. Isn't this rather jumping the gun? I persuade the wife to leave the room while we talk. I have always found it useful to divide people up before talking to them. The girl's presence has galvanised and disconcerted me. I am thinking fast, as when one used to come home to find Gregory on the sofa with a glass of gin and tonic in his hand. This is sheer provocation, I tell the doctor in a low voice. But Vanoli objects that on the contrary everything should be out in the open. His children have grown up. He owes it to his wife to bring his mistress along. I am perplexed. I was expecting to be consulted. If he has already decided, why invite me? The girl is less attractive than I imagined. Decidedly so. Vanoli is making a mistake, I tell myself. With all the pretty girls there are in Rome, this is madness. The short fashionable haircut frames a coarse face. Attractive only in youth, I tell myself. This is a familiar pattern of thought. The wife, on the contrary, has a noble face. Albeit scored by age and tears. I expected to be consulted, I tell Vanoli. I can't understand why you invited me if not to consult me. I am paying five thousand a minute. But Vanoli protests that he hasn't decided at all. Far from it. To bring things out in the open is not to decide, he says, just a necessary precursor of decision. We haven't decided at all, Mr Burton. We wanted your opinion.

Well, I'm on the sofa. I have a whisky in my hand. How pleasant, I reflect, crossing my legs on the sofa, a whisky in my hand, to be asked for an opinion! I haven't felt so at ease in years. To think of Vanoli, rather than yourself, going through a crisis like this, leaving his pleasant wife of noble physiognomy for a chit of a girl. A girl with nothing on Karen, for example. Imagining he can bring things out in the open like this, humiliating his wife like this, without seriously prejudicing the outcome of events. Nowhere near as beautiful as Karen. Is he Italian or what? And I lean forward, swirling my whisky, and quote Samuel Johnson: If marriage partners were chosen at random from the public registrar, I quote, the overall level of weal and woe would not be greatly altered. Samuel Johnson, I tell him. An important figure in my chapter on British character types. I sit back. The girl still hasn't spoken. Probably hasn't understood. Younger than Karen was. Definitely less attractive. To think of Vanoli of all people, Italy's foremost psychiatrist, making the mistake you didn't. This is an illusion, I tell the man. Rather brutally. I'm leaning forward again. Your wife is your destiny, I tell him. Do you see? The important thing is to think of her as chosen. By the public registrar for example. Not your responsibility. By some other power. You are not responsible for your unhappiness, I tell Vanoli. Even God. His beard is as well trimmed as ever, his eyes as small and clear. This has always annoyed me. Even if you leave her, Doctor, which I predict you will not, you will continue to feel that she is your destiny. Vanoli shows no sign of emotional stress. How annoying that is. You are hurting your wife for nothing. Understand? You should never have told her. You could have enjoyed this young woman and she you without destroying your wife. I have learned enough from Italians to know that. I'm surprised at you. Vanoli keeps his faint air of superiority. You merely wish to force a crisis for your own psychological well-being, I elaborate. You love your wife, I'm shouting at him. You are a team! Understand? Understand the word team? Vanoli is unflinching. I am in love with Nadia, he says.

Then I'm overwhelmed by the folly of it. This is folly, I tell myself. All around me people are committing the gravest of follies. Paola, Paola, Paola. Even the bathroom is like hers. I am just about to explain to Vanoli, who should know better, the nature of his madness, my reasons for prescribing Thorazine, that will do the trick, even if he will be sleepy for much of the day, when the guests begin to arrive. One two three four. They arrange themselves on rows of chairs. There's a crowd and music is playing. A hoarse voice. *Non posso non ricordarmi di te*. I have been invited to speak on the subject of national character and destiny. A decidedly hoarse singing voice. *Non posso pensare che l'amore non c'è*. How I love public speaking. Though nervous to start with. Montesquieu insisted on the importance of climate. The hoarse voice strains on. A radio presumably. And likewise Leopardi. I should ask them to turn it off. How is it, Leopardi asked, that the warmest and most vivacious of national characters, the Mediterranean Italian, is also the coldest and most calculating? Produced the likes of Machiavelli. The most calculating and cynical? These were Leopardi's words, I told my wife, not mine. More or less. I liked Machiavelli. A man much maligned. Paradox ties the knot at the heart of character. But what I am going to insist on today, I sip my whisky to make my audience wait, is the importance of language. Take this song for example. *Non posso non*, etc. – 'Can't help remembering you'. This false song, with its hoarse voice and tortured tribute to the great god love. *Non posso credere* . . . This fake song – 'Can't believe that love is gone'. Suddenly I am in a dark space, people are coming and going, the music coming and going. Footsteps approach along the corridor. A long, long corridor. *Non posso non ricordarmi di te*. Every time I return to Italy, I tell myself, I tell my audience, every single time, there is always a hoarse voice on a radio somewhere singing a hoarse and tortured tribute to love. Lost love. A fake tribute. Always. A voice that strains to strain. Every nation endlessly sings itself the same song, I tell the hospital staff arranged on a huddle of seats in Vanoli's front room. Do you understand what I'm trying to say? The momentum of national character is in the language, I tell these doctors. They are laughing. It surfaces, flowers, in certain songs, certain cadences. These hoarse and irretrievably false love songs – I am obliged to raise my voice – are entirely typical of the Italian mentality. Every time I am in Italy, I am immediately aware of these songs. Lost warmth cynically retrieved as merest rhetoric. Lost passion redeployed for merest self-interest. I am struggling in the dark with the words of the song coming and going along the corridor. This will be the burden of my second chapter. Language is of its nature a closed system, I tell the sniggering public. The same way the minds of each of your patients present so many closed systems. Do they not? Talking to themselves. Marco was forever talking to himself. Or rather: *being talked to by themselves*. Languages talk to themselves, I insist. Through us the language talks to itself. To explain Italian in English, for example, is always to have an English explanation. That is the folly of Gregory's book. Of all travel books. We are surrounded by folly. English elaborates Englishness, I struggle to explain. How can a man ever *explain* his wife, his foreign wife, or vice versa for that matter? But all wives are foreign. Or son? You cannot marry a woman in one language and think in another, I told Vanoli once. But we all do. Globalisation is meaningless, I insist. And I told Vanoli how the only affair I ever had that ever meant anything was with an English girl. We spoke English. Karen was much prettier than your blonde. Half black, I boast to Vanoli. Incredible skin. English mind, foreign smell. Whereas my wife spoke to her lover in French. A very Italian thing to do. A sort of ultimate rhetorical flourish, to speak to your lover in another language. Where the words are fresher even if the sentiment isn't. Gregory fell in love with her because he was speaking to an Italian woman in French, or so he told me. So he told me. Gregory actually *told* me. His French was better than his Italian. In a hotel bar in Palermo. A hundred paces from where a prominent politician was gunned down in cold blood. Andreotti may have been involved. I'm in love with your wife, he told me. The essence of Andreotti is that he may or may not have been involved in everything. A mystery. A closed system. You will be aware, Signor Presidente, that you are surrounded by a veil of mystery. But did you actively cultivate this? Your notorious secret files, for example. My wife kept a diary in French. Their love language. No, a proper knowledge of language, I insist to the doctors gathered in Vanoli's front room, is essential in the study of national character and national destiny. Psychiatrists should be linguists. Politicians should be linguists. The language *is* the national destiny, I shout. Its evolution, the future. I am yelling now. The doctors laughing. And with an overwhelming sense of frustration, a huge pain in my chest, I realise at last that I am speaking to my audience in English. Somehow my Italian – I had imagined it was Italian – is English. They are laughing among themselves, uncomprehending. Vanoli is cuddling his girl. I'm furious. My chest is bursting. And suddenly I am wide awake.

I am wide awake on the lower bunk bed in my grand-daughters' room, and my first thought on returning to myself from this strange and strangely vivid dream is that *Marco was always praised for being everything I was not.* My heart is beating fast. I need to breathe. I have not taken my heparin. Marco was always praised for being *in every way* different from yourself, I remember, immediately upon waking from this vivid dream. By your wife that is. As if his birth, I told Vanoli, were a question of *parthenogenesis.* My wife always spoke of his birth as a miracle. My wife bought an ex voto and placed it beside the Madonna in Santa Maria degli Angeli. A small heart-shaped shield with Marco's date of birth engraved in silver. That was understandable. I come to see you alone, I told Vanoli, because otherwise I would have to watch my wife seducing you. So you seduce me instead, he laughed. She would light a candle there, on his birthday. Every birthday. But why this thought after this dream? Parthenogenesis. Conception without fertilisation. And why this dream when it is the opposite of the truth: why Vanoli leaving his wife when it is I who have left mine? You have left your wife, I remind myself, amazed, lying on a child's bed in the dark. Left your wife after all these years. The shutters are closed behind a curtainless window, but in the socket by the door a nightlight spreads a red glow. From the bed above comes the sound of soft, even breathing. A child's gentle breathing. I am in my granddaughters' room. Why that thought, I ask myself, after that dream? The thought as vivid as the dream: Marco always praised for being everything you were not. Where are the connections here? The famous *bandhu*. And this the very morning after leaving your wife. I have left my wife. At least you didn't dream of your wife, I tell myself. At least you didn't dream of your son.

Your son has been taken to the *policlinico*, Mr Burton.

The rain had eased somewhat. My wife has this way of sending me on ahead, as though acknowledging that I am the more practical, only to storm in later when I fail to achieve whatever it is I should. There were storm clouds over low hills, a rolling mist. In staring twilight I hurried across a few yards of asphalt to the main steps. A seventeenth-century villa with a finely landscaped park is now a closed community for chronic schizophrenics. There is even a bell pull. I told the nurse I didn't understand.

For the post-mortem, Mr Burton. We don't have the facilities here.

The patients were eating their dinners. My wife has sent you ahead, I remember thinking in the stone-flagged entrance to this beautiful but unrenovated villa, precisely in order to storm in a few minutes later. You announce your wife, I thought. You go before her, like John the Baptist. This is part of her way of moving heaven and earth. Her relationship with you is part of her strength. And what greater telluric movement could there be, I reflect, lying here in the strangest of moods in my granddaughters' room, the soft red glow and slow gentle breathing imposing a fragile calm on an otherwise frantic mind, what greater movement than birth by parthenogenesis? Or raising a boy from the dead? Was Christ's birth a case of parthenogenesis? Conception without fertilisation. Certainly

71

it required sending someone ahead. Most likely it pointed to his resurrection. But these are facile connections, I tell myself. No, it is quite facile to go on generating connections that don't mean anything at all. To look for analogies that don't mean anything at all. And isn't it shameful that even your dreams contain no sign of grieving for your son? In your dream, I suddenly reflect, lying quite still in my granddaughters' room and at the same time intensely aware that in all likelihood my wife is still at his side, still at this very moment sitting in the mortuary in the *policlinico* in Turin, beside his body, weeping over our son's body, praying over his body, as once other women planned to weep over Christ's – but such connections are quite ridiculous, if not pernicious – in your dream there is no sign at all of your son – you could have dreamed this dream any night, I tell myself, any night you want – and above all no sign of his body, your son's body, which was so athletic, your wife always said, so unlike your own she meant. Did my wife, I am suddenly reflecting, miss even one of his basketball games? Ever? Did she ever miss lighting that candle? In Santa Maria degli Angeli. On his birthday. The miracle of his birthday. Basketball is a sport I never understood. Paola was hopeless at sport. Marco was everything you could never be, my wife said. Marco is obese, I told her.

He isn't here then? I asked. Voices echoed along the corridor. At any moment, I predicted, my wife would come storming in. Why had she stayed in the car, thinking as she did that the body was here, if not to storm in after the shortest of intervals?

Would you like to talk to Dottor Busi? the nurse asked. I'm worried about my wife, I said. My wife doesn't know it was suicide. Dottor Busi mustn't tell my wife it was suicide. Then my wife stormed in. Where was her son? There is a payphone in the entrance to this once noble villa, now a closed

72

community for chronic schizophrenics. Its orange casing is clamped to the wall beside a radiator. I have frequently called Paola from here – the line is better than from the mobile – while my wife walks arm in arm with Marco in the ample grounds. The grounds are very beautiful, Vanoli said. She always walked arm in arm with Marco, rested her head on his tall shoulder, caressed his hands. A number of my patients have made big improvements there, Vanoli said, though later I realised his intention had been to get the boy as far away from his parents as possible. I looked at the phone. Why on earth were Paola and Giorgio splitting up? I wondered as my wife came rushing in and demanded to know where our son's body was. Vanoli had reckoned without our travelling eight hundred miles in the car every week. Four hundred there, four hundred back. We saw him every week, I remind myself. Overcoming considerable obstacles. And how is it that others split up so easily and we do not? How many times have friends, colleagues, relatives, even strangers told me: My wife and I have just split up, My husband and I have just split up, as if this were the most natural thing in the world? And immediately I ask myself, And us? We stayed together to visit Marco, I tell myself, lying here in the red glow of a child's nightlight. To drive eight hundred miles a week. She walked arm in arm with him in the grounds, like a lover I often thought, while I made phone-calls from the hospital. There can be no point in our staying together now that Marco is dead.

My wife stood in red coat, green hat, demanding to know. She was trembling. Her make-up had smudged. She is as afraid as you are yourself, I told myself. She is biting her lips. I felt sorry for her. Afraid to see the body. But quite determined. A post-mortem is a necessary formality, the nurse said. In these cases. We don't have the facilities here. He's been taken to Turin. To the general hospital. And she repeated. Would you like to speak to Dottor Busi? We will go straight to the *policlinico*, I said. How could Busi speak to us without recalling that it was suicide? Without explaining what had happened. How was it my wife still hadn't asked what had happened, hadn't enquired as to the cause of death? It is rare for my wife not to attend to her make-up. Like many Italians she is a person intensely aware of her physical appearance, her physical attractions. I love her for that. I took my wife by the hand and pushed the door, and for the second time that day she allowed herself to be led like a child. As if under shock. For the second time that day I covered her head with my jacket. It was raining again. The reason you must leave your wife, I reflect, lying here in the soft red calm of my granddaughters' room, or rather, the reason you *have* left your wife, you left her last night, is that she generates such contorted thoughts in you, such a tension of love and frustration. Why didn't you tell her immediately that it was suicide? How could you not foresee the tension that omission would generate? Has she found out now, sitting beside his body? Giorgio looked at the clock on the dashboard. Twenty minutes, he said. Traffic permitting.

The floor is strewn with toys. In a moment I must get up to pee. My eyes have grown accustomed. There is some kind of xylophone. But I cannot interest myself in children's toys. Like cooking, I tell myself, lying somewhat uncomfortably in my granddaughter's narrow bed, toys were a territory your wife very early claimed as her own. Did I ever buy toys? Did I ever cook? I was encouraged not to, then blamed for having failed to do so. Your whole married life, I tell myself, turning on my side to look down on a pink clutter of dolls and crayon drawings, you would be encouraged not to play the family man, then blamed for not doing so, encouraged not to buy toys – I'll get the presents, I like doing that – then reminded that you hadn't. In the presence of Gregory Marks, perhaps, with his gin and tonic on the sofa. For years your wife showed no sign of minding your sleeping under Paola in the kids' room, in Marco's narrow bed, as now you are sleeping under Maria Cristina in Martina's narrow bed, your granddaughters, only to remark acidly on the fact during the otherwise gayest of dinner parties. Her dinner parties. They were excellent. Her determined social life. Oh, he'd rather sleep on his own in Marco's bed, my wife laughed across the dinner table. She flirted. Her raucous side. It was a considerable concession on her part to come to England. Never mentioning of course that she had Marco in hers. That it actually began with Marco in hers. Is that where it began? Was she aware of the hypocrisy there? Throughout your married life, I reflect, your wife has always underlined, in private conversation with yourself, the importance of your career, encouraged you to pursue your career wherever it might take you, whatever absences such a career might imply, insisted on the generosity of her support, on your need to fulfil a considerable talent, only then to show the most exaggerated respect and interest in a man whose work is clearly inferior to yours, his vision in every way inferior to yours, merely because he speaks passable French and is official correspondent of the BBC. In Rome. And thus a man in direct competition with yourself, a man who had taken a job for which you yourself were better qualified and in every way better suited than he. Only to tell you quite contemptuously in the corridor of the Policlinico di Torino that you never cared about anything but your work, your career. Where did this rancour begin? Why didn't you tell your wife it was suicide? She doesn't know what she wants perhaps, Karen would say. Dear Karen. Would she play photographer, if I had the courage to ask? Would she? And many years later I remember saying to Vanoli: Sometimes I think the problem with my wife is that she doesn't really know what she wants. And you? he asked. He was behind his big desk, which somehow reinforces the enigma of his smile. Do you know what you want? Then Vanoli said: She seems very clear about what she wants when she speaks to me, Signor Burton. She wants your son to get better. She phones you then? I asked. She makes an appointment from time to time, he said. Just as you do. I imagined you knew. We were supposed to be discussing the possibility of his giving Marco a reference for some menial job. So this must have been before the trial. Some hopelessly menial job. School caretaker I think. Vanoli looked at me from his small bright eyes, far away behind his desk, and as always he had that irritating complacency of one who is wondering when on earth you will begin to see the obvious. When she sees me, Mr Burton, it is quite clear that she wants Marco to get better, he repeated. After all, it is her life he makes a misery. It's she who has to wash what he fouls. Vanoli paused. Despite the Thorazine, our son was getting worse. My wife was too embarrassed to let the cleaning woman see the sheets. It would be more convenient, perhaps, Vanoli said, if we could all speak together.

I've left her, I told Paola. I was speaking from a payphone on the platform at Torino Porta Nuova. That was the longest lapse, I tell myself now, lying very still on the bunk bed beneath the elder of my two granddaughters, gazing at their dolls and drawings in the red glow of the nightlight, my heartbeat almost back to normal now. In a moment I must get up to pee. Between the *policlinico* and the phone on the platform. Almost an hour. *Cosa, Papà?* The line was surprisingly clear, but she hadn't understood. Presumably I had taken a taxi. I've left your mother, I said. Unless Giorgio brought me. Now, she asked? For good? And I repeat that question to myself, stretched out on this small bed in this tiny room in the nondescript suburbs of Novara. Now? For good?

What time is it now? She will still be sitting with Marco, she will sit all night with Marco. She won't even have realised I am not outside the door. My wife doesn't know her husband has left her.

We were directed, misdirected, through a maze of corridors. Giorgio had gone to phone the airport about the luggage. My heparin. The charger. When suddenly it occurred to me, quite inappropriately, what a different experience airports and hospitals are. Airports the world over, I couldn't help thinking as we hurriedly followed an orderly's directions, are the same bright kaleidoscope of neon and consumer goods, while hospitals the world over – the thought came to me quite uninvited as we turned first left and then right – are a dingy, under-funded maze of linoleum corridors, grey screens, white coats and peremptory warnings. No difference between England and Italy here, I thought. My wife was tight-lipped, deathly pale, rejecting the hand I offered. Our whole society I suddenly thought, offering my wife my hand – it was the kind of thing I would once have written an article about – could be understood in terms of the different environments we create in airports and in hospitals. Though before the illumination that led to my repudiation, my final repudiation, of journalism, any such article would have been a rather superficial and spurious thing. All my early work was superficial, I thought, following my wife down the twisting corridors of Turin's *policlinico*. How could it be otherwise? She is still wearing her red coat, her green hat. She still walks with the same brisk elegance. Spurious remarks on priorities and spending policies. I have often yearned for my wife when seeing her from a distance, walking with such elegance, brightly dressed, brightly made up. Spuriously endorsing the superficial notion that politicians could and should change the world. Until that evening in the Hotel Garibaldi with

Gregory. My illumination. Which came after a sleepless night thinking about my marriage and about Gregory and about a mafia murder and Andreotti. All my intellectual development has to do with my wife, it occurs to me. Or rather, the mystery of my wife. Airports and hospitals are at the opposite extremes of our aspirations, I thought, hurrying down a long corridor with frosted windows on one side and a maze of pipes on the other: the wishful departure, the ineluctable point of arrival. And now there is so little time left to do anything with what you have learned. The Andreotti interview is dead, I thought. You must get hold of some heparin. Suddenly my wife stopped. We were standing in front of a shiny Madonna, a heap of flowers at her feet. The flowers were packaged in shiny bouquets. Shiny with cellophane. Italians love cellophane. I had written that somewhere. In some spurious article. They love shiny surfaces and hoarse, love-struck voices. These are reflections I have frequently made about Italy: baroque the first example of kitsch, for example. Flowers not permitted in ward, read a peremptory warning, and I realised we were in Maternity. They had directed us to the mortuary via Maternity. My wife stood perfectly still. Again I tried to take her hand. She was already moving on ahead.

Your wife was remembering your son's birth, it occurs to me now in my granddaughters' room, still trying to understand into what situation exactly I have awakened. The floor is strewn with dolls. I need a pee. She was remembering the grace granted and the candles. The ex voto. But what exactly was said? I ask myself. What was said to make you choose such a moment to leave your wife? No, that *compelled* you to leave your wife. One does not choose such things. Surely if one chose such things, chose whether to leave or not, one would have left ages ago. Or at least chosen. Suddenly there is a lapse, a taxi ride perhaps, and you are standing on a platform in Torino Porta Nuova telling your daughter you have left your wife. You were compelled to leave your wife. But why? There is a clock that is an elephant's face on a low wicker chest. It is quarter to three. I won't be able to sleep again unless I pee. And absurdly I remember that the elephant never forgets. How difficult it is to be clear about anything, I remark, in a mind that never stays still. Yet I seem remarkably composed. Unravelling the past, I tell myself with remarkable composure, is like unravelling a lost dream. I don't know anything about Vanoli's marital status. Why did I have that dream? Why did I persuade a man to stay with his wife when I have just left mine? Remembering and forgetting amount to very little, I reflect, remembering my wife remembering the miracle of her son's birth, on our way to the mortuary. It doesn't amount to much. Not when it comes to understanding. As if by parthenogenesis, I would tell people, to make light of it, to turn it into a joke. My wife would be boasting at one of her dinner parties about how different her son was from his father. *A son in every way different from his father*, she said. It was my first thought on waking. His birth was a miracle, she claimed. You had nothing to do with your son, she shouted outside the mortuary. Nurses passing did not even turn. There was a radio on behind a door left ajar, the duty-nurse's room, and a hoarse voice, entirely fake, straining to regret. A son – the old reflection flashes back – who in *so many ways* became a weapon to be used against yourself. With that thought my composure is gone. That thought always terrifies me. You move from calm to terror in no time. But I told myself that yesterday. I need to pee. Your wife's relationship with Marco became a constant reproach, I reflect, staring at Jumbo's Play Clock, trying to decide if it is working. What should have been a blessing became a curse. Toys always have English names. Why? And why these thoughts on waking from that dream? Your son became a means of expressing your wife's rancour. That much I understand. But rancour about what exactly, if it began long before Karen? Long before. My wife never knew a thing about Karen. I would never have brought Karen home and sat her on the sofa. Her dark skin against my wife's pink sofa. It is curious, Vanoli said, that your wife would agree to sending your son to an English-speaking school, if, as you suggest, she saw the child as a means of vendetta against yourself. Ten to three. The truth is, I reflect, that we always vied to think of ways of showing our concern for Marco. How much we would do for Marco. In a way we did not for Paola. We had done so much for Paola just adopting her. And it was the vying that mattered perhaps, not Marco. Why was it so important, for you, I wonder, that your son speak English? Why did it matter so much? Paola doesn't speak English and you love her just the same. It has never occurred to you not to love her. It has never occurred to you to vie over Paola. And why were you so excited the day Marco began to speak English in the home, to *impose* English in the home on his *cara mamma* who had always refused to learn so much as a word? He came back from Milan for the weekend, from the university, his first and last year at university, and refused to speak to her in anything but English. Why do you laugh when you tell me that? Vanoli asked. Suddenly you were laughing with your son. The son you had given up for lost, given up as exclusively his mother's. I could not be interested in basketball. Football perhaps, but not basketball. And now his mother, who knew all the players in every team, was sitting there at the dinner table, deathly pale, tight-lipped, beaten. Your wife, I told myself, watching her across the table that day, that evening, is completely stunned by Marco's decision to speak English and only English in her presence. He is refusing to speak to her in Italian. With one simple, albeit quirky decision, I realised, your son has achieved something you have never managed. Your son has brought your wife into line. As if you were born by parthenogenesis, I joked to him, telling him the old story. We were in a bar in the Parioli. No one as yet had thought of his strange behaviour as a *symptom*. And in a perfect English that was at once an impersonation of my own, yet better somehow, more English than my English, posher anyway, he said, Oh, but I'm far more like you than her, Dad. I'm far more like you. You should fuck somebody else Dad, he said, the way she treats you. I was taken aback. But still thought it was just the drink. Father and son were drinking together. Beers. We were in a bar in the Parioli. When had we ever gone out to bars before? He had given up his basketball. University had changed him. He was more like me than her, he insisted. You should fuck somebody else, he said. I was silent. Mamma's always with your friend Gregory, he said. He leaned across the table. His face was getting fatter now he had stopped training. He is eating enormously, I thought. You should fuck who you want, he leered. It was unpleasant. Why don't you? For the first time I was afraid. I phoned Karen about it. Our lives are separate now, she said. You must think of me as just another person. It was shortly after that, I told Vanoli, from a hotel room in Palermo, that he began smearing the sheets with shit.

I have stood up to pee, picking my way between toys. My granddaughter is snugly asleep. How many times has one picked one's way between toys in the night, experiencing that celebrated cocktail of affection and envy on seeing a child's face in sleep. A combination of emotions widely celebrated in films and books. How can they sleep, you wonder, looking at the child's face, while the mind beside them, watching over them, is clanging with alarm? The smooth forehead, the lips just parted, the gentleness of the little girl's breathing. In here, the duty-nurse said. There was a large double door. I was surprised by the lack of occasion. We were to walk in and see our son's body, just like that, without ceremony or preparation. Later he'll be moved to the *camera ardente*, she said. They've offered you no preparation for this moment, I told myself, suddenly rigid with alarm now the event was upon us. We were to see our son's body. In the Turin *policlinico*. They must imagine you have spoken to each other, I thought, your wife and yourself, or to somebody else. To Busi. They must imagine you are prepared. When she discovers it is suicide, I told myself, her reaction is bound to be punitive. Then a voice called along the corridor. A doctor was standing by the half-open door, whence faint music, an elderly couple beside him. Bed three, the nurse said. But what preparation could there ever be, I ask myself, feeling for the light in a cluttered little bathroom, for seeing a son's dead body? Watching him in sleep? What can ever prepare consciousness for the absence of consciousness? In a loved one. What can prepare life for death? Not sleep. There is a sort of hum about a sleeping child, it occurs to me, waiting for the pee to come, my granddaughter's face still in my mind. As of electricity singing in a wire. The hum of the sleeping mind, the mind ticking over, rearranging the elements of its life in the kaleidoscope of dreams. Myself quoting Samuel Johnson to my son's psychiatrist. Vanoli posing the old conundrum of whether confession is a prerequisite for change. Should I have told my wife? When it ended with Karen? That was when your heart turned to stone. Should I have opened my stony heart to my wife? To my son? What did Marco understand from my silence? What did Marco ever understand about our marriage? Not sleep, I thought.

I don't want you to come in. It was my wife speaking. The nurse had gone. She shook off the arm I had tried to put round her shoulder. I wanted to protect my wife from the shock of seeing our son. Our dead son. There would be the wounds from the screwdriver. I don't want you to come in, she said. Go and see Giorgio about getting the suitcase back. For some reason the pee will not come. We were standing alone in the corridor by the double doors of the morgue. He was in bed three. Bed is surely the wrong word. Or had she actually said slab? I need to see him alone, she said. Her voice was extremely cold. I've things to say to him. He's dead, I said. I tried to be gentle. I didn't mention suicide. I've things to say to him, she repeated, alone. I don't want you to come in. And what are you going to say? I asked. She didn't say please, it occurs to me now, still standing over the loo in my daughter's flat. She didn't say, please let me be alone with him a little while. She presented it as an imperative. What did my son understand from the way my wife and I were together? Did he smell my fear? Are you going to tell him to get up and walk? I mocked. Are you expecting a miracle? I wonder why my mind moves in this way, why I am so gentle and then suddenly so brutal. She lowered her eyes. I don't want you to come in. I want to be alone with him. The voice was soft, my wife's softest voice, but the tone was one of command. She would not be disobeyed. Already she was turning to go in. He's my son too, I said. I have to see him. You can't tell me not to come in. But already – and for some reason I am obliged to admit this to myself, leaning over the lavatory in my daughter's house, waiting an unconscionably long time for this pee to come – already I was feeling the relief of sensing that I didn't have to go through with it. I didn't have to see the body. My wife didn't want me to. The whole question of suicide need not be discussed. As the whole question of unfaithfulness has never been discussed. Never, never been discussed. He's my son and I want to see him, I repeated. There's nothing you need to say alone to a corpse, I told her. I loved Marco, I said. I felt tears on my cheeks. Then my wife raised her voice. Her lipstick was orange today. Her mouth working. Though smudged. My wife's eyes are fierce. You cared nothing for Marco, she said. She raised her voice. You think of nothing but your career. She was shouting. Of your stupid book. Marco was everything you could never be, she shouted. She was suddenly shouting. I looked round, but nurses passing did not seem to have noticed. You did everything to get me away from him, she said. You got the doctor on your side. You care for nothing but your career, and England. You had him send us to England. And your ridiculous reputation. There is nothing honest about you, she was shouting. My wife was shouting at me quite openly in the hospital corridor outside the *camera mortuaria*. Two nurses walked right past us. Later they would move him to the *camera ardente*, the funeral chamber. After the post-mortem. And it occurs to me, leaning my hand on the tiled wall, wondering why the drops will not come, the pee will not flow, that we have never had a crisis quite like this before. There has never been a crisis where everything was said. Wasn't this the burden of that famous conversation with Gregory? The hotel in Palermo. Have it out, he said.

I said nothing. I was sitting on one of a row of chairs bolted to the wall outside the morgue. There was a coffee machine about ten yards down. I felt utterly exhausted, an unpleasant tension in my bowels. I cannot shit, I thought. And now I cannot even piss. Giorgio came. I was vaguely aware of music seeping from a nearby door. He had parked the car. How inappropriate all this is, I thought. Outside my head and in, everything is monumentally inappropriate. BA refused to fly your baggage without you on board, Giorgio announced. There were security regulations for passenger flights. I explained I was just sitting out for a few moments.

Then I'd go back in. My wife and I would take turns all night, I said. I felt quite exhausted, almost faint. I must find some heparin. You should go home, I said. They would be happy to send the suitcase freight, Giorgio explained, but I must decide whether I wanted it sent to Milan or Turin. What a dull fellow my son-in-law is, I thought, and very abruptly I asked him why on earth he and Paola had split up. I thought you were so happy. Your voice is still on the answering machine, I protested.

Giorgio stood in the corridor staring at me. His eyes are glassy. They bulge a little. His travelling rep's suit was crumpled. Giorgio was perplexed, I reflect now in this pokey lavatory, thinking back on something that had barely registered at the time, perhaps even shocked by your question. By its abrupt inappropriateness perhaps. When you should have been grieving over your son. Certainly there was a look of considerable surprise in his glassy eyes, under the neon in the corridor. I told them I'd phone back immediately, he said, to say whether you wanted it to go to Milan or Turin. Turin, I decided. Paola asked me to leave, he said, no doubt she will explain, and then I was alone in the corridor with the music still seeping from the half-open door of the duty-nurse's office. Unwillingly, I made out a few words. *Non posso non ricordarmi di te.* There is no end to bad music, I suddenly thought sitting uneasily on the chairs outside the mortuary. My wife had shut me out, cut me off from herself and our son. It was a hoarse voice, straining to regret. *Non posso pensare che l'amore non c'è.* Bad music flows from an inexhaustible source, I thought, the inexhaustible hypocrisy of the human spirit. If Benedetto Croce, I was suddenly thinking, sitting outside the mortuary where my son's body lay awaiting post-mortem, dreamed of an Italy purged of all rhetorical and sentimental romanticism, an Italy of unceasing but always constructive self-criticism, this could only be because he perceived that in nine cases out of ten the opposite qualities prevailed. It's not so much the words of this song that are awful, I thought, but the awful falseness with which they are being sung. And what's more a careless falseness. No, a flaunted falseness. But why on earth was I thinking this only moments after such an awful confrontation with my wife? Your brain suffers from a terrible inertia, I recognise, stepping back from the toilet bowl and sitting down on the edge of the bathtub. I am wearing Giorgio's green pyjamas. I presume they are Giorgio's. You go on thinking yesterday's thoughts as if the world hadn't suddenly and radically changed. As if your son hadn't killed himself, as if you hadn't finally walked out on your wife after thirty years of marriage. If Croce spoke so much of the need to rid Italy of the wrong kind of rhetoric, the wrong kind of sentiment, it was because he saw so well what a natural tendency the Italians had for it, knew even then that these false and horrendously hoarse love songs are entirely typical of the Italian mentality. Croce was familiar with these love songs, I thought. Could I ask Andreotti what he thinks of Croce? What his favourite songs are? Suddenly I was furious. I stood up and walked towards the duty-nurse's door, determined to have this music silenced. This music is obscenely inappropriate, I would tell the duty-nurse. I stopped. It is also obscenely inappropriate, I told myself, disorientated, that you are standing outside the mortuary thinking about Benedetto Croce instead of inside paying your last respects to your son. I was standing in the empty corridor, entirely disorientated, entirely frustrated. Then from nowhere, but in a soft clear voice, came the words: *What we do is always less and worse than what we are.*

The words had been spoken by someone else. Or at least so I thought. I looked around. No one. But despite that uncanniness, the idea was soothing. What we do is always less and worse than what we are. Repeating the words in my own voice, I felt soothed and steeled. My son, I told myself, picking up from that uncanny suggestion – where on earth had the words come from? – is better than the young man who has thrown away his talents and killed himself. This was obvious. My wife is better than the woman who flirts with everybody and is determined to exclude her husband from her grief. I had no doubt of that. Why would I love her otherwise? And you are better than the man who so often betrayed her, while terrified of betrayal himself, better than the man who didn't have the courage to tell her it was suicide, didn't have the courage to tell his wife that their son had savaged himself with a screwdriver. In what state of despair and self-loathing must one be, I asked, suddenly appalled to find myself face to face with the fact, to inflict such ferocious damage on oneself with such an unlikely weapon? With the briskness of one finally about to act, I turned away from the duty-nurse's door and back to the mortuary. I experienced – and I remember this perfectly now, sitting shivering here on the edge of the bathtub in my daughter's small flat – an extraordinary sense of clarity and urgency, turning briskly back to the mortuary door. An oneiric clarity. As when one sees oneself from some unimaginable vantage point in a dream. I must go in at once, I told myself, forming the words out loud, I must go into the mortuary and beg my wife that we behave like decent human beings. I could see myself doing it. Yes, the time has come for the great confrontation, I told myself. I sensed the drama. I must insist to my wife that I love her. I must remind her that she loves me. Why would we have tortured each other for so long if we did not love each other? I must beg my wife's forgiveness, I told myself, over our son's savaged body. Beg forgiveness for all the ways I have hurt her – was

87

this what Marco intended? Yes, and I must grant my wife, spontaneously and immediately, complete forgiveness for all the ways she has hurt me. It is over between us. I stood by the door. I must go in at once. I must.

Mi scusi, signore, a cracked voice asked, *è questa la camera mortuaria?*

I have turned on the hot tap. Perhaps a bath will help. Perhaps it's just extreme anxiety that does this to your bladder and bowels. I had forgotten about the Ferrantes. It was the Ferrantes made you leave your wife, I realise now, fishing out a small plastic boat, glancing through the various bottles for some bath oil. Theirs were the last faces before that longest of lapses. The lapse that ended with the phone-call to Paola from the station. Cedar Flakes. Nivea. Is this the mortuary? they asked. I told them it was. I think you are supposed to see the duty-nurse if you want to go in, I said. I pointed to the door where the hoarse voice had given way to the urgency of a news bulletin. Equally fake. The urgency of the voices that read us the news is just as fake as the voices that strain to regret. Later they move them to the *camera ardente*, I said. They sat down side by side on the row of bolted seats and at once their heads were together, arms around each other. I think you're supposed to see the duty-nurse, if you want to go in, I repeated as gently as I could. I immediately felt full of respect and tenderness toward them, so evident was their grief. Immediately the news gave way to the faint jangling of an advert. But the man shook his head. They were in their forties perhaps, the man almost completely bald, but sanguine, a look of drained vigour about cheeks and eyes. The wife's face must normally be prim, but was puffy now, and short-sighted, as if without her spectacles. Without her contact lenses perhaps. They held onto each other without any show. We're waiting for someone, the man said by way of explanation. Clearly it was useful for him to hear his voice. They haven't brought her yet. We have to wait. His wife pressed against him as he spoke, both offering and taking comfort. All this I remember very clearly. While in the background the radio was running through a sequence of ads. Why do we listen to things that are unsurpassably false? Our daughter, he said. The man needed to hear himself say these words. The wife held him tightly. Hear himself capable of saying these words. And for some reason I was reminded of the elderly couple at Heathrow who had offered us their seats. These people are a couple, I thought, stepping back from the door to the mortuary. They are a couple as we never can be. I am so sorry, I said. I pointed to the machine. Can I get you something? I asked. A coffee? Even before they shook their heads I knew it was a foolish offer. Why would they want coffee? But I was desperately eager to show my sympathy. Why is it, I ask myself now, slipping into the first shallow inches of hot water, that you were so desperately eager to show your sympathy for these two? So much so that you turned back from the mortuary door. Turned your back on your wife and son. On the great confrontation. The girl had been hit on her moped, the man said. A drunken bus-driver. Perhaps you read about it in the paper. Amelia Ferrante. They are a couple, I thought, turning brusquely away from the door. Whatever professions or confessions I make to my wife now, I told myself, turning away from what only a moment before had seemed the inevitable and decisive confrontation of my life, we can never become a couple like these two. There is nothing false or fake or rhetorical or sentimental in the suffering of this man and this woman, I told myself. And I realised that they had not even heard the radio with its tired grind of inanity. They weren't hearing it. A couple like this, I told myself, would never allow themselves to be distracted by something as inappropriate as a radio. At a time like this. So far are they from its falsity and inanity. One is what one allows to distract one, I thought. There is nothing false at all, I thought, or inane, in the way this man and this woman are suffering together. The woman was feeling in the man's coat pockets for some tissues. Whatever I say to my wife we could never be so candid, I thought. So genuinely supportive of each other. We can never make up for all the time we have lost, I told myself. And sitting here in the bath, the water steaming the mirror and tiled walls of this modest bathroom in the modest flat I bought for my daughter unbeknown to my wife who would never have agreed, who had fallen out so deeply with Paola that the two could not even speak, I realise, trembling, that it was this thought that did it: the lost time. The impossibility of reaching the candour I saw so beautifully exhibited before me. She had been in coma for some days, the man went on. It was in the papers. The woman's short-sighted eyes looked up at me, as if to see whether perhaps her husband wasn't speaking to the wrong person, to a person who would be upset, or who wouldn't understand. They are so lucky to have this intimacy in grief, I thought. And I wanted to tell them how lucky they were. The most appalling thing had happened to them – the doctors were now removing the kidneys to save someone else, the man said, and corneas – the most terrible and appalling thing, and yet they were lucky. Sitting in the bath, I remember wanting to tell them that. I wanted to interrupt the drivel of the radio to tell them how intensely I could feel their togetherness in this grief. How my wife and I would never achieve that. And, eyes shut now, sliding deeper into the water, I recall a book I read somewhere that claimed that one of the reasons why the mental patient tends to settle, irretrievably, into a chronic state after a period of four to five years is because any approach to sanity, at this point, merely makes the patient aware of how much he has lost. How many years had Marco been ill? I ask myself. Four? Five. A return to sanity, this book – one of the scores of books I have read on the subject – suggested, is a return to *the reality of irretrievable loss*, a truth so frightening as to be quite unbearable. The body would be brought down in just a few minutes, Signor Ferrante said. Did Marco kill himself, then, in a moment of sanity? I was suddenly asking myself. Standing outside the mortuary door. And not out of folly at all? On return from folly. To irretrievable loss. We would never be as this couple were, I thought. We are waiting to see her one last time, Signor Ferrante said. I repeated that I was sorry and fled.

I must have fallen asleep in the water. It is almost cold. Not sleep but that series of intense hallucinations from which the mind struggles to awaken, only to fall into the next. A slide show at first. You congratulate yourself on your control. Then the tumble into a world surely imagined by an alien mind. The bathtub full of worms and wood-shavings. Or I am trying to toss a line to a group of horribly misshapen children spilled from their rowing boat. The muddy river drags them off. What needless abundance and virtuosity in these images. What priceless pointless clarity. The last child's head is just a huge shrieking rotting mouth. Beyond the worst dreams of Hollywood. Beyond the most extravagant special effects. I turn on the hot tap. The room fills with steam. Perhaps I'll be able to pee now. I need to pee. I climb out of the tub, wrap myself in a towel, and then, moving to the toilet by the window, it seems I must be hallucinating again. Wake up! The steam is discovering letters traced by a finger on the window-pane. This must be a hallucination. Unless I wrote them myself. HELP ME. The letters slowly appear, called up by the steam. I watch fascinated, as I wait for my pee. HELP ME. In English. But surely I would remember if I had written them myself. Wake up! You *are* awake. Help me, someone has written on the bathroom window of the modest flat I bought some years ago for my daughter, my adopted daughter, and her dull but reliable husband. When I helped them to marry. Help me.

V I

It was the intuition of an infinite multiplication of detail which, while incarnating the spirit of history, or indeed reality, or even truth, nevertheless veils it, renders it forever opaque, or actually distracts the mind from it, that finally prompted my repudiation of journalism. This thought is darkly present to me as I sit at a table in Pasticceria Dante spooning the froth from a cappuccino and considering the face of a famous theatre director whose photograph is on the front pages of both *La Stampa* and *Corriere della Sera*. For years, it crosses my mind, glancing over the front pages of these two prestigious newspapers, or rather for decades, I daily reported on this story and that, analysing causes, motivations, repercussions, hinting at solutions, safeguards, appropriate sacrifices. The famous theatre director has died. Mine was the award-winning coverage of the Moro kidnap, mine the most revealing interviews with Sindona and with Gelli – published in Italian as well as English – mine the first photographs of the downed Libyan fighter presumably involved in the mystery of Ustica. One of the great geniuses of our time, the headline claims. I bite into my brioche. I was in Basilicata the morning after the great earthquake: I pulled corpses from the rubble, fed pastries to orphaned children, spent years stalking the relief funds. The Master Makes His Exit, says *La Stampa*. How predictable that is! I predicted Tangentopoli and the eclipse of the Christian Democrats. I exposed the incompetence behind Seveso and interviewed Pio Della Torre for *Time* only hours before his assassination. The Master Takes His Bow, says *Il Corriere*. It was inevitable one of the papers would say that. The mind is ever seduced by easy analogy. Until one spring afternoon, being shown the place where the pavement had yet to be sluiced of the blood of another assassination, the death of a politician known to be close to Andreotti, to this figure who more and more has come to be emblematic of all that remains obscure to me in a country that, though ever my sphere of operation, has never quite become my own, at this of all moments, this Palermo afternoon, precisely as everything I had predicted on the world's most prestigious pages at last began to happen – the collapse of the old regime, of which the victim that day was a prominent representative, the crumbling of one of the world's most elaborate and meretricious façades, whose shiny and enamelled surface the victim that afternoon had given his life to polishing – I suddenly lost interest. That spring afternoon in Palermo, shown the pavement and the blood, the outline where this lackey of Andreotti's had fallen, hearing the urgent voices of the reporters, the urgent voice of Gregory Marks, among others, addressing a camera, or cameras, the busy carabinieri forcing back the photographers, I suddenly understood that I had lost interest. What's more, that this loss had occurred some time before. Perhaps years before. Or at least I had lost interest in the details. I didn't want to tell the complicated story of shifting political alliances and oblique vendettas, didn't want to trace the victim's last movements or consider who was privy to his whereabouts. Didn't want to attend briefings, quiz colleagues, tease tip-offs from anonymous officials. Standing below a flight of steps outside a pompous public building, the blood of this prominent politician, arch lackey of Andreotti's, still thick on the pavement inside a cordon of carabinieri, I suddenly became aware of having no desire at all to speculate on consequences, analyse the present state of play in the war between the clans, pontificate on electoral repercussions, no desire whatsoever to find the urgent words journalism must daily find to feed the world's insatiable appetite for drama and for schadenfreude. And that this had been the case for some time. For some time, some long time, I told myself, you have been operating entirely mechanically, under the pressure of an old head of steam. Under the thrust of obsolete ambitions. But at last, that spring afternoon in Palermo, I understood that I was no longer interested. That these details were spurious. The blood the gun the motive. There was no end to them. There is no end to such details, I thought. There will always be more blood, better guns, nastier motives. You don't want to know who did it, I told myself, deigning no more than a glance at the blood almost black on the pavement before turning my back and returning to the hotel. No, the only thing I want to know, I told Gregory, finding ourselves, which was not unusual, together at the hotel bar late that evening, the only thing I want to know is what it is like inside Andreotti's head: when he attends mass early every morning and says his daily prayers, no doubt sincerely enough; when he appoints lackeys he knows are corrupt, no doubt astutely enough. What it was like, I said to Gregory, to be as Italian as Andreotti. How it was possible for the mind to entertain such paradox. Or rather to be founded upon it. Grounded in it. To get all its energy from it. From paradox. Nothing else interested me, I told my old rival. Gregory frowned. My candour has taken him by surprise, I thought. I have been drinking more than I usually do. More than even I usually do. This was before the bypass. Perhaps it was time to move on, he said, frowning. He seemed concerned. Vanoli would have laughed, it occurs to me this morning in the Pasticceria Dante. Vanoli treats you like a child who hasn't understood. But Gregory frowned, apparently concerned. Time you moved on, he said.

Unparalleled achievement, *Il Corriere* claims. How Italy loves its artistic heroes, I reflect, dusting sugar from my sleeve. The death of a theatre director would never have made the front pages in the UK. The banning of calculators from primary schools is far more important than the death of a theatre director. However great. In the UK. The greatest and loftiest theatre director of our time, says *La Stampa*. Italy needs to think of itself as producing men of genius, I reflect. This has occurred to me before. Writers and artists of genius. To compensate for the assassinations perhaps. Whereas England is happy to forget. Even theatre directors of genius. In England, it occurs to me, what really matters is that children do their sums in their heads, not that they become artistic geniuses. They have printed a poem this octogenarian theatre director wrote to his young mistress only a week before his stroke. It speaks of his premonitions of *la notte infinita, il silenzio eterno*. Predictably enough. The last card you can play to impress them, perhaps, is your closeness to the great divide. The thrill of imminent decease. An Ace of Spades. The great mind approaches the great divide. Would Karen go for that? Consciousness awaiting the extinction of consciousness. A call you might make? Here, from this café. Chat about the bypass. Our lives are separate now. How changed her voice was when she said those words. Drained of intimacy. Intimacy, I reflect, unable to shake the sugar from my sleeve, is something we generate with our voices, or fake with our voices. Singing into a microphone. Speaking into a mobile. Or simply exclude. With our voices. Stay to love me a little longer, the old man's poem concludes. The person with the problem staying a little longer, it occurs to me – I must get some heparin – was himself.

I have finished my brioche. A modest breakfast. I must find a doctor. What am I doing filling a stomach, however modestly, that will not empty? A bladder that will not empty. Help me, someone wrote on the bathroom window. Then the phone ringing at six a.m. I have taken my two granddaughters to school. And now for the second time this morning I am sitting in the Pasticceria Dante. Could I have written the words myself? For the second time this morning I am drinking cappuccino and eating brioche and reading the newspapers I affect to despise. A modest breakfast twice over. Like men who marry carefully twice. I smile. One affects to despise things, I reflect, but then continues to do them anyway. We are better than what we do. How strange that sense of being spoken to, as if from outside. In the nondescript corridor of a large municipal hospital. Was this what it was like for Marco? Voices outside, beyond control. Is this how one comes to write things on windows without being aware of it? Now there is a battle over the considerable inheritance. The woman who bore the genius theatre director's child, his only child, was lost to public attention many years ago. His first wife died in a car accident. Some claim it is not his child. His second, again childless marriage was annulled by the church but is still considered valid by the state. His mistress of six months' standing, a promising, they say, young dancer from a poor Polish family, speaks of a recent will in which he left everything to her. Why am I reading this article rather than the piece on the Andreotti trial? At least I might read something useful for my book. Why am I so eager to know what the motive for the marriage annulment was? My suspicion, I told Gregory, who had had his own marriage annulled, is that there is no communication between certain separate and sizeable parts of Andreotti's brain. This is his great achievement, I told Gregory, in the rather old-fashioned plush of the hotel bar in Palermo. The evening after the assassination. To have separated the right hand from the left. Irrevocably. As there is no communication, it occurs to me, between *La Stampa*'s article on the theatre director's achievements and, far more interesting, its exhaustive account of his private life. Unflagging pursuit of sublimity, says the first. Regardless of any will, the deceased's pension must be divided among the claimants in proportion to relative periods of cohabitation at whatever period of his life, remarks the second. A recent court ruling has laid down this principle. Two entirely contradictory motions of the spirit: sublimity, bureaucracy. That was Italy, I told Gregory quite late in the evening in the bar of an expensive hotel in Palermo. I was on expenses of course. Two entirely contradictory states of mind simultaneously entertained, I told him. A paradox that ties the knot of Italian character, I insisted. The sublime and the nit-picking. I wasn't interested in talking about the details of this assassination at all, I said. Time for you to move on, old chap, Gregory said. He seemed genuinely concerned. And my rival explained how his large and reputable organisation encouraged everybody to move on after four or five years, otherwise they lost their excitement in a place, their desire to tell, to narrate. This was important in journalism, Gregory said. It was a well-known phenomenon, Gregory insisted – we had both had quite a lot to drink – that after a certain period of time in the same place a journalist went stale. Your reporting went stale. You had to sound excited in broadcasting, he insisted. Urgent. In television. Why else would they have appointed him to his job when there were any number of people who knew Italy better than he? This was only his second assassination, he insisted. He was fresh. Yourself to start with, he confessed, earnestly. You know Italy far better than I do.

Gregory is a very earnest fellow, I reflect, wondering how I am able to sit and read newspapers in a pasticceria when my son is laid out in a nearby mortuary, when my wife, whom I have abandoned, is at this moment no doubt phoning number after number to find out where I am, when my health is on the brink of final collapse. A man ever intent on giving others their due. Gregory Marks. There is, I thought at the time and still do, a handsome, if unkempt candour about Gregory, a rugged, English, up-front frankness, qualities entirely compatible with the condescension inherent in giving others their due. It is not unlike love then, I joked. I was drinking too much. On expenses. A glow of interest slowly cooling, over what, five years, ten, until finally replaced by a single nagging irritation: what the fuck is going on inside her head? Time to move on! I laughed, as though entirely resigned, to disillusionment that is. Leopardi is good on disillusionment, I told Gregory. Journalism a sort of serial monogamy, I chuckled. Rome, Prague, Peking. Claudia, Sabina, Karen. I was laughing out loud. As though I had never expected anything better. The theatre director, it appears, set up the young mistress in his seaside villa, but then usually slept in hotels in Venice. But Gregory was not the kind to share in a little therapeutic misogyny. Oh you don't really believe that, he said. He looked intently, earnestly, into my eyes as only someone much younger than his age usually would. There is a terrible impertinence, I reflect, in insisting on looking into someone's eyes. On continuing to behave as if you were much younger than you are. As if eager sincerity were a staple of life, rather than a moment's gift, or aberration, sitting on a terrace, perhaps, overlooking the Bay of Naples. You just say that, he said, because it saves you from doing anything. You're not a real cynic, he said. Unsettled, I admitted perhaps he was right, though I still felt there was an analogy there. Analogous desires to go away, or go deeper. In journalism as in love. To repeat a superficial experience elsewhere or embark on a new one, however inscrutable, however unpromising, in the same place with the same person. The deepening of an old experience. All of a sudden I'm fascinated by analogies, I said. And like it or not, I boasted, my instinct is always to go deeper. I mean rather than to go away. Whether in one field or the other. It was a vain boast. Really, a lie. The challenge is to go deeper, I said, not to find another surface to slide over. I was quoting Montale, and proud of it. He wouldn't know that of course. I had drunk a great deal. We must go deeper, I insisted, quoting Montale, that's the thing. The BBC correspondent wouldn't know the Nobel poet. Until, having all the while stared into my eyes, Gregory said – and even as he spoke I was immediately aware, indeed a chill fell upon me, that my rival felt superior in his courage, proud to be the one who had finally beaten the culprit from the bush – Gregory said: Then I suppose at some point we shall have to talk about my being in love with your wife.

My wife had woken up Giorgio and got him to phone Paola. Having phoned and hung up twice herself, Paola said. At six and six-thirty. Martina was gathering things for school. Presumably it was my wife. Who else would phone and hang up so early in the morning? Maria Cristina appeared in bright pyjamas. A bright blonde little girl in bed-warm pyjamas. Brioches! Grandad's brought brioches for breakfast. From the pasticceria! Clapping of hands. Brioches! With cream! With jam! Grandad always knew how to get a kiss. I told him you were here, Paola said, but that you'd gone. My daughter, it occurs to me, wondering when I am going to move from my table in the Pasticceria Dante, my adopted daughter, doesn't look boldly into your eyes the way Gregory did that night, with the impertinent boldness of one determined to give you your due. But then nor does she refuse to look into your eyes, as your wife does, with that refusal born of fear and rancour, of having chosen to turn her bureaucratic side towards yourself and her yearning for sublimity elsewhere: to Gregory, to Marco, to the first Jehovah's Witness who comes to the door. No, Paola glances quickly at her father, her adoptive father, her eyes meeting yours for a moment, barely an instant, over the morning clutter of a child's clothes, to see how much can be said, to see if you are well, to say, I am here, but I don't impose, nor wish to be imposed upon. Was the problem that Giorgio imposed too much? I said you'd been, she said, but had already gone. You must have left terribly early. Paola has quick brown eyes. I didn't know where you were. The girls were tearing the paper bag with the brioches. My wife and I threw away the pleasures of family life, I reflect in the Pasticceria Dante, my mind's eye recalling the two little girls eagerly tearing open the bag of brioches I had brought them from this same pasticceria. A big white paper bag. Initially we wanted those pleasures, we moved heaven and earth for the right to have those pleasures, the pleasures of family life, but we grew bored. Moving heaven and earth was more exciting than the pleasures. We wanted something else. Then we wanted them back again. We needed them back. Those pleasures. But heaven and earth wouldn't move a second time. You move heaven and earth a first time, I thought, easily enough it seems in retrospect, but the second time you can't even imagine where to begin. To get back to what you got bored with. The girls were arguing over the biggest. Which is the biggest brioche? It is the thought of the wasted years that blocks the schizophrenic's return. I can't remember the title of the book I read that in. Probably mere speculation. I have read very little about schizophrenia that doesn't bear the hallmarks of the merest speculation. Paola said quietly: I suppose you left when you heard the phone ringing, Papà, didn't you? Her eyes came and went. If it had been you that answered, she wouldn't have hung up. Would she? Like the way she glances at your eyes, I reflect, there was nothing challenging about the way your daughter said this. It's me she doesn't want to speak to, isn't it? There was no accusation in her voice. And now you don't want to speak to her. I told her I hadn't been able to sleep. I had got up and gone out. The children's hair, over their pastries, was gold and brown. Only one, Paola scolded. You'll be sick Tina, she warned. Let them eat. I got them for you, I told my grandchildren. They're young, I told Paola. I see myself smiling, playing grandfather, generous grandfather. Try one with jam, Mari. One plays generous grandfather to hide one's cowardice, I reflect. One's inability to answer a phone-call. Or simply to compensate. As great theatre directors compensate for assassinations. A ridiculous connection. One must distinguish between the illuminating connection and the spurious. And I told my daughter I'd thought of getting an early train to Turin, then remembered they were doing the post-mortem this morning. No point in going before the afternoon, I said. They were moving him into the *camera ardente* in the afternoon. I went to the station and came back, I said. You did not, of course, tell your daughter that between seven and seven-thirty you wrote down the ten questions for Andreotti at a corner table in the Pasticceria Dante.

From my corner table, once again in the Pasticceria Dante,

I can just see a clock on the opposite wall that tells me it is now almost half past ten. The theatre director died in the early hours of yesterday morning. In his bathroom. It was his dog, not his mistress, who discovered him. How discreet 'in his bathroom' is! No mention of a screwdriver, though it must have been at almost exactly the same time that my son chose to kill himself. In a fit of folly, or lucidity? Or does the second generate the first? What do they show of a body in the mortuary? Just the head, the face? The rest covered with a sheet, please God. If only for my wife's sake. In the bathroom, *Il Corriere* repeats. I have never written on windows before, that I recall. And I tell myself that despite missing dinner last night, it would be foolish to order another coffee now. Another brioche. The dog is called Boccaccio. The mistress says she's determined to keep him. Another artistic genius. As a memento. He came to her room barking to wake her up. It was close to genius on your own part, I reflect, to write the questions to Andreotti on plain paper like that, and by hand. My mind is always sharpest early in the morning, however badly I've slept. Presidente, what would you say to those who suggest you have a split personality? Andreotti would warm to that. To the freemasonry of those too grand to engage with computers and the like. Those who preserve the mysteries of calligraphy. Writing things on plain paper on the table of a pasticceria. Only someone, he will reply – and it will be something along the lines of his famous remark, Power fatigues, but opposition more so – only someone – not realising that he is taking a bait, that he is saying exactly what I have already predicted he will say – who has never been obliged to think of more than one thing at once could ever make such an accusation. I can see his smile. Only the envious make accusations. That's always Andreotti's line. The line of the Italian leader accused of corruption. His hunched shoulders. Get power yourselves and stick your snouts in the trough, replied a certain southern mayor when accused of corruption. His cunning, short-sighted eyes. Another detail I reported.

Paola's eyes caught mine and immediately were away. I'm sorry about last night, I said. I must have frightened you. You were ill, she said. She said she had told Giorgio I was ill. There were pills I needed. He'd called about a quarter past seven. While I was scribbling down the questions. She was worried for me. That I might be wandering about catatonic. How intimate then when she smiled sadly, closing a cupboard door, leaning against it for a moment. The girls were wolfing their brioches. Papà, she said. She's not an attractive woman, but she has pleasant ways. She is not blessed with beauty. Papà. Shifting her weight as she stands, pulling out a strand of hair. In *Corriere della Sera*, photos of the theatre director's mistress show a raven-haired marvel of a girl. The annulled wife, whom he married in his early fifties, was a Sardinian bathing beauty, now turned minor politician. The first wife won a literary prize. Then drove off a bridge. Giorgio tells me you asked him to leave, I said. None as pretty as Karen, I thought. Then all at once in the Pasticceria Dante, thinking of the relative beauty of various women, of Paola, of my wife, of Karen, of the theatre director's young and decidedly desirable Polish mistress – there is a large and generous picture of the girl – I am overwhelmed by another great tide of emotion. My son was this girl's age. No, it is the same tide as before. My son never had a woman! My hands are trembling on the pages of *La Stampa*. A huge dark stream roars in my ears. For the last twenty-four hours, I tell myself, you have been hiding in an eddy, a backwater, while a huge dark stream of emotion floods by. You are trapped in a backwater. Whirling round and round like jetsam in an eddy beside a great tide of floodwater. This can't go on much longer, I tell myself. A tide you can never breast. Unless it has been going on your whole life. Your whole life you have been hugging the bank beside a huge, dark tide. Beside your wife. Who was it wrote Help me? Someone about to breast the tide. You told Gregory you wanted to go deeper, I reflect, struggling to regain control, determined not to allow another lapse, not to find myself brought, as last night, to my daughter's flat in a state of complete confusion in the car of a complete stranger, not even a taxi, yet you never do breast that deep tide. You never go away, as Gregory said you must, as reason has often counselled, and you never go deeper either, just mill in the shallows, the eddies, while your wife thunders by. What will she have seen in the mortuary? What do they let you see? When Martina jumped to her feet, wiping her wrists on her skirt, I said I would drive my granddaughter to school. It would be an honour, I said very determinedly, to drive my pretty granddaughter to school.

So for five minutes this morning, I remember, watching people come and go in the Pasticceria Dante, I sat beside a pretty six-year-old as I drove her to her school, then twenty minutes later I sat beside a pretty three-year-old as I drove her to her nursery. And both girls chattered as we drove and asked me how long I was staying and would I bring brioches again tomorrow morning. Mamma never brought them brioches. I watched Martina run into her school. She has a yellow back-pack on a red top. I should have reminded her to comb her hair. And it occurred to me, watching my granddaughter disappear in a crowd of other children, that now that I have left my wife I could stay a while with my daughter and her children. You could live a while with Paola, now that she and Giorgio have broken up, I thought, driving back from Martina's school. Is this what my dream was somehow saying?

There have been times in the past, I thought, when it was in the air that Paola and yourself could have lived together very happily without your wife. Times when you longed for such an arrangement. You could help her through this difficult period, I thought. At least logistically. It was odd that I had been in Paola's apartment in my dream. Odd how vivid the dream still is. Vivid dreams were always considered a basis for prediction, I thought. Then I was disturbed to find myself rehearsing an idea that once occurred to me years before: that I had only approved of Giorgio, of Paola's marrying Giorgio that is, because he was so dull, because he could in no way replace myself, my own privileged relationship with my daughter. Is that true? Is it pure coincidence that you left your wife only hours after hearing that Paola and Giorgio had split up, only minutes really after hearing from Giorgio that it had been Paola who sent him packing and not vice versa? But why do you insist on making such perverse connections? Such disparaging and unsettling connections? If dreams are considered a basis for prediction, I thought, and at the same time I was noticing that while Giorgio had kept the Mercedes Paola, predictably, was stuck with nothing better than a Fiat Uno, this only goes to show how limited our powers of prediction are. If we have to look beyond calculation, to dreams and astrology. You can do all the sums in your head you want, I reflect, and still have no idea how to behave, or how you will behave. Can anyone tell me what I will be doing later today? Can anyone tell me how I will finally leave things with my wife? Whom I have left.

Then ten minutes later I was driving Maria Cristina to her nursery. For some reason the little girl was wearing a pink party hat. Papà gave it to me, she said. You could help your daughter and granddaughters through this difficult period, I thought, substituting for the man your daughter has inexplicably pushed out. Perhaps precisely because too dull, because not a substitute for yourself. But I must stop making such connections. I must not interpret Paola's marriage in terms of myself. As it would be folly to interpret Marco's folly in terms of his parents' marital conflict. I was always ice-clear about that. And Vanoli never disagreed. He is a psychiatrist, not a shrink. I don't want to discuss it, Paola said, between my taking Martina and Maria Cristina to their respective schools. Okay, Papà? I don't want to talk about Giorgio. It's my business. She gave me one of her glances. Her eyes, like a beacon, establish contact, then immediately break it. She has no difficulty saying his name, I noticed. Papà gave it to me, Maria Cristina said, as I led her by the hand into her nursery. She used the other to clutch the pink party hat to her head. And the serenity, I thought, that would come from being around these delightful children and from feeling I was being useful at a difficult time towards people who are dear to me, really the only people who are dear to me, would enable me to start working on my book, would give me a feeling of belonging somewhere and of having something sensible to do. Three months of hotels has been extremely debilitating, I thought, both for myself and my wife. We have been living in a kind of limbo, I reflect, undecided how to give a rhythm to our lives without the visits to Marco every week, without the familiar surroundings of home, however much I hated that house, however badly it had been damaged. Marco offered a sort of ballast that kept the boat upright. I wasn't so stupid as not to have seen that. Perhaps one needs some pain or pathos to give one's life ballast. A sick son, a house to hate. To keep the boat upright in the flood. Rather than have the place repaired, I wanted to leave. I refused to have it repaired, just as my wife refused to have it sold: the house of ghosts. But at Paola's I would be able to get some work done. I must find somewhere to fax those questions from, I reflect. Otherwise what was the point of writing them? And I must buy some shaving tackle. Though obviously I won't be going to Rome. It will be a faxed interview. You haven't shaved, Grandad! Maria Cristina cried, turning her perfect face up to mine for a goodbye kiss. What clear eyes children have! I could hardly give them to Paola to fax from her office. You're all prickles! the little girl complained. With a pang, a real pang, it occurs to me how sad it is that my wife should have cut herself off from the pleasures of her grandchildren. From little girls who lift their little cheeks to be kissed. There is something lamentably self-destructive about a woman who cuts herself off from the consolation of her grandchildren, I tell myself. From those apple-perfect cheeks. Paola's testimony was not vindictive. The theatre director also cut himself off from his child, if it was his child, and hence grandchildren. The mother, now grandmother, was lost to public attention some decades ago. Clearly the old genius had other consolations. He is always photographed, I notice, this considerable theatrical genius, with his face tilted proudly upward, usually in profile, a noble nose, his wavy white hair flowing back over his collar. How he must have groomed and groomed that long white wavy hair. This great man!

But why am I sitting here reading the newspapers when I have so many other things to do and to think about? You'll have to think about the funeral, Paola said, dropping me in the piazza on her way to her office. You'll have to do that together. You can't just not speak to her. Why do I read the newspapers at all, I wonder, when I have made such an enormous issue of my repudiation of journalism? The burden of Dante's *Purgatorio*, I told Gregory that evening in the hotel bar, was that history was hell, and one should withdraw from it, one should set out on the pilgrimage to perfection. Dante repudiated history, and journalism with it, I reflect in the Pasticceria Dante, though his *Inferno* is one of the great masterpieces of history, and indeed of journalism, and universally recognised as much better than the *Purgatorio* or the *Paradiso*, which deal with the pilgrimage to perfection. Journalism is the endless description of hell, I told Gregory belligerently, some hours after we had left the bloodstained pavement. It was a surprise to have made this reflection. I had never thought anything of the kind before. Not consciously and with such clarity. The clarity of those thoughts that seem to be spoken to you from outside, that speak themselves ready-made. Its multiplication of detail is part of the hell it describes, I told myself much later that night. At a certain point one must abandon journalism, I had decided before dawn of the following day, as Dante abandoned Virgil on leaving hell, though Virgil was the best of guides and perhaps only hell is worth describing. Certainly my son's mind must be hell, I thought, lying in my bed in the Palermo hotel that night, mulling over my long conversation with Gregory Marks, correspondent in Italy for the BBC, trying to understand where it all began. As my relationship with my wife has likewise become a hell.

The only thing for you to do is to get out, Gregory said. I'm in love with your wife and she's in love with me, he said. You know that, he said. We were sitting at a table now. I can't remember how that happened. In an alcove. You must have realised. When you saw us speaking together. In French. She keeps a diary of our love. In French. She writes every day, he said. I listened to him talking. I stared at this earnest, avuncular, ruggedly frank man, perhaps five years my senior, perhaps ten, seeking my eyes across the table, telling me he was in love with my wife, talking to me with the enthusiasm of a teenager, the enthusiasm I might have unleashed myself if ever I had spoken to anyone of Karen. I spoke to no one. Perhaps the assassination has given us a sense of occasion, I thought. And if I could quote Dante, he was saying, though I had not quoted Dante at all, then he could just as easily quote Guinizelli. *Al cor gentil ripara sempre amor.* Thus the thirteenth-century poet. Gregory leaned across the table in our little alcove. There was low music, but no hoarse voice, thank God. Love to the gentle heart repairs, he translated, unnecessarily. Love ennobles, he announced, to a background of low music. It doesn't reduce a man to cynicism. Thus the BBC correspondent commenting on the thirteenth-century poet. Guinizelli. One of my wife's favourites. Certainly outside Gregory's range of reading. Or grasp of the Italian language. If he hadn't read Montale, he would hardly have read Guinizelli. She does speak some Italian to you then, I remarked. You must get out, he insisted. You're only doing each other harm. Thérèse and I had our marriage annulled, he put it to me, because we both agreed we had never loved each other. We were boyfriend and girlfriend for years. He sat back to explain himself, with the soft jazz behind. People expected us to marry, he explained. The whole thing was imposed. There was a sort of momentum, he explained, that we weren't old enough to recognise and reject. He leaned forward. But it came from outside, do you see, not from us. Gregory is being very eloquent about the annulment of his marriage, I thought. Presenting the case to the ecclesiastical tribunal, they had simply explained that the whole thing had come from outside, had been imposed from the beginning. Not chosen. They were too young. They had allowed a social inertia to sweep them along. They had not made a real choice. If it had been real love, Gregory said, coming from deep within themselves, it would have lasted. Do you see? As it was, we were only doing each other harm. Do you see? Love should ennoble, Gregory said, back with my wife's college-girl Guinizelli. It brings out the *virtù* in a lover, he insisted. All this to a background of soft jazz, the lift doors opening and closing. And instead we were doing each other harm, he said. He had tears in his eyes. We were – what's the opposite of ennobling? – I've drunk too much, Gregory admitted, but I am so glad we're having this out at last. His eyes were bright, staring earnestly into mine. Debasing each other, he decided. At each other's throats. We never loved each other, Gregory said with great emphasis. The priest we talked to could see that. He said he could tell with couples when they were being honest about their marriages. Then Gregory told me my wife had told him she couldn't leave me because of Marco. Marco was upset, was delicate, he wasn't well and it would upset him even more if we split up. I said nothing. But he had given her an ultimatum, he said. You two harm each other, Gregory said, leaning across the table again. The upholstery in the alcove was green. You're not happy, he said. You're forever at each other's throats. The lighting was red. I wouldn't be surprised if it wasn't that that was making Marco ill, Gregory said aggressively. This is something Vanoli never suggested, I reflect, still mulling in the Pasticceria Dante. Though I have no appetite for another brioche. I couldn't drink another cappuccino. Not until I have seen a doctor. Not until I've found some heparin. A laxative. She stays with you, he was telling me, because she's afraid you will lure Marco away from her. She's afraid she will lose him. Gregory is being very eloquent, I thought, on the subject of my wife's state of mind. Three years ago, this conversation, almost to the day. Certainly it was spring. It was shortly before the elections. When else do you assassinate a politician? You've never had it out between you, Gregory insisted. But you should. For your own sake, he said earnestly. He seemed genuinely concerned, as he had earlier shown concern about my difficulty in sustaining interest in my job, my journalism. For your own sake, he repeated, no doubt giving me my due. Otherwise your life is just a lie, he said. You're lying to yourselves, he said. I've given her three months, he told me. It was an ultimatum. I've waited a long time, he said, we are in love, but something must happen, or I'll go mad. Certainly he was very excited. You think you can't do these things, he started again, but you can. Thérèse and I had got to the point where we thought our marriage was, I don't know, necessary, he said. Part of the scheme of things. You know? His eyes gleamed in the red light. Fifty-five years perhaps? Fifty-eight? But it wasn't. You could even get an annulment yourselves, Gregory declared. We had both drunk a great deal. The upholstery was ghastly. You married so young, he said. Perhaps before either of you really understood. His hair is boyishly tousled. His wide handsome face, so prominently featured, I remember now, in the Heathrow Terminal One bookshop, always gives a convincing impression of frankness. The ruggedly frank middle-aged Englishman. Of candour. But why did he never tell me he was writing a book? And on my subject. Your wife's a real Catholic, he said. Like me. That helps me to understand her. Perhaps better than you do. She wouldn't want to marry again, Gregory said, unless her first marriage was annulled. Was he proposing? You've a good chance of getting an annulment, he said. Certainly, he had referred to our marriage as a first marriage. My wife's first marriage. If nothing else, the fact that you're not Catholic would be grounds enough, he said.

Rather than overwhelmed, I was amazed. The drink had slowed me down. *Corriere della Sera* has nothing to say about the annulment of the theatre director's second childless marriage, though I suspect in his case it had more to do with his wife's political ambitions and his own affiliations in the Christian Democratic Party. As it then was. I had predicted its downfall. That day's assassination proved me right. What exactly is the situation with Marco? Gregory now asked. I can't remember whether there was still music. Is he seriously ill? I didn't reply. Is there anything I can do to help? he asked. There are obviously limits to what your wife tells him, I thought. In her elegant French. *Amor e il cor gentil sono una cosa*, Gregory said, quoting another line from my wife's school-girl repertoire. How could he imagine I had never heard these words before? Love and the noble heart are one. How could he imagine my wife hadn't quoted me these lines a thousand times? She was still studying them when we met, for heaven's sake! And when we met was when we married. We ordered more whiskies. I mustn't order anything else to eat or drink until I have seen a doctor, I tell myself. Until I have some heparin. Then replying at last to Gregory's long monologue, I said I didn't understand annulment. Separation and divorce were simple enough. But not annulment. With annulment you denied anything had ever been. You pretended you had never been married at all. There had been no marriage to escape from. Talk about lying to yourself, I suddenly found myself shouting in the plush green alcove of the hotel bar. The same contradictory motions of the spirit, I lowered my voice, were at play in the annulment of a marriage as those I had described in the Prime Minister, in Andreotti. Sublimity on the one hand, a nit-picking bureaucracy on the other. Has Gregory used this notion in his book? I wonder. The red light shone off the green plush. A sublime belief in the sacredness of marriage, I told Gregory Marks, and a cynical, nit-picking, ecclesiastical bureaucracy that arrogates to itself the right to determine whether this sublimity has been achieved or not. There is no copyright on ideas. Talk about lying to yourself,

I shouted. It was laughable, I insisted under ghastly lighting. As if one solved the go-away-or-go-deeper conundrum by declaring: I was never there in the first place. I was never married at all. I was never in Paris. But it was just a going away in the end, I said. I was never in Bonn. Without even accepting defeat. Without even admitting one had got bored and was moving on. One couldn't talk excitedly about one's wife any more. One couldn't put any urgency in one's voice when one fucked her. So one moved on. As if every assignment was your first, I said. You had never been any-where else. Never reported from Paris or Bonn or Moscow. Every assassination your first. Even you are at your second assassination, I told Gregory Marks. Even you talk about first marriages and second. The barman, when we ordered more drinks, gave us that familiar look that says you have drunk too much already. The music had been turned off. The lighting was lower. This barman's long experience, I remember thinking as I became more and more animated, at last replying to Gregory's monologue, tells him you have drunk too much already. I have seen that expression on many a barman's face. And even as I spoke, having hardly spoken at all for the previous twenty minutes, having hardly opened my mouth from the moment my colleague Gregory Marks said: I am in love with your wife – perhaps because at the very back of my mind I had been tormenting myself with the question: is he going to tell me that they have made love, is he, have they, or have their absurd Catholic pieties, their candles and conclaves, restrained them in a paroxysm of romanticism and *dolce stil nova* poetry? – even as I spoke I was wishing some other colleague would come and interrupt us, hoping that some other journalist would turn up and put an end to this intimacy, so that I could then exchange a few last pleasantries and escape to my bed where I would lie and think about all that had happened inside my head that day, all that I had discovered, about myself and about others, since I was well aware that when you have drunk as much as this, when I have drunk as much as this, I tend to sleep only an hour or two, if at all, and then to wake with the mind racing, the racing mind furiously examining and re-examining all that has been said, or mis-said as it always seems in the small hours, in the course of a drunken evening. Annulment is absurd, I said. And, what's more, an Italian absurdity, I insisted. No colleague came. You're upsetting my grasp of national character, I joked. How can an Englishman, even if his wife was half French, do something so absurd as to annul a marriage? Where's the reason in it? No doubt, it occurs to me now in the Pasticceria Dante, re-reading the theatre director's poem to his mistress, which is not very good, no doubt Gregory quoted my wife the poems he had once quoted to Thérèse, his first wife. Or rather, the poems that Thérèse had quoted to him. Gregory is the kind who hears poems from others, I reflect, quotes poems that others have quoted to him. He doesn't read poetry himself. The theatre director's poem is really painfully poor, I tell myself. You're ruining my notion of stereotype, I laughed over my drink. I wrote better poems to my mistress, I reflect. It was a hollow laughter. Better than this famous theatre director's to his. But on that score, I went on, suddenly talking a great deal, talking far too much, when for the previous twenty, or even thirty minutes I had barely said anything at all – on that score I remember how disorientated I was when I first discovered there were Italian evangelicals, even Italian Jehovah's Witnesses. I've always had strong ideas about national character, I explained to Gregory – was I trying to change the subject? – and then one day I discover there are Italian Jehovah's Witnesses. How can this be? I laughed. Had he ever come across them? Has he put them in his book? I had to work hard, I told Gregory, to fit the *testimoni di Geova* into my vision of Italianness. I laughed. It was quite a setback. Then very deliberately and myself leaning across the table now, under the red light, against a background of green plush, I told Gregory how my wife had recently interrupted love-making to speak to a Jehovah's Witness. We were making passionate love, I told Gregory Marks – I wasn't changing the subject at all – quite recently, I stressed the point, and she broke off to speak to a Jehovah's Witness. I was at once boastful and furious and looking deep into his eyes to see what I could learn, to see whether his frank and criminally complacent eyes would tell me whether he and my wife had made love. We've always made passionate love, I said, speaking words I had never spoken before. Certainly not to Karen, certainly never to Vanoli. Certainly our marriage is sick, I conceded to Gregory Marks, to this man who claimed to be in love with my wife. But equally certainly it is a marriage. There was nothing imposed about our marriage, I told Gregory, rubbing in the words as hard as I could, pleased to read the first signs of disquiet on his face. But at the same time furious about the Jehovah's Witness. We were making love, what, three months ago, I said, though I had no idea how long ago it was, when this fellow rings at the door. I have only the vaguest idea when things happened in our marriage. Wanting to talk about the end of the world. You know the way they introduce themselves. Everything seems simultaneous, in marriage. By all means, my wife says into the intercom. Or at least in our marriage. Though I know what I'd be doing, she says, if I heard the world was about to end. We were making love on the sofa, I told Gregory. I insisted. This is in awful taste, I thought, but with not the slightest intention of stopping. I had drunk a great deal. And when he came up, little more than a boy, a pleasant young boy in an office-grey jacket with his copy of *The Watchtower*, in Italian, I don't remember what they call it, she starts to flirt with him. In just her night-dress, I said. *La Torre di Guardia*. She offers him champagne. We had opened a bottle of champagne for some reason. These were unnecessary details, but I wanted Gregory to hear them. Perhaps it was an anniversary. An nth anniversary. She poured him champagne. There are so many. I know what I'd be doing if the world was about to end, my wife laughed. Marco's birthday perhaps. She is a terrible flirt, I said. My wife. You must have seen that. She sat next to him on the sofa in just her night-dress, winking at me over his shoulder drinking champagne, talking about what she would be doing if the world was about to end. Fucking of course. I could read alarm in Gregory's eyes now. And disbelief. I could see from his eyes that he and my wife had not been making love. Or not often. He has not seen her raucous side, I told myself. She has been quoting Guinizelli. Something she hasn't done with me for so long. She has been talking about Marco. Her hopes and pain and prayers. But not about his smearing the sheets with shit. His disconnected speech and frightening hallucinations. Not his obscenities and obesity and violence. I can forgive her that, I reflect now in the Pasticceria Dante. No, I find no difficulty in forgiving my wife for that. For carefully editing the life she presented to her lover. Ours was a passionate love and a passionate marriage, I told Gregory abruptly. I stood up. My feet were firmer than I expected. It can end, I said. It may very well end, I said. Probably it will end, I shouted. But it can never be annulled. Good luck Gregory, I told him. And good night. And I turned to find the lifts.

As soon as I was up in my room, I remember, still marooned here in the Pasticceria Dante, still fascinated by these photographs of the great theatre director, his great nose tilted haughtily upward, fascinated by the thought of his messy private life and the sublime achievements of his art, and above all by the newspapers' complete silence on this point, on the contrast, that is, between the chaos of his private life and the sublimity of his achievements, I phoned my wife. Or would any headline have held me riveted this morning? It was almost two in the morning, but I phoned my wife anyway, the kind of thing I never do, in a fit of anger and of love. I was determined that something be said. Gregory was right in that regard. Something must be said. And it occurs to me now, here in the pasticceria, that perhaps every character has areas about which they are scrupulously silent. Is this what the complicated concept of lying to oneself means? I have never understood how one can lie to oneself. Can one know truth and tell oneself untruth? Or is it rather a conspiracy of silence between the contradictory parts of oneself? Might a person, a couple, a nation, I wonder, Andreotti for example, be best understood by the things they keep silent about, with themselves: their taboos, their *omertà*? Nationality a conspiracy of false consciousness perhaps? Language a conspiracy of silence? Certainly not a single journalist has put the question, what does it mean that this indisputably great artist conducted the most inexcusable of private lives? What are we to make of this? How can one lie to oneself, it occurs to me, except by keeping silent? Keeping parts of oneself apart. A contradiction unchallenged. Journalism hides the silence, I thought, by talking about the wrong things, by multiplying the details, chattering to fill the silence. I must talk to my wife, I thought, that night in the hotel. They had turned down a corner of green bedspread and put a Swiss chocolate on the pillow. The bedspread was green and the bedside lamp red. I must say the things that have never been said, I thought. Clearly I had had too much to drink. Obviously I was shaken. Assassinations always shake me up. The protraction of our relationship is a conspiracy of silence, I told myself. On both sides. I was determined to have this out. And I felt vaguely sorry for Gregory now. I had suddenly sensed, staring into Gregory's eyes as I recounted to him, perhaps overdoing it a little, the anecdote of the Jehovah's Witness, that my colleague was not going to get what he wanted. Had she really sat next to the boy on the sofa? No, our BBC correspondent was being lamentably ingenuous, I thought, giving somebody like my wife an ultimatum. Guinizelli didn't give his mistresses ultimatums, I thought. One might as well give an ultimatum to the mafia. To Andreotti. Though I knew nothing about Guinizelli. Only what my wife had quoted. It had been a mistake to imagine Gregory a serious threat, I thought. His book *Italian Traits*, I reflect here in the Pasticceria Dante from the few brief glances I have given it, seems quite inexcusably ingenuous. I tried the number again. My wife might move heaven and earth to keep him as a source of romance, I thought, a sort of dream, perhaps an occasional lover, but she had no more intention of running off with him than with the poor boy who wanted her to take a copy of *The Watchtower*. Why was no one answering the phone? And it occurs to me now, here in this pasticceria, ironically named after the greatest of all Italian poets, or rather, the piazza was named after the poet and then the pasticceria after the piazza, in a sort of anti-Platonic demonstration that names have no special relationship with whatever it is they denominate, that that moment, trying to call my wife at two in the morning from a hotel in Palermo, was not unlike the moment yesterday evening outside the mortuary. And indeed a whole series of moments in my life. I was determined to go into the mortuary, I reflect, and have the final showdown with my wife. Over Marco's dead body if necessary. As three years ago I was determined to tell my wife what Gregory had told me. To have the final showdown with her. Over a phone line from Palermo if necessary. How often have I planned the final showdown! To tell her Gregory had been quoting Guinizelli. To tell her about Karen. About my stony heart. Now bypassed. The assassination had created a sense of occasion perhaps. Andreotti is finished, I thought, now they have assassinated his number-one lackey in Sicily. The phone wouldn't answer. This is the end of his alliance with the mafia, I was thinking, and so quite probably the end of his political career. Suddenly I felt the urgent need to tell my wife that although this assassination was absolutely momentous in its implications, the fulfilment of something I had been predicting for years, I nevertheless had no intention of writing about it. I wanted to go deeper, I would tell her. And I would try to convey to her the idea: with you as well. I want to go deeper with you. Remember when I wanted to leave Italy, I would remind her, when I wanted to go to Moscow, and you said: but you haven't even understood this country yet. It takes more than five years to understand a country like Italy, you said. I suddenly remembered that it had been my wife said that. I should have told Gregory. I must talk to her at once, I thought. It had been my wife stopped me moving on. You'll never become an expert, she said, if you leave something after just a few years. I must tell Gregory that, I thought. And it wasn't just because my wife hadn't wanted to leave herself. Hadn't wanted to leave Rome, her family home, the house of ghosts. No, it was not that. Not at all.

Sitting by the telephone, I had worked myself up into a considerable emotional state. I cried. I took a shower while waiting to call again. I would tell her our marriage was sick, but that I for one wanted to go deeper, to go to the root of it. We must go deeper with Marco, I would say.

With Paola. We must stop these niggles, this point scoring, this marital bureaucracy. We must remember the sublime. Nobody was answering my call. The Ferrantes stopped you just as you were about to go into the mortuary, I reflect. And nobody would answer your call in the small hours from Palermo. I was perplexed. I could just about understand that my wife might still be out at one of her parties, one of the interminable after-the-theatre, society parties that constitute the only remaining trace of her semi-aristocratic heritage, an embassy dinner perhaps, or at least on her way back from such a party, the kind of party I met her at after all. But where was Marco? His drugs are making him sleep, I thought. He is sleeping through my phone-calls. But Marco refuses to take his drugs, I told myself, pacing up and down my hotel room, eating the chocolate they had left on the bedspread. He never takes his drugs. If only Marco would take his drugs there would be no problem. I tried again.

But had the call gone through, would you actually have said the things you planned to say to your wife? I am bound to put this question to myself this morning, here in the Pasticceria Dante, since behind it lies the further and more pressing question: Am I going to have it out with my wife, some time today, tomorrow, in the *camera ardente* perhaps, or am I simply going to leave her? Without a word? People do do that. Despite such pressing details as the funeral, the burial, the question of where we are both to live. People do just walk away. Just pick up and go. No, I must not, I tell myself, absolutely must not leave the Pasticceria Dante with everything still unresolved, with this momentous day unmapped. After all, how long were you standing outside the mortuary before the Ferrantes gave you the excuse to retreat? How long did you stand with your hand on the door? Before the image of the Ferrantes' intimacy and dignity in catastrophe allowed you to convince yourself that it was too late for you to beg your wife to see reason. The lost years prevent the lost from coming back, I reflect. Was this Marco's state of mind, not forty-eight hours ago? A moment of lucidity? The theatre director and his mistress slept in separate rooms, the Polish girl explained to the press. That was why the dog found him. In broken Italian, *La Stampa* claimed. Perhaps at precisely the hour Marco killed himself. No, you say you would have said those things to your wife from the hotel in Palermo that night, but most probably you would not. You're not capable of it. Most probably you would not even have mentioned Gregory's declaration. These occasions, I reflect – that assassination coupled with Gregory's declaration, and now, so momentously, your son's suicide – spark off the desire for a showdown, unleash an emotional flood, a great tide of wild feeling, but you never actually say anything. You flounder in the shallows. Beside the bank. Or you walk away. When you are most needed you walk away.

Two carabinieri walk into the pasticceria joking with the pretty *barista* and reminding me, absurdly, of my tax evasion. You are hereby informed that you are under investigation for tax evasion. You say you will go deeper, I reflect, watching the handsome young carabinieri, no doubt southerners, perhaps Sicilians, joking with the pretty *barista*, but then you just go sideways, crabwise, reading more and more, escaping more and more into analogies, reflections, without facing the enigmas head on: your wife, your son. You never faced the problems head on. First you went sideways into adultery, without facing the difficulties presented by your wife, your family, and later, when that ended because you refused to make it any more than a diversion, you went sideways into reading, this despite all your protestations to your colleague Gregory Marks about your instinct to go deeper, went sideways into an obscure and ridiculous project to write a monumental work on national character and the predictability of human behaviour. Though I do believe such a project is feasible. You went deeper where it didn't matter, I tell myself. Though I do believe such a book could prove a milestone. And what else am I to do with what I've learned? You couldn't even face your son's dead body, I reflect. You must go and look at you son's dead body, it suddenly occurs to me in the Pasticceria Dante. Now. The carabinieri are wiping the cream from their mouths. Stop thinking about Andreotti and go and look at your son. At least at his body. There is a crucifix above the pretty head of the *barista* in the Pasticceria Dante. As there was a crucifix in one corner of my room in the hotel in Palermo. And doubtless in the mortuary where Marco is lying. There is always a crucifix or a Madonna in Italy. Offering endless fuel for easy analogy. For escapes into analogy. The Madonna outside the maternity ward on our way to the mortuary. My thoughts of parthenogenesis and resurrection. My wife as Mary at the tomb. Unforgivably inappropriate connections. And between attempted phone-calls from the Palermo hotel, which was called the Garibaldi I think, thinking back over what had been said down in the bar, and in particular thinking over Gregory's piety about moving on, and about my wife's long-forgotten objection that I couldn't leave Italy before I knew it, couldn't go after only a few years or so, I was struck by the old revelation that you become what you know. I know Italy now, I realised, in my room in the Hotel Garibaldi. Italian hotel rooms are entirely familiar to me, I thought, with their heavily-framed mirrors and clunky plumbing. I had become Italian. At least to the extent that I was no longer interested in talking about the place. To the extent, I reflect, that after all those years castigating corruption, I had myself started evading tax. In Rome as the Romans. The following documentation must be sent at once to the above address by registered mail. So the letter said. You know your wife, I thought – the Biblical sense, profoundly, is the real one – and so ultimately you become like her. You eat into the apple, only to find it has eaten into you. You're not so English as you imagine, I thought. You have become Italian. You have become like your wife. You possess knowledge, so now it possesses you. So that if Italy, like your wife, remains obscure to you, that can only be because you yourself are obscure. To yourself. As she to herself. We are all obscure to ourselves. To become like someone doesn't mean to understand them. Knowledge brings to a blank, I reflect, as light the eye to the sun. Is it really possible that I have become like my wife? And I wanted to phone Gregory there and then and explain to him that he had lost his sense of pathos. Lost his grasp of fatality, of having become everything he knew, though still agonisingly separate from it, still fatally capable of knowing more, as I had chosen to know Karen when already fused with my wife. Fatally capable of rediscovering ignorance, losing one's sense of destiny. You should fuck somebody else, Marco said, six or seven years after the event. After that expedient had been tried. Over and over. His mind must be hell, I thought. Our lives are separate now, she said. Paola married to escape home, I thought, married desperately young, without having found a man to replace me, left when she realised that talk of our living together away from her mother was just talk, just dream-talk when I was angry. I should never have said that to my daughter, it occurs to me now in the Pasticceria Dante. That we should live together. Do I flirt perhaps as much as my wife does? Certainly Vanoli suggested as much. Does Marco take as much after me as her? Perhaps I behave in exactly the same way she does. I don't want to talk about it, Papà, my daughter said. She gave me one of her quick glances over the sofa. Then the eyes were away. Some of us are overwhelmed by what we know, I reflect, by what we are being obliged to become. By our wives, or fathers. We cannot breast the flood. Then suddenly the line was engaged. Instead of not answering, the line was engaged. At the tenth or twentieth try. It was four-thirty. I kept phoning. Rather than answering, I thought, my wife has taken the phone off the hook. I was furious. Unless she had just got back from some ridiculous party and was phoning Gregory. In the middle of the night. In French. Perhaps my wife will teach him pathos, I thought. Waking him in the middle of the night with her French. With her Guinizelli. My fury suddenly left me. I remember laughing. I was exhausted. My wife is good at that, I thought. At teaching pathos. You must abandon journalism, I told myself, at last lying down on my bed that night in Palermo. Then waking shortly after nine I phoned Dottor Vanoli on impulse. It all began, I said, when Marco started speaking to his mother in English. Why do you laugh when you tell me that? the psychiatrist asked. And he said this was merely a symptom. What he wanted to know was, where had it all begun? I put the receiver down and again dialled my wife, determined to put that question to her, to use that question as a way of telling her about my conversation with Gregory, of my repudiation of journalism, of my sense that even if our marriage was sick, still it was a marriage, and as such we must decide whether to heal it or kill it. How extraordinary, I reflect now, watching the carabinieri hurrying out of the bar, waved on their way by the wry *barista*, how extraordinary when she produced the word heal in the cab on the way back from Courteney's. No wonder you began to cry. Perhaps your wife's mind moves in exactly the same way yours does, I tell myself. She has become like you and you like her. I dialled the number. We must go deeper, I would tell her. We must face the fact that Marco is seriously mentally ill and not just upset, not just delicate, or whatever drivel she had been telling Gregory. We must break the humdrum back-and-forth of our recriminations, our competitive alliances with our children. Why had Marco changed sides so suddenly? Was there something I hadn't been told? I dialled. *Pronto*, a male voice said. A strange voice. A carabiniere, he explained. Your wife is under sedation, he said. Your son is under arrest. Marco had held her hostage all night. In the bathroom. They were treating it as a case of assault. Your daughter arrived and immediately called the emergency services. She wishes to press charges. Would you like to speak to your daughter? Help me, Marco said when I went to visit him the following morning. He spoke in English. Help me! And at last I'm on my feet. I'm paying for my breakfast. It was Marco wrote that on the bathroom window! My son. In my daughter's apartment. Help me, he said. There are things I have not been told. I must go to Turin. I must see my wife.

Fifteen minutes later I faxed the following questions from the main post office in Novara:

FOR THE ATTENTION OF PRESIDENTE GIULIO ANDREOTTI

Presidente . . .

1. A seven-times prime minister accused of collusion with the mafia? Where did it all begin?

2. You are surrounded by a veil of mystery. Did you actively cultivate this?

3. Despite all the instability, little ever changes in Italy. Did your long period in office

126

serve more to keep things the same than to improve them?

4. What are your favourite songs?

5. Shortly before his assassination, Moro described you as 'cold, impenetrable, devoid of human feelings, given over to the conquest of power in order to do evil'. Yet you attend mass every morning, edit a religious magazine and boast the friendship of popes and cardinals. How important is it for you to feel that you have behaved virtuously?

6. Has your wife played an important role in your career?

7. What would you say to someone who accused you of having a split personality and what do you understand by the expression 'lying to oneself'?

8. You are frequently praised for your flair for compromise, but equally frequently your coalition governments have been compared to dysfunctional families. Did it never occur to you that you were protracting a stalemate out of fear of change? Did you hope to die with the old regime intact?

9. It has been said that you have a talent for predicting other people's behaviour. Assuming you accept that this is true, do you, as a religious man, believe that this belittles them, or is it just the inevitable result of the prevalence of predestination over free will?

10. With which character in *I promessi sposi* do you most easily identify?

VII

It had been necessary to re-read *I promessi sposi* to establish the continuity of an Italian gallery of types, a kinship between the saints and tricksters of the *Inferno* and the *Decameron* right through to those of D'Annunzio, Pasolini and even Fellini. Not that any one figure or quality could be considered superlatively Italian, or even as holding the kernel of Italian national character, for one can no more be Italian or English on one's own, than one could be human, or indeed inhuman, on one's own, or a son without a mother. But that there was a constellation of types who made each other what they were, who became more and more obviously type figures when seen in relation to each other, and above all in action, in reaction, with and to each other. A sort of Italian dynamic, if you like. A complementary community of minds. A particular way of twining stories together, imagining available spheres of action, and thus of defining each other, of becoming oneself. To establish the existence, I had thought, I had long thought, of such a dynamic, to savour its extension and evolution, its openness to nuance and resistance to change, would be to discover new continents of predictability. To go deeper, in short. That was my goal. Far deeper than my journalism had ever gone. Andreotti was predictable, I thought, in so far as he moved in the world of Italian politics, defined by and defining those around him. Including the corpse on the pavement that decisive spring morning in Palermo. Brought up in Lytham or Lisbon, Andreotti would have behaved entirely differently. I myself would have behaved entirely differently, I felt – no, I was sure – in London or Los Angeles, or with an English wife in Rome. Or a Tibetan wife. In Rome. Thus, in re-reading Manzoni, it wasn't so much that I wanted to show what perfectly recognisable and even contemporary figures Don Abbondio and Lucia and the Avvocato Azzeccagarbugli and Don Rodrigo are, to name but four, but how they are so *in relation to each other*. And indeed to many others before and after them, real and imaginary. Destiny is a thing we do together, I thought.

Such, in any event, was the idea I was seeking support for on reading, re-reading, among a score of other books – it seemed no more than my duty given the task I had set myself – *I promessi sposi*, when I came across the story of the Nun of Monza – I hadn't thought of it for years – and above all I came across that chapter opening where Manzoni says: There are moments when the minds of the young are so inclined that any request for a gesture of seeming goodness or sacrifice is met with immediate compliance: like a freshly opened flower the young mind settles softly on its fragile stem, ready to grant its fragrance to the first breeze that blows. Such moments, Manzoni goes on – though I quote, I translate, imprecisely and from memory – such moments, that others ought to wonder at in mute respect, are precisely those the selfish and crafty know to wait for, and seize upon, thus to bind a will that is as yet without defence.

Why was I overcome by a sense of terror on reading

those lines from *I promessi sposi*? On re-reading the story of Gertrude of Monza's monstrously manipulative father? I had not tricked my daughter into becoming a nun against her will, thus condemning her to a life of duplicity. I had not manipulated her, or even encouraged her when it came to marrying Giorgio. I had no personal interest in the matter. I had not denied her a dowry. On the contrary, I paid through the nose to set them up. Against my wife's wishes. And even had I wanted to, I could never have manipulated my son Marco in any way at all, since Marco fell entirely within his mother's sphere of influence. That was obvious. And jurisdiction. Marco is still entirely attached to his mother's sphere of influence, I would say to myself as I travelled from one Italian city to another, reporting on this or that scam or tragedy, consolidating what many were beginning to speak of as a very significant career. She controls his whole life. He is hardly my son at all, I would think sometimes, in this hotel or that. It was a time when people were beginning to speak of me as the foremost authority on contemporary Italy. When is he going to grow away from those apron strings? I wondered. I had called home from some party convention only to have Paola tell me that my wife and son were out together. It annoyed me that Marco went so regularly to mass. With his mother. She has seduced him entirely, I thought. I can hardly be proud of his basketball and brilliant maths results, I felt, despite an intense desire to feel otherwise, since he is hardly my boy at all. I don't even know the rules of basketball. No doubt she speaks ill of me to him, I thought. My maths was always hopeless. A son in every way different from his father, my wife insisted, at her many and amusing dinner parties. Had I spoken ill of her in his presence he would have stuffed his fingers in his ears. He was loyal. It annoyed me to see Marco make the sign of the cross. To see him fall so tamely within his mother's sphere of influence. He has none of my vision of the world, I thought. I haven't influenced my son at all. Let alone manipulated him. Yet when I reached the page where Manzoni describes how at the last the Nun of Monza is walled up in a cell for years of living death, I knew it was Marco I was thinking of. Marco too is walled up in a cell, I told myself. I can't remember where I was when I read those pages, when I said those terrible words to myself, but I suspect at home, for the book is too large to carry around comfortably. *I promessi sposi* is a large book. Marco has been walled up for years, I thought, sitting at home in the house he half-destroyed that night I phoned and phoned from Palermo. His mother's ancestral stairway sledgehammered to fragments. In a single night. Those pages of Manzoni's, I remember now, that terrible and terribly Italian story, induced a sense of horror such as I had rarely felt before. It was the image of the beautiful Gertrude hopelessly trapped, walled away irretrievably from all company, that frightened me. It is a frightening image: a beautiful, sensual woman twisted and destroyed in her inmost self, as a result of circumstances at least initially beyond her control. Her youthful dutifulness exploited by a manipulative father, a complicitous mother. Why had Marco turned against his mother? In the story of the Nun of Monza, I thought, there was all the age-old clash of established custom and wayward individual. The way the two call to each other to form a single destiny. National character warps the character, I thought. Though they cannot exist separately. There are no individuals without society. Gertrude bows but rebels. She does her duty, then rebels. Was there a moment when the apron strings became a noose? For Marco. Gertrude takes the veil, against her will, but behind it rebels. She can't breathe behind the veil. Should I have untied those strings? Could I? But behind a veil you can rebel. She loves, fornicates, kills. She has all the rancour and cunning of somebody rebelling from behind a veil. She would still like to be dutiful, as when her young mind sacrificed itself to her father's will, bowed like a fresh young plant on its fragile stem, but she is suffocating. All her father wanted was to save himself the dowry, the cost of marriage. The veil is smothering her. She is smothered by her father's greed. Whereas I was happy to pay for my daughter's apartment. Destroyed by his disinterest for her most intimate needs. She breaks her vows, loves a man, kills a blackmailer. She is betrayed. She is punished. She is walled up in a cell. He was such a gentle boy, my wife wept at the trial that followed. We had fallen into our routine of moving heaven and earth. I barely had to ask and he obeyed, she sobbed. There were very few people in court. You cannot imagine a more amenable child, she insisted. She was wearing her green jacket, a lipstick almost scarlet, a thick powder over bruises that would not heal. He was always extremely gentle with me, she pleaded. The police had photos of the hole smashed in our bedroom wall, of the broken slabs on the stairway. I didn't want them repaired. Invited not to press charges, Paola refused. For your sake, Papà, she insisted. For Marco's sake. He has always been extremely well behaved, I said quietly at the stand, feigning embarrassment at my wife's emotion the better to confirm her evidence. We're an unbeatable double-act. No, and I repeat, I said quietly, I know of no incident of any kind such as those recounted by my daughter. We must at all costs avoid a prison institution, Vanoli had warned. The trauma of the prison institution can be decisive, he told us. Marco is walled up, I thought, on reading those pages by the great Manzoni, the appalling story of Gertrude of Monza. Not so much in Villa Serena as in his mind. A story absolutely without relief or catharsis, I thought. This image of a woman walled up, of a woman who *accepts* to be walled up, she *accepts*, because still locked into the group vision of her crime and its punishment. She *chooses* her punishment. Marco was allowed to leave Villa Serena for brief spells under certain conditions. But rarely did so. He was walled up in his mind. As surely as the murderess nun. Smashing his mother's ancestral home hadn't helped at all, I thought. What consolation can there be in such a story, I asked myself, turning the pages of Manzoni's great book? Gertrude was walled up, I thought, from the moment her monstrous father tricked her into taking the veil, manipulated her young woman's readiness to please, the better to bury her forever, merely to save himself the dowry. Marco was buried forever, I thought. There is a momentum in such things. But it was ludicrous to imagine I was responsible, the way Gertrude's father clearly had been. Why do I draw such analogies? He imagines I run some international spy ring, I told Vanoli. That I'm all powerful. Apparently that's why I travel so much. One moment I am moving vast alien armies to destroy him, the next I am his only hope of protection. He claims his mother has killed his pet dog. He never had a dog. Suffocated his pet puppy. I don't remember any puppies. He claims she pulled the animal under her dress and suffocated the thing. Every time a different story. All my travelling has to do with the way I control world climate, I laughed nervously. I bring his mother children to eat. Or Paola is his guardian angel. His saviour sister. Though it was she who accused him. He has seen her giving blow-jobs at Stazione Termini.

Vanoli was in a hurry that afternoon. I was speaking quickly, reading as instructed from notes I had taken on our first or second trip to Villa Serena. After the trial. Our long drives north. Marco was really beyond Vanoli's care now, after the trial, the move to Villa Serena, but I still went to see the man. He smiled. These were precisely the kind of things a schizophrenic did say, he said. And hardly remarkable. That was what schizophrenia was, he said. But I knew that. I must just go on calmly repeating the truth, he said, the true story. That we were his parents who loved him and wanted him to get well and come home.

Just keep repeating the truth, Vanoli said, calmly and above all consistently. Just keep reminding him how the world really is. And check that he takes his medicine. At least we've managed to avoid the prison institution, Italy's foremost psychiatrist said. Villa Serena is a civilised place. Something of a miracle actually, given the evidence your daughter gave. And he is taking his medicine again. Obviously there were things I hadn't been informed of, Vanoli said. Your wife put on a remarkable performance though. He was clearly impressed. There are few people my wife cannot impress. Or seduce for that matter. She had had her hair freshly permed for the occasion. Her glorious hair. Many of my patients have made dramatic improvements at Villa Serena, he said. Dottor Busi is an excellent psychiatrist. But on returning home from Vanoli's office on the Lungotevere and re-reading the story of the Nun of Monza, I was overwhelmed. That was not the truth at all, I thought. I didn't want you home at all, I tell my son now, sitting here beside his body. That was a lie. I wanted your mother to myself. At last. I wanted you out of the way. Our lives are separate now, Karen had said. I have decided to stop travelling, I told my wife. At last. It had taken two years for those words to sink in. I am giving up journalism, I told my wife. I'm needed in the family, I said. I want to be with you. How flat and dead Karen's voice was when she spoke those words. I never had the stairs repaired. I shall write a book, I decided: national character and the essential predictability of human behaviour. But on re-reading the story of the Nun of Monza, walled up for ever in her cell, I was appalled.

Why had I started thinking of this, remembering this – *I promessi sposi*, the Nun of Monza – those few precious minutes in the *camera ardente* before being so cruelly interrupted? Was it the candles? The religious iconography? The thought of a body about to be walled up? Was it my tricky question for Andreotti? What will he answer? Or just a general and absolutely absurd feeling of guilt? An absurd and masochistic *bandhu*. Linking myself and Gertrude's monstrously manipulative father. A connection that didn't connect. Paranoia, no less. Marco is less remarkable in death than in life: that was my first thought on being shown into the *camera ardente*, those few minutes before being so cruelly interrupted. I was surprised and I suppose relieved to find my wife not there. Very surprised. I took a seat. To my immense relief he was dressed. The corpse was dressed. My wife wasn't there. Dark trousers, blue sweater. Villa Serena must have sent his clothes, I thought. How kind. The nurses had dressed his body, hidden his wounds. How generous. Sitting down I was surprised and moved by this generosity. They had dressed the boy after the post-mortem. There were candles at the head and feet. It was the *camera ardente*, not the mortuary. There were two or three heavy pieces of dark wooden furniture and a Sacred Heart on the near wall. A public space that apes the private, I thought, or the imagined private of a distant past. That saves you taking your late beloved home to lie under halogen light by the television. A more meaningful past of coffin-like chests and sideboards with Sacred Hearts. But in an under-funded public hospital. I sat down on a straight-backed wooden chair with red upholstery. Our parents' past. I sat down. Or their parents'. It was definitely Marco. Definitely his face. He was laid in a sort of shallow coffin whose darkly polished wood matched the other furniture glimmering in the candlelight. There was a crucifix, a Sacred Heart. These objects conjure an illusion of meaning, I remarked. Less remarkable in death than life, I thought. Less wild. More like the dutiful Marco who knelt beside his mother every Sunday at mass. How that irritated me! Not her religion, which I respect, even envy, but his docile mimicry. The diligent Marco who walked forward to take the host at his grandmother's funeral, while Paola sat behind in the pews with me. Aren't you going up to take the host? I asked my daughter. It was her grandmother's funeral after all. She held my hand and sat in the pew while the others went forward. I remember her face being especially foreign that day, especially set about the lips in the dim light. Was it this religious iconography, in the *camera ardente*, that reminded me of the Nun of Monza? Of Gertrude's monstrously manipulative father, her terrible destiny of being walled up, as Marco quite definitely had been walled away in his mind and now is beyond all walls.

You must be paranoid, I thought. I had barely taken my seat in the *camera ardente* before I was overwhelmed by feelings of guilt. You must be eager to think ill of yourself. Perhaps it was the English school, I once suggested to Vanoli. Really the only way I had influenced my son at all was the English school. Perhaps that was the mistake. And I explained to the psychiatrist that whereas I was always being mistaken for what I was not, German in Italy, American in England, and while my wife was never mistaken for anything other than what she was, Italian, or rather Roman, whatever language she was speaking, however fluently, Marco – I explained to Vanoli – Marco had the uncanny knack of being taken entirely for English in England, entirely for Italian in Italy. His English was a perfect impersonation of my own, I said, only without that element, whatever it is, that makes people imagine me American in England. His Italian was his mother's. His mother's exactly, I said. Geoff Courteney had remarked on

Marco's excellent English, his excellent manners, over dinner only the evening before last, it occurred to me now, taking my seat in the *camera ardente*, wondering why my wife, who had sat the night beside him in the cold of the mortuary, was missing this opportunity to be here now, now that he was properly laid out, that is, with the candles and the darkly polished furniture in the funeral chamber. In an appropriately religious aura. We should really be together now, I thought. As a family. One says appropriately. My wife should be here beside me. Paola should be here. Our family is radically split, I thought. It was radically split the day Marco went to take the host and Paola did not. At their grandmother's funeral. He'd been so sorry, Geoff Courteney said, to hear from Gregory about our son's illness. My wife's ears strained. It was a considerable sacrifice on her part to come to England, to hear Gregory's name without understanding what was being said. He is dead, I thought. His skin is cold. Your mother could not raise you from the dead. A stupid thought. I hadn't even asked for the results of the autopsy. She felt alien to English, she told me. I told Vanoli. English is hostile to my spirit, she laughed. This in the days she might still have quoted Guinizelli. To me I mean. Or Foscolo. *I sepolcri*. Her ears strained at the sound of those names. Marco's name, Gregory's name. My wife has such a thrilling laugh. Nobody better placed than yourself, Geoff Courteney conceded, just the evening before last – though he hadn't offered a contract – to write a comparative study of national characters. Is this a clue? To what went wrong. This language thing. But now of all moments, you must not be distracted, I told myself calmly but firmly. I had only just sat down in the *camera ardente*. Now, of all moments, you must concentrate, I told myself. You must look at the body. It was only minutes after all, though I could hardly have known that, before I was to be so farcically interrupted. You must not think about the Nun of Monza and Vanoli and languages. Your various ideas. So convenient for not looking at things. You must look, I told myself. Look at your son. Look now.

I looked. When Marco spoke English, I thought, he was English, he thought of himself as English and was acknowledged to be so. Summers spent in England. With the Courteneys. Likewise when he spoke Italian. I looked at his pale lips. Is that a clue? Two entirely disconnected thought patterns, I told Vanoli. Was this what we should never have imposed? My wife finds them hostile, I told him. She has always refused to learn English, I said. Things you know in Italian, I tried to explain to the psychiatrist, that you'll never know in English. Things you become in English that you'll never become in Italian. Two different ways of telling yourself about yourself, I said. Was language the beginning of the schismatic process? Half the world is bilingual, Vanoli smiled, with no adverse effects. He dismissed the idea. He is a psychiatrist, not a shrink.

But is it even useful, I suddenly asked myself in the *camera ardente*, quite exhausted, but equally surprised, at least thus far, by my calm, by my lucidity, the coherent working of my mind, to search for clues, to think of this thing in terms of guilt and causality? Was there any point at all in trying to understand what had happened? I felt completely exhausted, and decidedly ill, in pain even, but much calmer than I had expected to be in the presence of my son's body. I was surprised that my wife was not here. Where was she? He was so much less remarkable in death than in life. I felt uncannily calm. And lucid. He had been ill, I reflected. Courteney used the right word there. This illness. I felt grateful to Geoff Courteney. There can be no guilt attached to a son catching the flu, I thought. Most recent thinking puts it down to virus mutation, Vanoli said. Unless you've locked the poor child out in the cold of course. Why do thoughts like that keep recurring? Walled him up in the cold. And I wondered if my wife were about to burst in. Demanding to know where I had been. People left in the cold do catch the flu virus. Hysterical over what would now be the last vision of her son. Of my son. She couldn't move heaven and earth this time. She cannot raise him from the dead. Your wife will burst in at any minute, I told myself. I must concentrate now.

Then at last I laid my hand on his forehead. I forced my hand to rest there on Marco's cold forehead, as one lays a hand on a sleeping child to check his temperature. He was ill, that's all. A virus. Here you are beside your son's body, I thought. You have done it. Beside Marco. It is Marco. Marco's face, Marco's jaw. It is Marco. You are not a coward, I told myself. There is no smell but the smell of candles and polished wood. You have come to see him. Poor Marco. Despite the possible presence of your wife. You are touching him even. Despite your fear of a smell of decay. Though I never feared such a thing as a journalist. I have smelt the decay of rotting bodies as a journalist, quite unimpressed. And I leaned forward until my lips were brushing his ear. Where was she? The skin seemed ochre in the candlelight. The fever's passed, *ciccio*, I whispered, my hand on his forehead. She called him *ciccio* when she took him in her bed. *Ciccio, ciccietto. Principino.* Our terms of endearment were all hers, I thought. It's passed now, kid, I whispered. Fever's gone. Then, just as the emotion I had been inviting rose with astonishing promptness to fill my throat, to flood my eyes, an emotion bound, it suddenly seemed, to sweep me quite away beyond any place I had ever been swept before, beyond any return to the person I was, at this very moment another voice spoke out quite clearly, even coolly, and with great authority: To recover this in all historicity, this voice suddenly announced into the thick of

139

my tears, is beyond you. It was a rather formal voice. It formed the words on my lips. Though historicity is not a word I remember my lips forming before. Nor was I quite sure, in that moment of bewilderment, what the words might mean. Such a task is beyond you, the voice repeated. There was an odd metallic ring to it. All the same, for one hour now, you shall tell yourself the story of your son. Immediately the flood subsided.

You were not shocked, I reflect now, so soon after that cruel interruption, back once again in the *camera ardente*, to hear that voice intervene as it did. They have given me fifteen minutes. On the contrary you were relieved. The flood of emotion was immediately calmed. You called the emotion into being and immediately, automatically almost, the voice calmed it, prevented you from being overwhelmed. You will tell yourself the story of your son, I told myself. I was amazed how swiftly I had recovered my composure. You will recover his life. The voice spoke once and was gone. With your hand on his forehead. Much as Vanoli told you to keep repeating the truth to him, the true story. Keep telling him the simple truth, preferably while establishing some basic physical contact. A hand on a hand, or round a shoulder. You must keep re-establishing reality as it is, normality as it is. A normal story, Vanoli said, of a normal mother and father and son, and nothing to do with controlling the climate and suffocating puppies. Don't even bother contradicting such inanities. The problem was virus mutation. Something that could probably be predicted if only we knew the mechanisms. Or there might even be a vaccination one day. Why then had he spoken to me of Italian mothers and their sons, I demanded, of particularly Italian forms of schizophrenia? And again I was surprised to think how much this corpse *was* my son. Not the shell, I had expected. Not the mask of horror. Far more your son,

I thought, than the last time you spoke to him alive. Less remarkable. I was relieved. In a way less frightening. You will spend this precious time telling yourself the story of your son. He can't hallucinate now, I thought. My hand seemed glued to the clammy skin of his forehead, which had itself been so feverish with voices on that occasion, that last occasion we met. There is no smell here in the *camera ardente*. Except of candles. They began when I went to college, he claimed. The candlelight flickered. But he frequently changed the story. He had had problems with room-mates. With girls. Who will ever know the truth behind those stories now? Who doesn't have problems with girls? He was convinced girls made fun of him. The fever's passed now, I whispered, only minutes before being interrupted. You were a darling child, I whispered. Always in your mother's way and the apple of her eye. She loved you and scolded you and kept you in her bed, I whispered. It sounded trite, but I was obeying the voice as best I could. I had sensed its authority. A last ditch authority. What more can one remember of those days? You were a good kid, I said. I can remember very little of his early childhood. A photograph here and there. Elba. Rimini. Suffolk. An infant body smiling from a big bucket. Summer snaps. At the Courteneys' Suffolk house. Was that where we first met Gregory? You were a good boy, I whispered. You were obedient. What story can a tiny child have? If not his parents' story? I wondered what my wife had felt the need to say to him yesterday. When she insisted on seeing him alone. Where was she now? You were very obedient. Mamma loved you. I wasn't jealous. I was so pleased for your mother. So pleased she had been able to have a child of her own. It meant so much to her. Travel as much as you like, she told me. She gave up the work she was doing. That came as a surprise. Her beloved PR. The big hotels. The society. Don't bother about presents, your mother said, I know what he wants. She had enjoyed the social aspects of her work. I know what my *ciccino* wants. Paola was jealous. That was natural. Did they smooth his face? I wondered. Was it horribly distorted when they found him? I must ask for the results of the autopsy.

You look so calm, Marco, I suddenly said out loud. Unexpectedly I looked up at the candles. The windows are curtained. Where was I? It is uncanny to turn and find somebody still in exactly the same position. Paola was ill. She was weak. That was when Paola was ill and you were healthy, kid. *Ironia della sorte*. Your mother was disappointed with Paola even before you were born, I told my dead son, my hand on his forehead. They would give me the death certificate at reception, the doctor said. Presumably that would indicate the cause of death. Thank God he is dressed. How generous of them. I looked at his big hands laid by his side. Bigger than mine. Basketball hands. There is no need to look at the rest of his body, I said out loud. When you say goodbye to a person, you don't need to see their bodies. Where had he stabbed himself? Not even lovers. You don't want to see their bodies again. Your lives are separate now. Why must you keep challenging yourself like this? I wondered. It's the face you say goodbye to. The closed eyes. My hand was as if stuck to his forehead, in the clammy candlelight. If candles are more solemn than electric light, it's because they can flicker and die, I thought. What exactly had they done at the autopsy? Candles consume themselves, as we do. Cut him open? The light in the eye is the fire that consumes the mind, as the flame the candle. I had read that somewhere. I said out loud: Marco's eyes are closed forever. That light is extinguished forever. But I must not get distracted now. If I allow myself to be distracted, I thought, the emotion will rise up and carry me off. Thinking of those dead eyes. Or the voice will cut in

142

again. The authoritative voice. Fleetingly, I was furious with myself for seeing the pun in last ditch. Perhaps you've passed it on to me, I whispered. I moved my mouth very close to his face. My dead son's face. Perhaps I've got your fever, kid. I was smiling. I heard a voice, I said. I would never look into his eyes again. You must get through these next few days any way you can, I told myself. Any way you can. Some voices help, if you let them, Marco told me. I can't remember on what occasion. They decide for you, he explained. But what was it that my son found so difficult to decide? Move in with Paola if you're unhappy, I told him. You're not far from Paola's. It's a difficult time when one leaves home, when one starts at university. What was upsetting him? Less than an hour on the train from Milan. Move in with your sister. You can still attend classes from Novara. She won't mind. Giorgio won't mind. All this, just moments before being interrupted. Trying to commune with my dead son. Finding it easier than I had feared. If not altogether convincing. But when had it ever been convincing? When is it ever convincing communing with anyone? Certainly easier than the last time I saw him. Or even oneself? When he kissed his mother on the mouth. Then rubbed mud in her hair. What did that gesture mean to you? I suddenly asked the corpse. I'm leaving your mother too now, I said. He rubbed butter in my hair, Paola testified. And pinned me against the wall. I do love Marco, she said, but he has made our lives hell for eighteen months. He lived with us for eighteen months in Novara, she explained. Myself and my husband. I feel he should be in some kind of institution. He said I was a replicant, Paola testified. At the trial. That I wasn't real. He is convinced people have been substituted by aliens. His mother and father in particular. He is convinced that if it had been the real me, I would have saved him. As it was, he would have to kill me. The aliens have to be

143

eliminated. He tried to rape me, Paola testified. Her voice never trembled. He used force, she testified. He said he was a replicant himself, otherwise he wouldn't do such things.

Your mother was disappointed with Paola, I whispered to Marco, my lips close to his ear. She didn't get any change from Paola, she said. *Non mi da corda*, she said. I can't remember what age we're talking about. It all seems simultaneous to me. And immeasurably distant. You were breast-fed for three years. I slept in the lower of the two bunk beds. Later we moved into the big house, your grandmother's house. Your mother was determined you wouldn't be damaged as Paola was. I lowered my voice. She breast-fed you for three years. My lips were almost brushing his cheek. That was it, Marco. That was the beginning. Yes. Or one of the beginnings. That was why she left her job. Your mother was determined you would be *saved from Paola's fate*. She would give you all the love Paola hadn't had from her real mother. She found it hard to love Paola. Paola didn't know how to be loved, she said. That crucial stage in life had been denied her. The first two years. The orphanages in the Ukraine. But she would have breast-fed you forever if that would have helped. Paola's dour, your mother said. She's damaged. We had arguments about it. It can be hard to love even your own flesh and blood sometimes. The mother was a Kazakh whore. But Paola always babysat for you when your mother was off at her various functions. When I was off travelling. Your mother is religious. We know that. And of course there were her parties. Her set. She likes to see people. She missed her work. I had to travel. She likes to get involved in projects. It is odd, though, it suddenly occurs to me now, once again back here beside my son's body, still trying to gather my thoughts after that farcical interruption, still wondering how on earth I am to behave in response to what has happened – it is odd how my wife has always managed to occupy both extremes of every polarity. She is religious and flirts. She is strong and independent and desperately needs to be with people. With me even. She plays mute, but she wants to be involved. It is because he suffers disillusionment so early, Leopardi wrote, that the naturally passionate Italian becomes so irretrievably cynical. They have given me fifteen minutes. Because disillusioned early. Certainly our life was less romantic than she hoped. Whose is not? But I have lost my concentration. There is nothing wrong with social functions, I was telling Marco a few moments before being so frighteningly interrupted. I liked your mother for her busy social life, however irritating it could be sometimes, I loved her for the way she brought life into the house, even though you must have seen the irritation on my face from time to time, you smelt my fear I suppose. There is no smell here but the smell of candles.

Paola babysat. I tried again to tell my dead son the story of our family, of himself. Paola babysat. We had moved into the family house on via Livorno. The house of ghosts, your mother called it. Joking. The family house. The generations. Who died there. Her own mother was dead at last. Perhaps I wasn't so jealous of you, Marco, because you had drawn your mother away from her mother. For centuries they died there. The endless weekends with her mother. Though her father was shot down over Malta of course. Your mother's father. There is no grave. No trace. He was called Marco too. Shot down by the British. There was no corpse, no tombstone. It was his father killed himself. Your great-grandfather killed himself. Paola babysat in the family house. She loved you. She was very jealous. But how can I know what the relationship between you and Paola was? Things get out of hand. I was away. Once I heard you calling her Xenia. But that wasn't her Ukrainian name I don't think. You know, I can't remember

145

Paola's Ukrainian name. I was frequently away. I felt your mother was right to rename her at once. To make her ours, to make her Italian. How can I know what went on between yourself and Paola? Her friends made fun of you. But all older girls make fun of little boys with their sticky-out ears. I could hardly be expected to see danger there. I can hardly deny I was attracted to some of Paola's friends. When they came with her to babysit you and I had to drive them home. That was a funny period. Did I let it show? How can a father know what best to say to his children in puberty? Especially when attracted to his daughter's friends. You seemed so sensible at school. So accommodating. Much more so than Paola. We couldn't have sent Paola to an English school. She was so far behind, so slow. It seemed the right thing to make her a hundred per cent Italian to give her a feeling of belonging somewhere. How can I know what went on between you both when you stayed in Novara? I was so busy. That year. Why did you think staying with Paola would help you escape the voices? It was the last year of the old regime. Of my journalism. I was working impossible hours. These illnesses always begin at the moment when one strikes out for independence. Late teens, early twenties. Staying with Paola didn't help. The literature is clear on that. But then many ordinary illnesses take place at particular times of life. Paola had offended you, your mother said. Kicked you out of her Novara flat. It seemed to me more likely that it was Giorgio had asked you to leave. I couldn't afford to get them a bigger apartment. Your mother wasn't to know. But I certainly didn't shirk a dowry. The trial was a revelation to me, Marco. I never dreamed Paola would say the things she said. I didn't know. Your mother was keeping you to herself. Perhaps the problem had been going on for years before I noticed, before you gave up basketball, before you suddenly insisted on speaking English. I hadn't noticed anything till then. Till those dramatic changes. In the end, we only went out drinking, what? three times, or four, before you blew apart. Before you destroyed the house. Before your mother and I were forced together again to find some help for you. The important thing was to avoid a closed institution, a prison. Vanoli was very clear on that point.

I stared at my son's face. At the gaunt profile of the nose. It's not that I betrayed you, Marco, I've explained this. Just that I suddenly realised you were ill. That the position you'd taken with me was sickness. I didn't see that at first. I was angry with your mother. I thought you had genuinely seen my side. Finally come round to my side. Was there something I should have said those times we went out together? Could I have said something? No doubt I said things I shouldn't have. Against your mother. I've always been content to be left in the dark, Marco. You must have sensed that. But the literature also makes clear that it is an entirely chemical alteration. A virus mutation operating on the enzymes. You've been ill, kid. My relationship with your mother always made me feel it would be unwise to look into the heart of things. I am perfectly capable of reading a little French if I have to, but I never looked at her famous diary. Nor read the famous correspondence with Gregory. Nor ever found out exactly how it ended between them. It did end. Very shortly after the trial, after we moved heaven and earth to avoid the prison hospital. I presume it ended. We can get through without looking into the heart of things, I thought. The shock just made her lose interest, I suppose. We understood we had to be strong for you. Strong together for you. To see how something works, you have to break it more often than not, that's what I used to think. And I didn't want to break it. We made love when you and Paola were at school. Your mother and I. Though at the same time I often spoke of the need to go deeper. That night with Gregory in the Hotel Garibaldi. I am afraid of being a coward. I love your mother, I told my dead son. I nursed the illusion that I was the kind of person who liked to go deep, but I was too afraid to look into the heart of things. Then I said out loud: and now it is over.

Withdrawing my hand from my son's head, only seconds away from being interrupted, I whispered: I can't remember you at all, Marco. And I asked: Why did you change sides? Were the apron strings suddenly too tight? Was it you who wrote help me? In the steam on the bathroom window? Did you leave Villa Serena when you weren't supposed to? Did you kill yourself because they forced you back? Because Paola phoned to have you taken back? But then why didn't they tell me? Why hasn't she told me? Do you know why Paola and Giorgio have split up? I suddenly demanded of my dead son.

I had withdrawn my hand from his forehead. I was looking straight at my dead son's face. The skin is lustreless and the eyes sunken. I would not dare to peel back an eyelid and look into an eye. They have combed his hair. It is ridiculous I suddenly thought, that your mother used to speak of us as being so different. Of birth by parthenogenesis. Your profile is exactly my profile, Marco. Overnight your eyes have sunk to my depths, I told him. At last I was speaking freely, honestly to my son. Your nose has come out like mine, I told him. I almost laughed. This could be me dead, I thought. It should be me dead. Though better dead than a life walled away in a cell. Actually I would say he looks rather like you, Vanoli remarked when I told him that story, when I came out with the word parthenogenesis. Though I never had your physique. Why do you think your wife chooses to be so provocative? Vanoli asked. And I said if schizophrenia was a purely biological question then I couldn't see what the relationship between myself and my wife could possibly have to do with it. Why did he bother to ask me these questions? Which were entirely unconnected with my son's illness. Perhaps it's because you're so interested in talking about them yourself, Vanoli laughed. And now you look even more like me, I told Marco. And my body functions seem to have stopped too. Just like yours. Since more or less the moment you died, I told him. My bowels haven't moved since you died, kid. My bladder refuses to empty. I remembered the dog and the theatre director. Who would find me? Would both Sardinian wife and Polish mistress be there at the funeral? I'm in an agony of cramps, Marco. I must get some heparin. How many times have I fantasised Karen at my funeral. It's only the mind racing round and round these things that stops me screaming, I told him. Suddenly, sitting on the straight-backed chair in the candlelight of the *camera ardente*, I felt extremely confused. I half got up, sat down again. The room flickered. The *bandhu* survive death, that book said. There was clattering outside the door. I can't remember the title. The connections the mind makes survive its physical decease. I was looking directly at my son, his head on a purple cushion in a shallow coffin, I was feeling extremely confused and absolutely certain that nothing survives death. I suppose I was weeping. When the door banged open, the candles guttered wildly. We were interrupted.

Giorgio! A few moments later I was at a payphone in the corridor. There are payphones by the stairwell. Paola had given me the number of his mobile. She didn't tell me anything, he said. From his cautiousness it seemed he must be with a client. But they've come to take him away, I insisted. To Rome. They want to take him now, this minute. Giorgio said he couldn't help. He didn't know what she had in mind. The family tomb presumably. Down in Rome. My suitcase would be at the airport in Turin by now, he said. I'll have to go to Rome immediately, I was saying. The digits on the credit display were counting down extremely rapidly. I had forgotten the family tomb. Did I still have the original ticket, he asked, with the baggage sticker? They would need to see the baggage sticker. Where is she? I demanded. I couldn't wait for him to finish speaking. There was a pause. My credit was evaporating. Are you well? he asked. Paola said you were ill this morning. She was worried for you. I was frantic. Is she coming back to the hospital, or isn't she? He didn't know. Have you seen a doctor? he was asking. Then my cash ran out and the line was gone. How is it, I demanded, hanging up the receiver, that these two recently separated people can mention each other's names so casually, so reasonably, as if there were no rancour at all between them? As if their marriage had been little more than an amicable agreement. And how was it that Italcom could charge so much for calls to mobile phones? Five thousand lire had gone in a flash. From public places like hospitals. An article proposing subsidies for calls from hospitals? As I hurried back along the corridor a hoarse voice, a radio behind a door, was singing a song of lost love. Italy, I thought. This is Italy. This is where I have spent my life.

They had negotiated the coffin on a trolley alongside the hospital's shallower version which I now realised must be some institutional stand-in for families who hadn't yet had time to purchase their own. Pushing the door I heard the word Juventus. My wife has found the time to purchase a coffin, I thought. And energy. How resilient she is! The undertakers were talking football. You felt sorry for her – you were letting her down terribly – and she calmly went out and purchased a coffin. Again they repeated that they hadn't realised there would be mourners. Football is less inappropriate than second-rate love-songs, I thought. They were under strict orders to drive to Rome. Even if they left this minute, the older of the four pointed out, they wouldn't make it much before nine. They would have to find a hotel. On whose authority? I demanded. I was the father. Only I had the right to decide what was to be done with my son. The man was in his fifties, tall, with a ski-slope suntan, a clipboard. These people are used to death, I thought. The others were just well-dressed boys. Perhaps death is less remarkable than we suppose, I thought. Perhaps it's quite easy to get used to death. I had seen a good few corpses myself after all. I was perfectly used to death. I had seen the dead piled in heaps in Basilicata that time. One boy leaned forward over the empty coffin and shifted it very slightly back and forth on its trolley. I have seen any number of murder victims. Though one sees one's son's corpse only once.

It looked an expensive coffin at a glance. A wheel squeaked. Almost a luxurious coffin. If one can say such a thing. This is absolutely typical of my wife, I suddenly thought, quite furious, then immediately conceded what, until only a moment before I had forgotten: how quickly they bury people in Italy. A day, two days. Today was Tuesday. The football matches were on Sunday. If Marco had been interested in football I would certainly have gone to see him. Certainly I would have watched Juventus with him. I like football. My wife knew that. She knew I liked football. The theatre director was to be buried on Wednesday afternoon, in Bari, despite all the prestigious guests who must be invited, the expected clash between his various women. Then I remembered that this was the exact same time I was supposed to be seeing Andreotti, though of course I knew I wouldn't see Andreotti. It would be monstrous for me to go and see Andreotti in these circumstances. My son had died at almost exactly the same time as the theatre director, thirty-six hours ago. He might well be buried at the same time, exactly. When I was supposed to be seeing Andreotti. On whose authority? I repeated, taking a second glance at what was clearly a very expensive coffin. The undertaker pulled out a mobile and called his office. From the *camera ardente*. Everybody has mobiles now. Even undertakers. They call from funeral chambers, beside corpses. Or from ski-slopes, no doubt. Nobody was looking at Marco. My wife has interrupted my mourning, I thought and at the same time I was ludicrously aware of an Italian comedy film I once saw where a heart surgeon drops his mobile in his wife's coffin while kissing the corpse goodbye and hears it ringing as they are burying her in the family tomb beside his three other dead wives. This is absolutely typical, of my wife, I thought, my only wife, and I thought how many times Marco had simply sat or stood or even lain, on the sofa, while others quarrelled over him. Could he have a moped, or couldn't he? Was he to go to Milan to university, or stay in Rome? One of the very few battles I won. I influenced his life very little. We played power games over Marco. In a way we never did over Paola. It has never been clear who has the power in our home, my wife's family home. I should never have agreed to live there. Until that weekend he took it into his head to come back from Milan, from Novara, and destroy the whole house. Sledgehammer the masonry, as if it was that walling him in. The house of ghosts. And she would never sell up now precisely because Marco had left his mark on it. Had added his ghost to theirs. Marco is part of my wife's family history, I thought. She will never sell up her family house. Not of mine. He locked her in the bathroom and took a sledgehammer to the place. The unburied airman and so many others. Her grandfather also killed himself. His ghost will haunt the stairway with a sledgehammer. Still, it suddenly occurred to me, I *had* walked out on her. What could she do but order a coffin? And why shouldn't it be luxurious? My wife is in the utmost distress, I thought. The least one can do is to buy an expensive coffin.

Two of the young men went out and immediately a smell of cigarette smoke drifted under the door. Their voices chuckled. Distractedly, while the undertaker spoke on his mobile and the smoke drifted in under the door, I recalled that there was a chapter in Gregory's book entitled 'The Paranoid Peninsula', full of ideas stolen from myself. I had leafed through it on the train from Novara. One must do something to kill the time. Even when going to wake one's son. To wake one who can never be woken. I haven't even had five minutes with him, I protested to the man still speaking into his mobile. She said she was the only mourner, he told me, not even bothering to cover the phone. There was no suggestion we might have to wait. *Sì, c'è un problema*, he told the phone. And only an address to take it to, he turned to me. Via Livorno, I thought, then realised when he nodded I must have spoken out loud. No mention of the funeral or burial place, he said. Was I announcing other thoughts out loud? He snapped the mobile shut. I imagine the local authorities will take over after we've delivered. That's the normal thing. Give me fifteen minutes, I said. Please. Then all at once a fit of pain returned my intestines to centre stage. Unbelievably fierce. There was a stabbing. I felt nauseous and might have tottered. It was deep in the innards. As if the gut had twisted. I'm turning white, I told myself. How can one avoid distraction when one has intestines? When one has a body? At the same time, suddenly and inexplicably, I was back on the straight-backed seat the other side of the coffin. I called to the undertaker who had reached the door now: But will they bury him if it's suicide? As he ushered the last of his assistants out, I noticed he had a limp. Somehow this seemed extraordinarily felicitous in an undertaker. For a moment my vision blurred, then came back. I mean in the family tomb, I said. In consecrated ground. An undertaker limps because he has one foot in the grave, I thought. Quite stupidly. He doesn't ski at all. Don't they have rules, I asked, about suicides? One of my reasons for living in Italy, I used to joke at my wife's dinner parties, and hence Gregory must have heard it at least once, if not many times, was that it was a place whose group paranoia was so evident, so laughable that I felt it was healthy for my own. Nobody would notice an Englishman's poor paranoia in Italy, I said. A country of mafia and *omertà* was necessarily a country of deep paranoia, I once wrote more seriously in an article. My wife believes in the evil eye. Certainly Marco became paranoid, believing I could manipulate vast armies, control the weather. And Gregory had stolen the whole idea word for word. I read it in the train. He had stolen it. They would never bury my son on consecrated ground, I thought. My wife would be destroyed. And I said, *Mi scusi?* Because I realised I hadn't been following what the undertaker was saying. I believe it depends on the individual priest, the man said, perhaps repeated. He was trying to be kind in the face of what was no doubt an irritating hiccup, a day that promised to be endless. Turin–Rome is a long drive. They rarely raise objections these days, he said. Not in his experience. On the other hand, I thought, an undertaker should be used to dealing with the distressed. I'm distressed, I thought. He has a limp. I have been distressed for years. My wife must be distressed beyond all consolation. Fifteen minutes, he said. Presumably I nodded.

For almost fifteen minutes then I have been sitting here in the *camera ardente* staring at my son. In death he does look remarkably like me. The sunken eyes, the nose rising from the face. Less remarkable than in life. This is the last time

I shall see him. My thoughts have collected somewhat. I shall never see this face again. His eyes I saw for the last time some months ago. They were wild then. I dare not touch his eyelids. I shall have to leave it to a later date, I reflect, a little more calmly now, to form any more coherent memory of him. But I do remember our last encounter at Villa Serena. There was a scuffle when he did the business of rubbing dirt in her hair. Wishing well, the shadows lengthen, he said. His eyes were wild. He must have said it five or six times, chuckling to himself. Wishing well, the shadows lengthen. All the literature remarks on the schizophrenic's pleasure in cryptic remarks. You made fun of us, I mutter in the candlelight. His face is quite still and smooth. Perhaps because we made worse fun of you. The shadows are indeed long in the *camera ardente*. It would be impossible to say how much I wish him well, and how far he is beyond any wishing well or ill. Wishing well does not seem to improve anybody's lot, I reflect. Though no doubt a good thing in itself. Was there sense then to his expression: Wishing well, the shadows lengthen? His mother wished everything in the world for him. And he said: Giving today, giving tomorrow, goodnight to the players. That was an Italian saying, from some play or other, but odd and strange in English. I tried to explain to Vanoli that this habit of giving literal translations of Italian idioms was his way of demonstrating the incompatibility of the different sides of himself. Idioms his mother used, spoken in his father's language. You want the wife drunk and the barrel full, he shouted. An Italian idiom was madness in English, I explained. You don't give me rope, he laughed. You never give me rope. *Non mi dai corda*, I translated. Why was it you would only speak English in your mother's presence? I mutter to the corpse. I had to translate everything you said for her. It is uncanny to sit beside a person who simply will not move.

Even a sleeping child moves. There is a sort of hum behind the eyes. Even when you said: Sodomise, damn your eyes, lobotomise, it's only wise, I had to translate. Your mother insisted. I'll kill you when I get out, you said. I'll give you rope and no mistake. And I remember how he said it almost casually, breathing heavily, overweight, and immediately my native paranoia has me wondering, can one die on purpose to haunt and hurt someone? And wall them in? He was obese again. Can one die to come back? To make them pay for their crimes? I had read somewhere that suicides become vampires. Am I already being haunted? I'll make you a wooden overcoat, next time I'm out, you said. Another idiom. I translated. Your mother wept in the car. She said she would come to England after all. And now it's you has the wooden overcoat, Marco. And a luxurious one at that. With a purple lining.

Sitting in the *camera ardente* these fifteen minutes, whispering in candlelight beside the face of my dead son – a face, now it is still, so much more like my own than I ever imagined – I am making a huge effort to collect my thoughts, to be straightforward and above all to be coherent, something to which I have always attached the greatest importance. Your mother is arranging for you to be buried in the family tomb, I tell him. I am sure of it. Beside your grandmother. Though I would have preferred a cremation myself. I am trying to concentrate on his face. There is a certain cut the lips have which is all his mother's. In my journalism I always put the highest premium on coherence. Yet the forehead is mine. The nose is mine. There are two spare places, I tell him, staring at a face that might be my own. Bar the lips. But you know that. Or from another angle my wife's. Bar the nose. When you toss ashes in the wind, I reflect, there is no sense of confinement, no sense of being walled away. Don't you think? The fifteen minutes are almost up. I find myself waiting as if for a response. The story of my son escapes me. That's the truth. I know Andreotti's life better than my son's, I reflect. That's a terrible thought. The closer you come to something the less you understand it. He will compare himself to one of the minor political figures in Manzoni's story, no doubt. A predictable false modesty. Or one of the church administrators. A wry smile on his lips. Your story escapes me, I tell my son. I could not write it up. But the story of myself and your mother is overwhelming. Is all the other stories together somehow. Is all I know. She has arranged for you to be buried in the family tomb, I tell him. Beside your grandmother, your aunt, your great-grandmother. I am breathing slowly, speaking softly. That was predictable enough. And I have given way again, Marco. You have seen that before. I have let her have her way. Again it was predictable. Presumably I could have told these men they had no right to take you away without my consent. To bury you in my wife's family tomb. Without my consent. I would have preferred cremation. But I didn't. No doubt she is planning to keep the place beside him, the last place, for herself, I reflect. To deny me, even in death, the place beside her. She has arranged to have you taken to Rome, I repeat, but I made only a token objection. I don't want that place beside her. As last night, you will be aware, I made only a token objection when she wanted to see you alone, when she told me I mustn't come into the mortuary. I could perfectly well have insisted on coming into the mortuary. Perhaps my wife wanted me to insist. Perhaps it was my duty to do so. But I didn't. I keep pausing as if for a reply. But Marco has become entirely predictable now. Eternally silent. The extraordinary thing about the story of the Nun of Monza, I reflect, is that it offers absolutely no room for comic relief or catharsis of any kind. Just an appalling socio-psychological dynamic that leads a young woman to be walled up forever in a cell, food passed through a hole in a wall, excrement on the floor, waiting to die, but really dead already. Death pushes back the horizon of predictability to the infinite, I reflect. There is no longer any danger of getting things wrong. My son will never move again. There can be no doubt about a reflection like that. There is no hum behind his eyes. Such certainty is hardly a relief. Really, Marco, I never made anything more than token objections to the idea of your sleeping in our bed, her bed. I could have objected, I tell my son, but I didn't. It began there perhaps. I was furious when I came to our bed to find you already in my place. I was tired, worried, and there you were in my place. I was deeply frustrated. But I made only token objections. Cremation would be my preference, the ashes in the breeze, but I can see no reason for imposing it. That's the truth. I see no reason for imposing myself. I ironise over my wife's religion, but have nothing better to offer in its place. Nothing that would have helped you. I criticised politicians, but made no policies of my own. I chuckled at the evil eye, the ex voto, the Italian paranoia, but had only a vague unfocused anxiety to offer in its place, a vague unease that leaked out in worried articles about democracy and the environment. At least your mother has faith, I tell my dead son. You mustn't blame her. Fuck somebody else, you said. I did, but it was never an alternative to your mother. To her energy. Just part of the general eclecticism, a general detachment I have. I never thought of imposing my mistress. I never considered bringing her into the house and sitting her on the sofa and saying, okay let's talk about this. However much I might have loved her. Your mother has all the energy, Marco. That's the truth. That's why she is so obscene, so scandalous, so attractive. I'm attracted to her and repelled. The mistress was just a mistress, Marco. Who would I be without your mother? I suddenly find myself demanding of my dead son. I am nobody. I find this *camera ardente* ridiculous. Its Sacred Heart. Its crucifix. It is ridiculous, when you think about it, to imagine that corpses have to be surrounded by dark wood and candlelight. But I can imagine no alternative. Nor any reason for imposing my view. I find Italy with all its old traditions, its superficial idealism, its gauche bad taste, its puffed up national pride and Catholic paranoia ridiculous – Italy is quite ridiculous, I am telling my dead son, the way people here believe in the evil eye and are always convinced there are conspiracies against them – but I would not swap it for anything I have to offer. For an Englishman's empty and pragmatic eclecticism. Why did I never have any vision to oppose to my wife's? To help you grow up. England is a nation without plans, I had insisted to Geoff Courteney the other evening. He was ludicrously enthusiastic about Blair. A nation that says, maybe we'll join this, if it's convenient. Maybe we won't, if it's not. A nation without vision, I insisted. Even the wrong vision is better than no vision, I told Courteney at his dinner party. We were arguing over Europe. Give me the delirium of a destiny, I told him. He was praising the wait-and-see approach. Any destiny, I insisted. While at the same time reflecting that all my life had been wait and see. Wait in briefing rooms. See the scene of the crime. The corpse on the street. Wait and see if our marriage improves. Your mother had plans, I tell Marco, quite abruptly, almost angrily, as if still pursuing the argument with Courteney, Geoff Courteney who has the power to publish my book. Your mother had endless plans. Hair-brained plans. I loved her for them and they went wrong. They went terribly wrong. I loved to think how dynamic she was, Marco, but I seemed unable to assist with her plans. I watched them going wrong, but seemed unable to assist. Courteney is irretrievably smug, with his talk of hedged bets and cautious good sense.

I was perfectly aware when it all began to go wrong with Paola. That is journalism after all. You wait and see and get the opportunity to watch things going wrong, *Inferno* in the making. I remember very precisely the moment when your mother realised Paola would not be beautiful. That is the bird on the Vedic tree who watches the other bird eat. Myself and your mother. I had no vision to substitute for hers. Even when the plans went wrong. It was the day Paola got her glasses, and your mother realised, in an instant, that she was not going to be a beautiful woman. She was immensely disappointed. She let it show. Your mother occupied both sides of every polarity, Marco. She took you to church and flirted with you. She prayed with Gregory, and committed adultery with him. She was generous to Paola and cruel to Paola. For some reason I am standing up, leaning over the coffin. My face is only inches from his. From my son's. But when it came to the poles of reflection–action, Marco, when it came to who actually did things, and who just thought about doing them, who just tagged along, who just offered a voice that was at best an echo, there we stayed at opposite extremes. What was it my son couldn't decide about, I wonder, when everything went wrong, in Milan? Could I have helped? What was it drove him to thrust a screwdriver in his veins? Without kissing him, without waiting for the knock on the door, without deciding to go, I am gone.

Dottor Vanoli? I have bought another phone-card. You have all my sympathy, he says. I am so sorry. Busi informed me this morning. I was hoping you would be in touch. It is . . . They have put suicide on the death certificate, I announce. I am standing in the busy foyer of the *policlinico*. Suicide. My wife doesn't know. I'm afraid they won't let him be buried in the family tomb. She will be distressed. There will be a scene. She will be wild.

I have bought a stack of phone-cards so as not to be cut off again. I have spoken to Giorgio again, and heard nothing but the blandest of disclaimers. I have spoken to Paola who says she does not see how she can come to a funeral in Rome. She is afraid my wife will make a scene. She ought to come to the funeral, she says, but she can't. She refuses to use the word mamma. Your wife, she said. There was something cool about Paola's voice when she refused to come, I tell myself now, listening to Vanoli's commiserations, when she refused to use the word mamma. Paola is determined to establish a distance from you, I tell myself, listening to Vanoli repeat what the undertaker said about its being extremely rare for priests to raise objections. Perhaps there is something dour about Paola. But surely your wife has been informed, Italy's foremost psychiatrist asks. I have left her, I tell him. There is no point in our being together now Marco is dead. It is over between us, I announce. Now I am listening to him worrying if I am well. How can I broach with Paola the question of my going to live with her? Or was her coolness to do with what was written on the bathroom window? With something she is hiding? These feelings of desolation are commonplace in bereavement Vanoli says. Am I looking after myself? Am I eating? He is telling me my feelings are commonplace. That I must not be hasty. Why don't you come and see me if the funeral is going to be in Rome? Perhaps I can prescribe something, he suggests. Then all at once I am shouting: It's not a question of prescribing anything. It was never a question of prescribing things. I substitute one phone-card for another, I am determined not to be cut off this time. Mr Burton, you are understandably upset, he is saying. It is ludicrous to imagine you can help me by prescribing something, I am shouting in the foyer. It was utter folly, I shout out loud in the hospital foyer, to imagine you could help my son with Thorazine.

With a mere medicine. For somebody out of his mind. It was our fault, I shout at Vanoli. It was my fault. My fault for letting things slide. For paying no attention. For having no vision. No, let me say what I think for once. Mr Burton . . . It was our fault and you knew it. We drove him mad. We made it impossible for him to live. And you knew it. We walled him up. As surely as with bricks and mortar. You knew it. I came to you – there are still four thousand lire on this card – to *avoid* clearing up the situation between my wife and myself, to *avoid* a doctor who would suggest his illness was anything but clinical. You *knew* that. You knew why we came to see you separately, why we didn't come together. You even asked the appropriate questions. We are totally responsible for what happened to Marco. That's the truth Dottor Vanoli. You knew it and did nothing. You were never frank. You were seduced by my wife's pleasant façade. You asked questions and never followed them up. All you did was prescribe things. You can't prescribe things for people like us. You should be ashamed of yourself, I tell Italy's foremost psychiatrist. Then suddenly I feel completely and utterly exhausted. It is my third wild phone-call in succession. Two thousand six hundred. Two thousand four hundred. All at once I realise he is smiling. Six hundred kilometres away Vanoli is smiling his knowing smile. But I don't have the energy to start again. Mr Burton, he says. There is a pause. I am sorry, Doctor, I'm sorry, I lost control. Mr Burton, if I may say so . . . Forgive me, Doctor. Please, Mr Burton, if I may say so, the habit of assuming ourselves responsible for everything that goes wrong is a particularly modern and western aberration. His voice is as calm and even as ever. But leaving aside the question of your son's pathology, might I suggest two things, both as a doctor and, after all these years I hope, as a friend. I wait. I am sure he is smiling. This isn't affecting him at all. There is still a thousand lire. First, I suspect that you are indeed in urgent need of medication. You do not sound yourself, Mr Burton. Second – he pauses. Second I do feel that the person your anger is really directed at, Mr Burton, is your wife. I am watching the money blink away. Mr Burton? Long distance calls cost less than calls to mobiles, I reflect. Something I have never understood. Vanoli is smiling, exactly as he always used to, in his office, in my dream. What I am trying to say is that it is perhaps your wife, not myself, you wish to be shouting at. And if I could just warn you, in that regard, I do feel that at this delicate moment . . .

Without waiting for the cash to run out, I replace the receiver. How can the man talk about prescriptions, I wonder, and then offer such a frighteningly accurate analysis of my state of mind? I let my feet carry me to the main doors, the steps. I am entirely predictable it seems. To a man like Vanoli. As predictable as a corpse. To an important psychiatrist. My face turns up to a bright blue afternoon. And to myself as well for that matter. I will shout at anybody but my wife.

VIII

I have been offered a pardon. Or rather, I have been invited to apply for a pardon that all have been offered. Suicide may be a somewhat misleading term for patients exhibiting this particular pathology. It was Busi speaking. He was slightly slumped on a swivel chair. The official term is *condono*. I have a pile of papers on my lap, the same pile Busi handed me across his desk, without bag or box. A patient exhibiting this particular pathology, Busi was saying – he is a nondescript young man, but courteous and no doubt competent – frequently fails to perceive his identity as coterminous with the moments of birth and death. I was finding it difficult to grasp what he was saying, I still haven't quite grasped what he said, so surprised was I to find a sheaf of letters addressed to myself and to my wife. The uppermost referred me to a table detailing different levels of payment to rectify different improprieties. And the verb they used, the word my eye settled on in this first letter of the pile, was *sanare*, to make healthy, to heal. They have used the word heal, I thought. To heal your improprieties – how did Marco come to be in possession of these letters? addressed to myself and my wife? – and Busi said: Such patients, that is, frequently imagine their identities, their selves, as beginning before birth and continuing after death. The patient's mind isn't normally embodied, we might say. I stared. Busi has used these words before, I thought. Indeed, the body may actually be perceived as an encumbrance, as alien even. Busi has given this explanation before, I told myself, this dissociation of mind and body. The man has a pleasant face, if a little nondescript. Hence when a patient exhibiting this particular pathology engages in some gesture of masochistic self-abuse, Signor Burton, he may not intend or understand it as an attack on self, or indeed as in any way threatening the normal protraction of individual identity.

It occurs to me now that the question I should have asked Busi here was, what about pain? Surely a source of pain is an unequivocal pointer to selfhood. Where can pain come from, I asked myself later, pushing painfully through the ticket barrier at Torino Porta Nuova, if not from oneself? I had no ticket but nobody stopped me. This much I had been able to predict. How can you feel pain and not recognise where it comes from? From your self. You must be catheterised at once, Busi had said, otherwise it may lead to serious damage. It may be a threat to the protraction of individual identity, I thought, studying the departures board. What time was it? He had mentioned the kidneys. Who are we and what do we identify with if not our pain, our distress? I wondered, looking around for the platform, for the twenty-one fifty-five. All is mysterious, except our pain. Was that Foscolo or Leopardi? That's what I should have asked him. My wife would know. For some years now – I could have quoted Busi this as the obvious example – my wife has been nurturing her identity, twining her most intimate self around the cross of unhappy motherhood. My wife has become The Mother with the Sick Son. I could have told Busi this. That's how she sees herself:

the personification of a pain, a sorrow. Not around the trivia of being Gregory's lover at all, the euphoria of romantic illusion. My wife never thought of herself, never defined herself, as Gregory's Lover. Does he realise that? Is that what his letter is about? In French. In the pile on my lap, handed to me across Busi's desk without bag or box. Across the station concourse bright neon announced FREE SHOP, pink on black. As once my wife saw herself as The Woman Unable to Have Children, The Woman Bereft of her Womanhood. Not my lover and wife at all. Not Mrs Burton. It is disappointment gives us our identity, I thought, momentarily dazzled by that neon. FREE SHOP. Disappointment and pain. The fact of not being able to have children was more important to my wife than the fact of being my wife. The FREE SHOP was selling sandwiches and soda. It's distress confers selfhood. FREE SHOP is a ludicrous name, I thought, a paradoxical name. As pink and black are two colours guaranteed to scream. Italians play with English, I thought, as Gregory and my wife played with French. It was only playing. Only word games. Whereas the shock provoked, it occurs to me now – I suddenly have a very clear impression of it – the shock provoked by thrusting a screwdriver deep into your skin would surely warn you clearly enough where self was. Nothing playful or mysterious about that. I can feel the metal point penetrating my skin. Self is in pain and distress, I thought. That much is obvious. I decided not to buy a sandwich. Stigmata our past. Why do the Italians play with English like this? I wondered: FREE SHOP, AUTOGRILL. Pain intensifies our sense of self, I thought. I must not eat or drink anything. The urine may be forced back into the kidneys, Busi said. Though monks wore hair-shirts, I remembered, walking down the platform now beside the long, gloomy train. They too saw the flesh as alien. It was an old *espresso* that would creep through the night, creep through the night to Rome, to the family tomb. Christians in general do not believe that selfhood ends with death, as Buddhists, I believe, do not believe it begins with birth. The mad are in good company, I told myself. Disembodied, Busi had said. Words to that effect. I even laughed, trying to decide which carriage I should get on. It was a long gloomy train. One mortifies the flesh to liberate the soul, refusing to recognise identity as coterminous with birth and death. Now I've got it. The *bandhu* survive death. That thought keeps recurring. The mind and all its analogies. Though I am sure it is not true. Suddenly, walking along the platform, I experienced the most compelling and immediate image of my son's face in death, of the eyelids that will never open. Never never open. Hence suicide, Busi concluded – he was sitting comfortably on his swivel chair in his cavernous office – suicide, Signor Burton, in the commonly accepted sense of deliberate extinction of self, is probably not the appropriate term.

The doctor had fielded a premise, established a syllogism, brought it to a conclusion. It was suicide, but then again it wasn't. Or not for patients exhibiting this particular pathology. Busi likes that expression. He swivelled slightly on his chair. As manslaughter isn't the same as murder, he said. At least he didn't smile though, I noticed. Which is why we never find suicide notes or letters of explanation in cases of this kind, he went on. His self-satisfaction on establishing this distinction, on defining the nature of cases of this kind, is free from any condescension, I thought. He has said these words before, and clearly he has been through the papers he gave me, seen Gregory's letter, seen the offer of a tax pardon – how could he know there was no suicide note otherwise? – but he genuinely does not appear to derive any complacency or sense of superiority from his competence in this field. It was a professionalism I could warm to. But didn't the boy feel pain? That is what I should have asked the doctor. Wasn't he warned by the pain? Pain would have told him where self was. Can't we at least predict that much? Even about patients exhibiting particular pathologies. All is mysterious except our pain. Suddenly I stopped, finding myself reflected in the shiny green and white panels of a Eurostar. Where had that come from? That wasn't my train. But you yourself are ignoring all kinds of warning pains, I said out loud. You are wandering aimlessly from one side of the platform to the other. You are in pain, but ignoring it. Trying to ignore it. This is the wrong train. You almost got on the wrong train. It was that image of Marco's face did it. Wandering across the platform. From the right side to the wrong. In pain. No, you yourself, I repeated – I have been in considerable pain for several hours now – are taking all kinds of risks with the protraction of your individual identity. Is this suicide? Ignoring your self in pain? Possible kidney failure, Busi specified. Though it wasn't his field. Then I remembered reading somewhere that analgesia is a widely recognised symptom of certain mental disorders.

Are you all right, Signor Burton? the doctor asked. The Eurostar is a beautiful train, I thought, with its shiny green and white panels which reflect the passing crowd. But now a whistle was blowing. My gloomy *espresso* was *in partenza*. Where did he come by these papers? I demanded. I gripped the pile on my lap. They were mostly letters addressed to myself and my wife, some recent, some less so. There was Gregory's handwriting. In French. Perhaps Busi didn't read French. Certainly I had never seen this particular letter from the tax office before, inviting me to apply for a pardon or face prosecution. It was dated three months ago. Its deadline is long overdue. The doctor was sitting patiently on his chair, slightly slumped – he has bad posture – occasionally swivelling a little this way and that. His hands, softly laid on the lap of his white coat, were absolutely without tension, I noticed. He is conceding you the interview that is your due as a bereaved father, I thought, though whether one thinks of it as suicide or not, my son is beyond the man's expertise now. Beyond Dottor Busi's expertise, his years of training. This interview is a courtesy, I told myself, a gesture of human solidarity, and should be accepted as such. A routine kindness. Like dressing the corpse. His working day is officially over. They had told me that when I arrived. Dottor Busi goes off duty at six. Busi is not defensive, I thought. You were lucky to find him. His conscience is clear. There's nothing Busi should have done but didn't. For my son. Why press him then about these papers? Or shouldn't have done but did. His hands are perfectly still. He is trying to be kind, speaking to you after hours, after his long day's work is officially over. Whereas my wife's sharp nails constantly pick at the skin round their borders. My wife is constantly nervous with her hands, her painted nails. I have no idea, he said. She likes to paint her nails the same colour as her mouth. He leaned forward: what papers are they? Can he really be so sure there is no suicide note, I wondered, as not to have even looked through the papers my son left? That was hard to believe. Perhaps there *is* a note. The nurse would know where he got them, Busi said, if anyone does. He sat back again. What papers are they exactly? Since Villa Serena remains unrenovated, the consultant's office is a cavernous, tall-ceilinged room where fragments of fresco still crumble on the walls: a leg here, there a martyr's face. Italy is full of such places. Schizophrenics tend to be very secretive about the most unimportant things, he said. They hang on to the oddest things. Busi is being extremely dismissive about these papers, I thought. I was shuffling quickly through to see if there was anything in my son's handwriting. What for you or I might be quite unimportant, Busi was saying, could take on a mystical significance for patients exhibiting this pathology. Nothing. I looked up. Just above the doctor's head was a woman's hand. A slim white hand. Is it possible, Dottor Busi, I demanded, that Marco was at my daughter's house the night before he died?

Passengers must purchase a ticket and have it stamped before boarding their trains, the p.a. is announcing. It's a routine announcement recorded in various languages. The *capotreno* tells me to get on anyway. *Faccia presto*, he tells me. Is there a chapter in Gregory's book, I wonder, that deals with the contradictory imperatives, the daily double-binds that form the staple of Italian life? The taxpayer is not permitted to apply for a pardon for improprieties for which he is already under investigation. Thus the small print of the printed enclosure. With reference – thus the cover letter – to the current investigation into the above-mentioned improprieties, the inspector of taxes suggests that the tax-payer apply for the tax pardon offered under the terms of DL/783/97 (see enclosure). Or face prosecution. Either Marco got somebody to bring our mail to him, I reflect, or he somehow got out of hospital and picked it up himself. Ignoring pain, I slump into a first-class seat. Both scenarios are equally unlikely. These are fine spacious seats, with deep, grass-green upholstery, no doubt designed many years ago to convey the strongest impression of luxury. As the Eurostar today. These seats, this first-class environment, were designed to give the traveller of twenty years ago the strongest of reasons for believing that Italian State Railways could offer the maximum of comfort and competence, I reflect, taking my place, in pain. Why am I ignoring this threat to my kidneys, to my self, no less? Without a ticket I may as well sit in first as second. Why am I not terrified? As a doctor's professional words, his polished and comfortable words, also seek to leave you no room to doubt his competence, no reason to question his assured analysis. Though the passenger knows perfectly well that the opposite is the case of course, I reflect. I have not spent a lifetime travelling up and down this peninsula without being aware that Italian State Railways are very far from offering the maximum in comfort and competence. Anything can happen on Italian State Railways – the patient knows that – whether your train be a gloomy *espresso* or a sleek and shiny Eurostar. There is something that doesn't add up here, Dottor Busi, I insisted. Something I haven't been told. False impressions and contradictory imperatives are the order of the day, I reflect, settling in my seat. Free Shop indeed! There is something behind this death that is being kept from me, I announced. I suddenly stood up. In pain. How could my son have come by these letters? I demanded. Something must have happened, I told Dottor Busi, to bring my son to this drastic decision. Perhaps to do with these letters. Offered a pardon, I face prosecution. Or with my daughter. He didn't just accidentally kill himself, I said. He knew perfectly well that pushing a screwdriver into his veins was life-threatening. Something tipped him over the edge, I insisted. However mad he was, my son was not a fool. Perhaps our absence. His parents' absence. Perhaps the break-up of my daughter's marriage. He was at my daughter's flat the day before he died, I told Dottor Busi aggressively. I'm sure of that. I know it. I have evidence.

Only now do I realise that all the seats in this first-class compartment are reserved. I am moved along by a polite young German who gestures to his ticket, his seat number. Then I am moved again by a man fatter than myself, a jolly smile on his lips, a mobile glued to his ear. *Non esiste*, he is saying while he smiles at me. *Non esiste*. That can't be so! He's laughing. Once again I get up and shamble down the corridor clutching at the papers Dottor Busi gave me. There is a letter to my wife from the International Professional Women's Association asking her to handle the PR for their annual spring reception. There are pages of Gregory's dismayed French. *Pourquoi n'as-tu pas repondu? Pourquoi tu ne veux pas m'écrire? J'ai été toujours fidèle. Non esiste,* laughs the fat man half out in the corridor as I come back down the carriage again. The signal is always better in the corridor. There is an invitation to contribute to the *European Liberal,* a magazine to suit all tastes. Perhaps I should have gone out to the airport and got the charger for my mobile, I reflect. Perhaps there was a late flight I could have caught. Not to mention the heparin. Two days without heparin. Rather than spending the night in the train. My heart. What kind of night can I expect in a train? With Italian State Railways. Despite the whistles we still haven't moved. I sit down and stand up again. I will not sit next to chatterers.

Your daughter was a frequent visitor, Busi acknowledged. He had been getting round to this, he said, but it seemed important to consider the nature of the deceased first, to clarify the question of suicide. Please do sit down, Signor Burton, Dottor Busi said. You are understandably fraught. Actually, I had imagined that at this point your daughter would have told you about all this. I wasn't aware you still didn't know. But it's quite straightforward. Your daughter was a frequent visitor, Signor Burton. Marco was her brother after all. However, we, the staff here, in liaison, I might say, with Dottor Vanoli, since he has a longer experience of the case than any of us, agreed with her, your daughter, and her husband, that it would be best not to let you know of these visits, since it was felt your wife might intervene in some way. She might not approve. I sat down. Paola hadn't said a word. She was hiding things from me. I had been offered a pardon,

I thought. A pardon! But the deadline has lapsed. We were concerned about your wife's reaction. I watched Busi speak. I face prosecution. The fresco must have been one of those jumbled crowd scenes where a saint is martyred. There was a head by the doctor's left shoulder. A woman's hand, a man's head. Will they pursue me if I return to England? Then on three occasions recently, Busi said, when we felt Marco was stable enough, we allowed him a day out with your daughter, if and *only if* accompanied by her husband of course. I stared at the supine head. As I said, we agreed that these outings would be strictly confidential as it was clear that given the animosity between various members of the family this development might upset someone, Marco's mother in particular, and perhaps prompt her to intervene in some way, or even to return to Italy before the experiment of your absence had been properly explored. It was impossible to say whether it had been severed. Our assessment was that that experiment was yielding results. In particular, I should say – perhaps it was just the broken surface of the fresco – your daughter was concerned that your wife would feel that in taking Marco out she was deliberately exposing him to situations which would put her in a position to make false accusations that he had assaulted her. How real that convoluted worry was, I don't know, but under the circumstances and given what had happened in the past I felt it wise to accept your daughter's request for confidentiality.

I was flabbergasted. I *am* flabbergasted, sitting in a second-class carriage, staring out at the still-stationary station. I have found a decidedly second-class compartment with a mature and wise-looking woman who will not talk, a woman reading a serious financial magazine to which I was once a regular and respected contributor. At least I have found the right compartment, I tell myself, albeit sacrificing comfort for peace and quiet. The décor is dismal. The light is dim. And what flabbergasted me was that after all that had happened, after all she had suffered, assuming her testimony was true, Paola was still willing to do Marco this kindness, to visit him in this institution forty kilometres away, and Giorgio too had still been willing to make this generous gesture, to take his schizophrenic brother-in-law out. He killed himself because these visits had to end then, I announced. Because Paola and Giorgio have broken up. It was obvious. We had been in England and there was no one left to take Marco out. The rules at Villa Serena were strict: patients are allowed out only if accompanied by *two* responsible adults, preferably relatives of the patient. Marco was walled up in Villa Serena. HELP ME, I remembered the writing on the bathroom window. It was his. He had just been told they had broken up, that this was the last time they would take him out, the last time anyone ever would take him out.

Busi was shaking his head. I appreciate that I am somewhat younger than yourself, Mr Burton, but please do allow me to give you the benefit of my experience in bereavements of this kind. For a man who has been working long hours Busi seems remarkably free from nerves, I thought, watching him from my armchair, his body is still absolutely without tension. He swivelled slightly on his chair. He gave the impression of one thinking how to put a difficult thought, though of course he will have said what he is about to say many times before, I reflected. He will put it to me as he has put it to many others before. After the event, Busi began – there is nothing unique about my experience, I thought – I mean after a death of this kind, Signor Burton, parents, brothers, sisters, loved ones in general, naturally try to understand why the tragedy has come about. I watched him, the woman's slim hand above, the supine head beside. A man's head.

The compartment has drab brown seats, black-and-white photographs of tourist destinations. They feel the need to exorcise the event, or to place the blame somewhere. You might even say that they need a story to tell themselves that will explain it all, explain who is responsible perhaps. It's an understandable reaction. Perhaps it is the human reaction *par excellence*. But as we have discussed before, Signor Burton, cause, effect, and above all intention, are concepts not easily applicable to patients exhibiting a pathology of this variety. Fortunately one would have to stand up to look in the mirror provided. Let us recapitulate. Your daughter and her husband took Marco out for some hours on the Sunday. As indeed they did on two previous occasions at intervals of a month. More or less since you left for England. There seems no harm in discussing this now. And suddenly, as a younger woman slides the door back and comes into this drab compartment with its cracked upholstery and gloomy photographs – for the train still hasn't moved – suddenly it occurs to me that the reason Paola didn't mention this outing, this outing the very day my son killed himself – I can see his face, the supine head, the closed eyes – the reason she agreed with Giorgio that they would not speak of it was because she was afraid that I wouldn't be able not to mention it to my wife who would then shift all the blame for his death onto her, Paola, onto that last outing of brother and sister who weren't really brother and sister. Such was the story my wife would no doubt have told herself, I reflect, putting together these fragments, picking at the skin round the borders of her nails. Busi was right there. Your wife conditions all your other relationships, it occurs to me. With the stories she invents. Your daughter cannot talk to you because of your wife, because you would talk to your wife and she would put the blame on her, on Paola. And of course it is quite possible that I would indeed have told my wife the

175

story, talked to her about the outing, if only to persuade her that Paola's heart was in the right place. It is with Paola that my allegiance lies, I tell myself. How can I put it to her that my presence would be a help through these difficult months to come?

Your daughter explained to me that she and her husband were separating, Busi was saying, but as I understood it they had decided not to interrupt these outings with your son. I know your daughter's husband had the greatest affection for Marco. He visited alone on a number of occasions and played chess with him. Again I was flabbergasted, I knew of no relationship between Giorgio and Marco. Not once had Giorgio mentioned Marco in the long drive from the airport. Dear dull Giorgio with his long hooked nose, his balding pate. Paola had told him not to. He is not an attractive man. Though reassuring. Not once had he spoken of playing chess. I was surprised he was capable. He had never played chess with me. In any event, Marco returned from that outing at the regular time early Sunday evening, Busi said. He seemed in a sensible mood. He ate his dinner. He was more than manageable. Your daughter reported to the duty-nurse that they had had a pleasant day. They had eaten in a pizzeria. They watched television at her flat. He had taken a bath it seems. Frankly, we were all very pleased with the progress he was making. He seemed better able to relate to others and at the same time more independent. There was a time, after all, Mr Burton, when your son was quite unable to take a bath alone. In short, we were optimistic. Busi paused. Then the next thing we knew, Signor Burton, he was dead.

Busi stopped. You have all my sympathy, he said. I am very very sorry. Who found him? I demanded. I was sitting up in my chair. Busi continued: It goes against the grain for a scientist to say this, but we are looking at purest enigma here, Signor Burton. You cannot know why he did what he did when he did, or even if he knew what he was doing when he did it. You must put your mind at rest. For myself I can only say that up to that point your decision to move to England had appeared to be a wise one, a courageous one – no doubt it was a considerable sacrifice – and we had every hope that the outcome would be positive. Who found him? I repeated. I couldn't help but remember the dog, Boccaccio, the curiosity of the theatre director's not sharing a bed with his delightful young mistress. The duty-nurse, Busi said. It was a matter of no importance. His voice is quite without tension, I thought. He is perfectly calm. Why didn't my daughter talk to me about this? I demanded. Where did he get a screwdriver? Surely you don't leave lethal things like screwdrivers lying around a mental hospital? I had raised my voice. Why am I surrounded by people who won't talk openly about things? I shouted. Standing up, I fainted.

After frequently looking at her watch, the younger woman asks both myself and the older woman what time the train was supposed to start. Simultaneously, and overcoming an immense inertia that is transmitted to the passenger as a sense of strain and resistance to strain, of conflicting energies doing battle around a static point, the *espresso* begins, with a groan, to roll. The older woman looks up over her glasses. Twenty minutes ago, she says, she smiles, but she considers it a miracle when any train starts at all. A miracle. Comes a stab of pain when the carriage jolts. The younger woman, who is not unattractive in an eager, practical way, remarks that certain trains are more reliable than others. She has a generous mouth. It's a question of knowing your train. Brightly painted. Bright brown eyes. The pain is deep in the abdomen. The older woman closes her prestigious magazine. Entirely predictably, the two fall into a conversation about train experiences. One says fall into a conversation, I reflect, as one says fall in love. My face is suddenly sharp in the polished black glass. We're out of the station. That loss of self. Loss of control. Pain does give a sense of self, I reflect, seeing a reflection I would never have sought in the mirror, but you are ignoring it. The train is out in the night. You are ignoring Busi's advice, ignoring a steadily worsening pain. The older woman is convinced that things are getting worse. Declining service, higher prices. And the government refuses to confront the unions on the issue of overmanning. *Ma i nodi stanno arrivando al pettine*, she declares. It's another idiom Marco liked to use in English. The knots are arriving at the comb, he would say. He made me translate for his mother. I'll make you a wooden overcoat, he threatened. But I couldn't translate the madness of his saying it *that way* in English. Now he's made one for himself. The younger woman believes the left-wing government is improving matters. But things take time. The nineteen-ten *superrapido* is never late, she says. They talk on. She usually takes the nineteen-ten. I thought I'd got in the right compartment, I reflect, a quiet if not so comfortable compartment, a desperately drab compartment in fact, but quite predictably I was wrong. An entirely predictable conversation develops about train experiences, about the present political situation. The lighting is dim. I who plan to write a book about the predictability of human behaviour should rejoice in this predictability, I tell myself, in the predictability of the conversations people have on Italian trains. The older woman – reading-glasses hanging round her neck – studiously adopts postures, tones of voice, suggesting experience and wisdom. Is this why I mistakenly imagined she was wise? Just because I saw her reading a magazine I used to write for? Things are predictable but quite predictably one makes mistakes. I'm in the wrong compartment. I don't have my ear-plugs, don't have my heparin, don't have the charger for my mobile. It can't go on, she says, *i nodi stanno arrivando al pettine*, she repeats. I have heard this a thousand times in Italy. I have prophesied it myself a thousand times. Wrongly. The knots are always arriving at the comb in Italy, but they never actually get there. Replacing Andreotti and company did nothing to solve the problems of Italian State Railways. Andreotti, I reflect, was the great architect of tax pardons, of the dubious ethics of tax pardons. But without him they go on all the same. Even the left-wing government has tax pardons. The women are proceeding warily now, they have appreciated that they are at different ends of the political spectrum. One says political spectrum. The older woman rehearses the sceptical wisdom of she who votes to the right, the younger the informed optimism of she who votes to the left. There is no difference between them. Both feel the need to chatter. About high-speed trains. About the quality of Swiss and German carriages. It is a cause for national embarrassment, the older woman is saying. Her voice becomes a trifle shrill. Her grey hair is permed to a helmet. I am fascinated by the predictability of this conversation. And at the same time walled up in my pain. She is shaking her old head, but her lacquered hair doesn't move. How Swiss citizens must groan when they realise they have to board an Italian carriage! I should take notes. There is a well-rehearsed theatricality about the older woman's positing of a national embarrassment. She isn't embarrassed at all, I reflect. Italian carriages aren't that bad. Quite the contrary, she rejoices in this opportunity to complain. What would any of us do without an opportunity to complain? I am fascinated and repulsed by the appalling predictability of this conversation. The battles between yourself and your wife were appallingly predictable, I tell myself. How your wife loved to complain!

Late or early, fast or slow, our arguments ran on metalled rails. But so do you. You also love to complain. From Rome to Turin and back to Rome again. Complain about England, complain about Italy. Marco's death has broken the predictable back-and-forth of our quarrels, I reflect. I have left my wife. Left the woman around whom all my old complaints revolved, the pain that gave a sense of self. Even if it walled you up. Marco has broken the spell. The older woman raises and lowers her glasses, pretentiously refers to an article in her financial magazine. The younger woman is playing the eager *studentessa*, eloquently disagreeing, but showing theatrical respect for the other's theatrically presented age and experience. I am only going to Rome for Marco's funeral, I tell myself. For the family tomb. Not to return to the metalled ways of my arguments with my wife. Not to interview old fox and seven times prime minister Giulio Andreotti. Why do we imagine the old are wise, I wonder, just because they read prestigious financial magazines? Just because they have been prime minister seven times? The pain is constant now. Deafening. You are walled up in another pain now. Will he dust off his remark that the deranged either think they are Jesus Christ or that they can *sanare* the finances of Italian State Railways? I should have phoned the fixer about the faxes. Perhaps he has already replied. Heal the terminally ill. Andreotti was the architect of the tax pardon, I reflect, of a society where, in the secular as in the religious, all would be sinners and all would be pardoned. All would be at the state's mercy and discretion as every Christian is ever at the Almighty's mercy and discretion, sinners queuing for pardon. But who can pardon me for the way I have behaved with my son? The way I have behaved with my wife? The deadline is past.

You mustn't torment yourself, Busi was saying. He helped

me back into my seat. It won't help anyone to make yourself sick, he said. Will it now? Your wife needs your support, he said. These things are not explicable, he repeated, and seemed more convincing now than when he talked about patients exhibiting particular pathologies. All is mysterious. It was Leopardi. Except our pain. *Arcano è tutto fuor che il nostro dolor.* The insistence on finding an explanation for what happened can only bring you pain, Busi said. It's as if he were talking to a child, I thought. You can't know that, he said. Then when I explained my pain, he said I must be catheterised at once. Otherwise there might be serious consequences. But these were simple mechanical things, Signor Burton, he said as he helped me along the corridor. The bladder, the kidneys. Though not his field. These things require no more than common sense and the right tools to do the job. Sometimes he wished he did work in a different field. A field where all you had to do was introduce a catheter and pain could be relieved. If you could introduce a catheter into the mind, he joked. Think of that! It's as if he were speaking to a child, I thought. I didn't tell my wife it was suicide, I announced. You mustn't torment yourself, he said. You must support each other all you can. I was in a chair in some sort of infirmary. He was on the phone. The last time the patient passed water was midnight, twenty hours ago. I was a patient. He claims to have drunk nothing since then. Just two coffees. The duty-nurse will be here in a moment, he said. Other people are taking over, I thought. I'm a patient. I'm ill. Walled up in pain. I'll just go and write you a prescription for some heparin, Busi said. Not something we stock, but the nurse will be able to tell you which pharmacies are open late. She'll be here in a moment with the catheter. As soon as he had gone, I opened the window and tumbled down four or five feet onto the gravel drive.

The older woman is talking about the immaturity of the Italian stock exchange. Two black girls walk by along the corridor, glancing into the compartment. Prostitutes no doubt. The supposed wisdom of the old is nothing but sham, I reflect, nothing but the theatre of wisdom. Suddenly I am wildly impatient with these women's voices, these ridiculous reflections on the stock exchange. Perhaps if they get off, you can have a prostitute, I tell myself. A man planning to write a monumental book on the predictability of human behaviour should rejoice in the fact that in Italy at the present time one can be ninety-nine-per-cent sure that two black girls walking the corridors of a night-train are prostitutes. In the prevailing social conditions, in mini-skirts, you can be sure of that. Surely these chattering women will get off at Genoa. Middle-class women don't travel through the night on Italian State Railways. Not on their own. Not without a couchette. The couchettes are full, the *capotreno* said. *Faccia presto*. Even though I had no ticket. Somebody must fuck these black girls, I tell myself. But how can you even think of having a prostitute when you have been unable to urinate for the last twenty hours! You are in considerable pain. Twenty-four is the limit, Busi said. You are heading for a deadline. Give or take an hour or two. Oddly, it's given me an erection. Either it is forced out by mere overflow, Busi explained, or it backs up in the kidneys. It's painful. That's the danger. A death-line then. Though he couldn't begin to explain my son's death. And now they are complaining about the scandal of tax evasion. The older woman's reading-glasses hang on black strings around her high collar, her powdered neck. She is well dressed. Discreet diamond earrings. Why isn't she in first? It's a national scandal, she says – definitely diamond – a cause of national embarrassment. My wife's earrings are never discreet. And even as she says it – my wife always travels in first – I know that she too evades tax. Likewise the earnest young girl who is convinced the new government is working on the problem, is preparing new mechanisms to trap tax evaders. She too evades tax. I'm sure she does. Tax evasion is a form of original sin in Italy, I tell myself. One can be ninety-nine-per-cent sure. How else do these people afford their jewellery? My wife would never spend so much to be discreet. Their prostitutes? We must all ask for pardons. That was Andreotti's genius. To make it impossible not to need a pardon. There is a deep complicity, it occurs to me, beneath the scandalised surface of these conversations. As beneath the arguments between myself and my wife. Our arguments were always a way of leaving things as they were, I thought. Andreotti was determined to leave things as they were. I must pin him down on that point. To keep everybody evading tax. Every change he made was to keep things the same, to keep them evading. I too would apply for the tax pardon if only the deadline hadn't passed. If only my son hadn't sequestered my post and kept it from me. I too would go on evading tax, safe in the knowledge that there would always be a pardon. Why did he do that? Only four hours now to another deadline. A death-line. Only four hours before something awful happens, I tell myself. For the hundredth time I flick through my son's papers. Unless it's merely incontinence. I merely begin to drip and dribble. The light is dimmer in second-class compartments. How clever of him and how pointless to get our post redirected. There is a letter from an American friend with suggested reading on genetic drift in pre-colonial North American populations. He wanted control over our lives, perhaps, as we had had control over his. Perhaps that was the point. A battle for power. There are moments when it suddenly becomes quite savage, great waves of pain. Something never resolved in our family. Didn't Rousseau have the same thing? Constantly catheterised. I have trouble reading in the dim light. The younger woman is outraged by the fact that her plumber never gives her a receipt, never pays his taxes. I am impatient for silence. It's their talk, not the light, that makes it hard to read. I am furious with their stupid conversation, their bitter complaints about tax evasion when obviously they evade themselves. Rousseau too had trouble with his plumbing. Simultaneous outrage and complacence is an entirely common phenomenon, I reflect. I refuse to read the whole of Gregory's letter. What my son did, presumably, was to write to the post office in mine and my wife's name, forging our two signatures and ordering them to redirect the letters. Is that possible? Then finally there is indeed something in Marco's own hand. A dozen lines in fact. I missed them before because they are written in the lightest pencil in the spaces of a circular letter inviting me to attend a conference on Italy's First World War Experience: the Forging of the Contemporary Italian Consciousness. In the familiar child-like print he regressed to in his illness, I find my son has pencilled the following lines. Villa Serena is the coming together of a considerable diversity of human minds. Why do schizophrenics always revert to print? I wonder. It is always very surprising to me, my son has written, as one of the patients here, the variety of the minds I have come across in Villa Serena. It truly is a remarkable fact, he has written, in English, perhaps it is the grace of God, that all of us at Villa Serena can live together here under one roof and eat together here at the same canteen and sleep together here two or three or even four to a room, when you consider the enormous diversity of our many minds, not to mention our very troubled condition, for we are all people who have had serious troubles. When I think about this extraordinary fact, then I also think, if this can happen here at Villa Serena, if all these different and difficult minds can live together here in one place, then why not world peace? Why not?

I am struck by the banality of it. My son's note tells me nothing at all. They write in print to disguise themselves, obviously. The older woman is now remarking that the problem is that the taxes are absurdly high, the rules absurdly complicated. To cast off their personalities. Nothing about why he killed himself. I could have written that myself, I reflect. No wonder people evade taxes, she insists. In some dull article somewhere. In England it is easier and less onerous to pay one's taxes, I would have written, but there are no pardons if you decide not to. Why should Marco care about world peace? Then, turning the page, following an arrow across a poor illustration of a First World War soldier silhouetted against a mountain top (*Caporetto*, the caption reads, *Italy discovers herself in disaster*), I find my son has added a few more words, in caps this time: PERHAPS IT IS BECAUSE HERE IN VILLA SERENA WE ALL TAKE OUR MEDICINE! Even as the two women launch into the long-awaited attack on southern corruption, into the predictable excuse of the impossibility of resolving things in the north while the south remains so lazy and corrupt – this is common ground across the political spectrum – I climb painfully to my feet and crash out of the compartment.

The train slides through the night. Across points. It has momentum now. Slides easily across a tangle of points, finding its metalled way. Was that meant as a joke? The cold of the window against my forehead is a relief. An unhappy joke: PERHAPS BECAUSE IN VILLA SERENA WE ALL TAKE OUR MEDICINE! The train slips into the tunnel. World peace with medicine. I have stopped taking mine. And an exclamation mark. Then out again. With tranquillisers and child-like print. In and out of tunnels along the dark Liguria coast. Dark glimpse of the sea. Could it be that when he reasoned with himself, Marco's thinking was perfectly sensible, even banal, occasionally witty? These comments on Villa Serena, on people living together stuffed with tranquillisers. Serene indeed! Written on a leaflet about the First World War. The exclamation mark has its comedy. Perhaps it was only with others that he coded his messages. With myself, with my wife. That he spoke in the wrong language, or delivered Italian idioms in English, or invented enigmatic phrases: wishing well, the shadows lengthen. To avoid conflict perhaps. To avoid confrontation. You will not be able to endure this pain much longer. Certainly not as far as Rome. Returning to Rome was always a return to marriage for me, I reflect, a return to conflict and decisions never taken. I have always felt gloomy on returning to Rome. The family tomb. Light-hearted on leaving. I saw Karen in Naples, though she lived in Rome. To avoid conflict Marco became ill, walled himself up. Is that a possible scenario? To wish this schizophrenic virus upon oneself? Thus peace. With tranquillisers. What was the decision he said he couldn't take? He became elusive. You too are becoming ill. You too need tranquillisers. Who can blame you for not settling matters with your wife if you are lying in hospital with kidney failure, walled up in pain? Or dead. Walled up in a tomb. It will have been twenty-seven hours before we reach Rome. Beyond the deadline for a swelling bladder. But why must you think in terms of blame? In terms of pardon? We are on some kind of viaduct now, spanning the chasm between two tunnels, the great engineering feat of the Torino–Genova. The sea glows a moment. On more than one occasion Vanoli suggested that if I insisted on feeling responsible for having in some way mismanaged relationships at home, if I insisted on imagining my wife was responsible, then by the same token Marco was also responsible for having foolishly become involved in the conflict between his parents. Then all three of you would be responsible, he said. All three of you to blame. One day you wish the problem to be entirely physiological, Vanoli laughed, the next you fear it may be entirely your fault. Or your wife's. Vanoli laughed. If it was my fault, I could be pardoned, I reflect. I would know where I stand. But if I was pardoned, I would know it was my fault. The freshness of the window on my forehead masks the pain in my belly. For a moment. Your anger is directed against your wife, Vanoli said, not myself. As the pain in your bladder masks the unpredictable enigma of the day to come. We are proud of our technology, I reflect, as the train shoots into another tunnel. It is going downhill now. Proud of our great engineering feats. Our communications. Our predictions. But it is the enigma that calls to us. The feats, the predictions, only mask the enigma. *Arcano è tutto*. Pain is an old friend. An old reliable. But you should take pride in adventuring beyond. Was that what he had in mind, screwdriver in hand? To go beyond? To go deeper? To push the metal deeper, beyond pain? A technical solution leading directly to enigma? The enigma of death. Suddenly, standing at the window of this gloomy train, I feel entirely lucid, entirely free from those waves of emotion that have tossed me hither and thither throughout this long day. I could contemplate my son's face now, I tell myself, without emotion. This lucidity, I suddenly find myself announcing, is the borderline of sanity. The words speak themselves out loud. They mist the glass between myself and my image, my face sliding over dark hills. This clarity – I say the words out loud – is the profile before the plunge, the soldier on the mountain top.

Amore. A black woman is standing beside me. Sex? You

want? Her face is grinning in my slab of glass. I am still clutching a sheaf of papers. Her friend stands a few yards along, skirt tight on big African thighs. Fuckie, she says. I seem to have lost Gregory's book. Where did I leave Gregory's book, *Italian Traits*? My mobile? I have nothing but this odd collection of papers. A deadline missed. My soiled clothes. The theme of the conference will be that Italy discovered its identity in the débâcle of Caporetto, in the extraordinary and unpredictable reaction to imminent catastrophe. She has a leather skirt, a shiny mauve blouse. Would I like to speak on the issue? The defence of the Piave. National sacrifice. *Amore* she repeats. She has her arm in mine. Perhaps I should read the whole of Gregory's letter. Did it traumatise Marco in some way, to read a letter from his mother's lover? I'm ill, I tell the girl. Another time, I mutter. She's tugging at my arm. Something Gregory said there perhaps finally made life unliveable for Marco. Something about Marco's mother, to whom the boy was so attached, despite the night with the sledgehammer. I have a girl at each arm now. Or they have me. These black girls. They are tugging me along the corridor. They will keep tugging me until I resist. To a bathroom. Or to some compartment somewhere. Why am I not resisting? How typical of me. They have an arrangement with the *capotreno* perhaps. Get on, he said. Though I have no ticket. No doubt there will be a fine to *sanare* my position. Anything can happen on Italian State Railways. Any impropriety can be healed. Andreotti's genius. You never even put up a fight, Marco said. Why am I so predictable? Fuck somebody else, he said. He was ill. I'm ill, I tell the girls. This is grotesque. I pull them back more determinedly, feeling faint, oppressed by the crushing pain in my abdomen. My belt is tight. It's grotesque that I have an erection. Sudden streetlights flash down the corridor. Their faces are at once smiling and anxious. Two rough, big-boned black girls. Black from Africa. Suddenly I realise they're friendly.

Karen said once: If you don't want us to live together, if you don't want to leave your wife, why not just go to prostitutes? It's perfectly respectable, she said. Then you wouldn't have to be romantic. Karen had a way of confusing respectability with normality. She cried. It was the room I rented in Sant'Elena, overlooking the bay. I was so generous, she said, so affectionate. I was too affectionate, she said. Why do you make so much effort, if your life is elsewhere? With them. With your wife and children. Give your affection to them, damn it. She wept. Go to a prostitute if it's sex you want. Did she believe me when I told her I had no interest in prostitutes? That I had never been to a prostitute? Prostitutes didn't even tempt me. I love you, I said. We always met in Naples. In Sant'Elena. No danger of meeting people you knew there. Rome was my wife. Naples my mistress. Prostitutes wouldn't have been punishment enough. I didn't say that. When you can't say something, then you know it's the truth. I love you, I insisted. We had a rule that we must never mention my wife, never meet in Rome. So the day she started to speak like that I knew the end had begun. Give your affection to your wife, she said. That was the day I fell into despair. One says fall into despair as one says fall in love. I had fallen in love with Karen. Nothing else would have been punishment enough. Our lives are separate now, she said. It was immediately after that that I began to think of demonstrating the predictability of all human behaviour. I began to read far and wide. We all fall at thirty-three feet per second per second, I wrote. It was one of the first notes I made on the subject.

What you want? *Amore*. One girl stands guard outside. The other is cuddling against me. Another drab compartment. But empty. I'm ill, I tell her. I got condoms, she says. What happens between a man and a prostitute is among the most predictable of all human exchanges. Fuckie. *Figa. Baiser.* The prostitute is polyglot. Necessarily. No, seriously ill. The girl is caught between puzzlement and irritation. Her smell is fierce. I could say I'm a Jehovah's Witness, discuss the end of the world. We are sitting flank to flank. That can put a damper on things. She is chewing. I haven't got all night, she says. I'm in the same position. A fierce and foreign smell. But I must do something. The pain is changing spreading swelling. She puts a hand to my trousers and at once I jerk away. I'm sweating pain. White. I must. Before I pass out. The girl is suspicious. They do this job because there's nothing for them otherwise. Paola's mother was the same. I can't remember her Ukrainian name. You're hard, honey, she says, but without conviction. For a moment I see her face very clearly, her cheap earrings, her frizzy hair. I see them very clearly. I see how the hair's ironed out, how it's fiercely pegged back in a green clasp. The lucidity before the plunge.

The girl gets up to go. Stop. I grab her wrist. I'd imagined I would just sit and wait it out. The death-line. The terminus. My heart is beating far too fast. This is not what I expected. That I should act like this. Rushing lights bring out the polish in her cheeks, a certain rugged handsomeness despite the brash clothes, despite the ridiculous lime-green party purse. You're in a train compartment with a prostitute and your bladder is about to burst. Sit down, I tell her. Sit down. I'm insisting. This is not what I would have predicted. I'll pay you, I tell her. She's thick about the waist. I already have a hundred-thousand note in my hand. The girl sits down at the far side of the compartment. She puts her hand out. Get your friend. Get your friend in. She stands up again. I empty my wallet onto the seat beside me. I'm about to faint, about to succumb. A great tidal wave of pain. This is me. I know I am. No doubt. Suddenly I am myself. *Caporetto*. The girls are wide-eyed, though they must have seen worse. I'm able to make that reflection. That a prostitute must have seen worse. I must have been in a daze all day, careless and confused all day. Now I'm amazingly lucid, right on the border. The catastrophe. You must tell the *capotreno*. My voice comes in grunts, but it is recognisably my voice. It's me. Please. I can be persuasive. Tell him to get me off at Genoa. I'm ill. I haven't pissed. I'm blocked. There's six-hundred-thousand. Understand? More. Take it. I don't know. Tell him to get me to hospital at Genoa. At Genoa. We're in a tunnel. Rattling through. The girls have gone. A strange chemical light creeps back and forth over the drab walls of the compartment. A roaring in my ears. Will they come back? I must get to my wife, I tell myself. I must get to my wife. She needs me.

I X

Where do you plan to be buried? I demanded, and what do you expect will be written on your tomb? I took a taxi from the airport. The midday weather dazzled the city. I have lost my sunglasses. From every granite surface the quartz sparkled. I tried to get my bearings among the dead. I hate you, I told her, I hate you and hate you and hate you.

I was struck by the pomp of the tombs. The preposterous dead, under this numbing blaze of light. As in the taxi, seeing the city glutted with light, sated with light, I was struck as ever by its pomp and by its squalor. This is a city of tombs, I told myself, of cenotaphs and mausoleums. A flight of swallows chased and turned in the dazzled air. No other city in the world gives so much prime space to ruins and to tombs. I had written that in an article somewhere. The traffic was moving fast. In no other city does one have such a strong sense of moving among the dead, of walking on layer upon layer of dead. Their grand achievements. Everywhere stones and obelisks. Their triumphs. The dead appropriating the dead, the dead commemorating the dead, the dead anticipating the dead: what you are we were, what we are you shall be.

And all above and around, the superficial squalor: asphalt and neon in the glittering heat, a stink of cats, a superficial bustle waiting to be death in the sating midday shimmer that bakes the stones, the monuments. There is a kind of madness in monumentality, I told myself, in the taxi from the airport. Two or three swallows turned in the dazzled air above the Tiber, careless of domes and columns behind. The only point of the monument is to spur us on to emulate the great deeds of the dead. Thus Foscolo, the days when my wife still read me poetry – *I sepolcri* – when our love was full of promise and of poetry, my ears sated with the softness of her voice drawing me to a language that would never be mine. Italian was never your language, I thought, vaguely aware that the taxi-driver was complaining. Though in many ways it has been your career. *Al diavolo*, he was muttering. But who remembered them now, those great deeds, those imperial acquisitions? It was your wife gave you your career, I thought, gave you Italy, gave you Rome, this city of tombs and monuments. I caught an echo of her voice of thirty years ago. Gave you your life really. Who thought them great now? The emperors and popes. Who cared? *All'inferno, cazzo!* For some reason the taxi-driver was furious. Did I personally know anyone who wished to emulate the great deeds of the dead? These days. Did I know anyone who even conceived of greatness as something one might aspire to? The greatness of those whose tombs cumber the city? Grandeur is the delirium of grandeur, I thought. Then I understood it was because I only had a credit card. I signed. My name. *Merda*, he muttered. There is something infantile about ordering monuments, I reflected, passing under the great arch of the cemetery. About having one's name engraved on monuments. They are mad and infantile. *RESURRECTURIS.* Two shrouded figures knelt beside a scroll of stone. There is something endearing even in their ingenuousness. In those emperors ordering their imperial tombs. Those bishops. Look on my works, ye Mighty. The petty aristocracy. And despair! Something charming almost in their vanity. The onyx and lapis lazuli. And now the middle classes. With their credit cards. One orders a monument with one's credit card, it occurred to me, remembering the taxi-driver's fury, the undertaker with his mobile. Vanity is as endearing as it is mad, I thought. A granite angel blew a trumpet. As if anybody remembered these dead now, these monumental dead. I had always loved my wife's mad vanity. It was her vanity perhaps that charmed me. I read a name that meant nothing. Her lipsticks and extravagant clothes. *Celebratissimo attore.* As if anybody believed in great deeds now.

The midday glare cast no shadow. The cypresses offered no shade. I was in a sea of monuments becalmed under the vertical glare of the sun, a hallucinatory multiplication of angels and Madonnas and Christs, a terrible ocean of hard stone, unanimated even by superficial squalor. No birds. No traffic. No cats. Only the quiet crunch of my steps, grunt of breath. And on every glittering slab the flattering photos of the dead. The flattering oval photos taken years before decease. My wife chose her photo years ago, I remember. Why do they have to be oval? It was madness to think of writing a monumental book, I told myself. I stopped, stifled by the heat. Where was the family tomb? I had forgotten. I had forgotten how stifling the heat of Rome can be. In Naples at least there was always a breeze. The very idea of monumentality is infantile, is illusion cherished beyond the age of reason. What had I meant to prove? Monumentalising the dead is just one more manifestation of the madness of life, I told myself, coming face to face with a risen Christ. I agreed with my wife's choice of photo. All life partakes of madness,

I thought. I had taken it myself after all. Only the dead are reasonable: what you are we were, what we are you shall be. Mute speech in stone. Between preposterous lines. *LUX PERPETUA.* There must be no more monuments, I suddenly said out loud, finding myself becalmed between preposterous lines of Latin. *LUCEAT EIS DOMINI.* No more polished stones. I said the words out loud. A man saved *in extremis* by two black whores on the Torino–Genova should not be thinking of becoming a monument. I shook my head. The sun was vertical. Where have I left my sunglasses? A man emptied like a sewage can in the middle of the night would do better not to think of immortalising himself. Marco should have been cremated, I thought, his ashes flecking the Tiber beneath the birds, Rome's ancient birds, wheeling in the dazzle, oblivious of monuments behind. She was very beautiful in that picture. Even after death, I let my son down, I thought. I left him to his mother's devices, to be walled up in a tomb, a monument, another manifestation of madness and vanity, her desire for possession. I hate you, I said at last. I hate you and hate you and hate you.

Somebody had given her a chair. I recognised the saccharoid cherub at the fork in the path, the broken cypress, the little girl's grave. I found my way. Cemeteries should be seen in full and pitiless sunshine, I thought, not in a grey elegy of twilight, offering repose, suggesting sleep. She must have heard my footsteps. Death has nothing to do with sleep. There was a smell of fresh cement. The great stone had been sealed. I saw a neat damp line of fresh cement. Even Christ could not have rolled such a stone aside, I reflect now, going over and over the scene in this room full of busts and bric-a-brac. Inevitably there is a crucifix. But I am still thinking of that huge polished slab, of the family name blazoned in great gold letters. DE AMICIS. My son lay beneath. That stone is quite immovable, I tell myself. A great granite slab pressing onto white shale surrounded by a low railing. Marco was below. Nobody could move that stone. The risen Christ himself, it occurs to me now in this elegant reception room, would never have shifted that great polished slab of black granite. Those huge gold letters. That monument. She must have heard my steps on the shale, but didn't turn. He would have suffocated in his shroud and all his illusions with him. She made no move. There was a mad multiplication of risen Christs in the cemetery, I reflect, while all the dead lay unmoved in their graves. Unimpressed. An unpitying light cemented the scene. I stopped. Her face was in her hands. She sat bowed, as on the bus to the airport, as in the plane to Genoa, her face in her hands. You'll make yourself sick, I said. Sitting in the sun like this. Somebody had given her a rickety chair. She had sat the same way in Giorgio's car. Bowed, face in hands. You'll make yourself ill, I said. A heap of white flowers was already wilting. The cypress offered no shade. I'm so sorry I missed the funeral. I've been in hospital. Very briefly, she looked up. At least they'd given me my heparin. But not at me. My heart is safe. She was powdered, white, ghastly in the sun, her dress black. There was no acknowledgement. She is fashioning her identity around this new pain, I told myself, around this bereavement. She is becoming her bereavement. I felt a familiar frustration. I took the first plane, I said. I came as fast as I could. Then I was aware her body was exploding with tension. In the still, glaring air I could feel the violent tension of her body under its black dress. When had she ever worn a black dress before? There was something theatrical about it. She still has a slim body. If not a young one. The only sound was the picking of her nails. She is bursting with tension, I told myself. But she won't speak to me. She sits by the grave picking at the skin round her nails. I should have been there, I repeated, I'm so sorry. The familiar rancour began to rise. Why was I apologising? He should have been cremated, I said, scattered in the wind, not walled up here under a huge slab of granite. In spite of myself, I cannot get that stone out of my mind, the weight of it, the huge bright letters of a family name that once dominated some southern province. A foreign land to me. Italian was never your language. Christ himself couldn't have moved it, I tell myself. A ridiculous connection. He would have rotted in His tomb. The veil would have remained unrent. One can move heaven and earth, I reflect, from time to time, but not a tombstone. The mind makes these connections from time to time, I reflect, but they leave the stones unturned, the dead unmoved. For some reason the slab's bevelled elegance made its weight all the worse. The elegant gold engraving made it all the weightier. And there were oval photographs, large photographs: her mother, her grandparents, a great-uncle. Life-size faces. As they do in Rome. Six places, five occupied. One says life-size. For the photos of the dead. My wife's photo shows her smiling brilliantly at the lens. It hasn't been enlarged as yet. The one she has chosen. I loved to take her photograph. I find all these monuments obscene, I told her. Her face returned to her hands. My wife will be neither comforted nor provoked, I thought. You always imposed on me, I muttered. She always had a brilliant smile for photographs. Then I raised my voice. You deliberately arranged the funeral so soon to exclude me, I said. That's obvious, I insisted. I was speaking very precisely now. Why did it have to be this morning? I demanded. My voice was almost clipped. Why the haste? There was a long silence. And sitting in this reception room, examining an inscription that tells how the small silver box it is written on was the gift of the Nigerian ambassador, I savour once again

– there is a bust of Pious IX, Pontifex Max. – the sound and taste of those words in my mouth, those words spoken at last and after so much turmoil: I hate you, I said. I hate you and hate you and hate you and hate you.

Marco committed suicide, I said.

I am sitting in the reception room of ex-prime-minister Giulio Andreotti. He greeted me briefly on arrival – the man is a corpse, I thought at once – but has some work to do while waiting for the photographer. He was cordial but busy. The man is a pale and broken shadow. He is finished, I thought. Though cordial. He will chat to me later while the photographer is taking his photos. The man's back was vulture-hunched, his face a spirit-owl. And he handed me his written responses. I could read them in the meanwhile, he said. Before the photographer came. Apparently we had agreed to do things this way. I could read his responses while I waited. The fixer had agreed this on my behalf. Then he would clarify anything that might be unclear. Where do you plan to be buried? I demanded, the papers in my hand, and what do you expect will be written on your tomb? But Andreotti had turned away. Do you expect it to be a national monument? He was already leaving the room, accompanied by a maid, a bodyguard. The man was armed. He didn't hear perhaps. His hearing is failing. Or perhaps I only muttered the words. Perhaps I didn't speak them at all. For forty-eight hours at least – I'm perfectly aware of this, sitting here in a comfortable armchair in a spacious reception room waiting for a photographer who will never come – for at least forty-eight hours it hasn't been entirely clear what I've said and what I haven't. Out loud. Nor can every single minute be accounted for. Though at least I have peed now. I have shat. I hate you, I said. I have taken my heparin. That much I did say. I hate you.

He stabbed himself with a screwdriver, I told her.

My wife looked at me now. Oh, I had got her attention now. She too is a corpse, it occurs to me. The chair she sat on looked like it had done long service in some café. It shifted when she looked up. She too is a pale and broken shadow. Her brilliantly preserved attractions are gone. As likewise Andreotti's charm. The charms of vanity are gone. There was a letter from Gregory, I said. He got hold of our post somehow. A love letter. Her eyes held mine. I had made her look at me. Something must have pushed the boy over the top, I said. He killed himself. She was weeping, but quite still. A love letter, I insisted. I hadn't read it. Amazingly, I was unafraid. She was exploding with tension, but I knew I was going to press on. I knew I was beyond the point where some interruption, some reflection might make it all seem pointless. It *was* pointless of course – I knew that – but now I would press on anyway. No, I would be carried on, borne on. You are in the storm now, I told myself. It is out of your hands. The current had me. I would say what I must. Paola was visiting him regularly, I said. I hadn't planned to say this. And Giorgio. Perhaps it *wasn't* pointless. Giorgio saw him regularly and played chess with him. They took him out together, I insisted. I could see my wife had stiffened. The tension inside her might explode at any moment. A corpse still capable of explosion. Swelling up. But I was unafraid. Perhaps precisely because I hadn't planned to say any of this. I was in the storm, in its grip. I was the storm. A dam had broken. Myself. Something has broken, I realised, changed. But not for my wife. The light glittered on the granite. The tomb was sealed. Still she wouldn't speak. Sealed by the light it seemed. A pitiless, unforgiving light sealed every surface. Whereas the ex-prime-minister's reception room enjoys a curtained repose, it occurs to me now. Yes, there is a pleasantly curtained penumbra, it occurs to me now, about ex-prime-minister Andreotti's lavish reception room. Which gives repose. They loved him, I told her. They cared for him. Despite what happened. Paola and Giorgio. They were visiting him. He was improving, I said. There was something frighteningly punitive in my voice. But I was unafraid. Something quite unnecessarily aggressive. Then something happened, I said. Something pushed him over the edge. I was aware of an extraordinary unpleasantness in my voice. She took him out on the Sunday, I said. On the very day he killed himself.

Paola, my wife muttered. Paola. What? I demanded. Suddenly she was on her feet. She began to blame Paola. You're mad, I said. Of course she had guessed it was suicide. What else? But she couldn't think about such things. She couldn't bring herself to think how he had died. How could she? How could I? Paola did everything to destroy him, she said. You're crazy, I told her. She was stamping her feet. Her fists opened and closed. It was Paola. The stony shale crunched. The dead would be as unimpressed by our shouting, I thought, as by the risen Christs. I was surprised to find my mind some distance from the scene. The dead will be unimpressed by your rancour, I thought. Her mouth was working. It was Paola! You're crazy, I repeated. Only the dead are reasonable, indifferent. I didn't back down. Perhaps precisely because I suddenly seemed some distance from it all. Paola was always jealous of him, my wife said. I couldn't tell whether she had sobbed or choked. Pity always made you back down, I reflect, sitting quietly and comfortably here in Andreotti's reception room. In the past, that is. Another place full of mementoes. Pity and fear made you back down. But not this afternoon, not beside the family tomb. Marco lay beneath. Paola never accepted that I had had a child of my own, my wife said.

This afternoon you were pitiless and distant as the sun, I reflect. Pitiless as light itself. Upon the boy's grave. There are things you know nothing about, she was shouting. You were never there. Paola was kind to him to destroy him, my wife insisted. She seduced him to destroy him. To turn him against me. The way she turned you against me. Can't you see? We adopted an evil child, my wife was shouting, standing beside her family tomb. DE AMICIS. She was wild with anger. But my own fury was steady. I was in the storm. I had breasted the wave, the great flood-tide that had always eluded me. Without actually having chosen to, I had done it. I had become it. A steady wind in the still air. Curiously, it gave me a sense of distance. You won't back down this time, I told myself. Engagement brought distance. Brought relief. That was odd. Our backs to the tomb, I finally said it. I hate you, I told her. You deliberately arranged this funeral to shut me out. You always shut me out. I hate you. All my life – I spoke compulsively, fluently, as if at last giving vent to words I had been rehearsing for years – you have shut me out. For years I had been formulating these thoughts, these words, and now at last I was actually saying them. And I was incredulous, almost hallucinated in the scaly brightness of the light, and at the same time unimpressed, distant. Your words were not impressive, I reflect. On the contrary, they were old hat to you. I felt far away. All my life you have drawn me in, I told my wife, repeating words I had thought a thousand times, then shut me out. You have made me love you and then refused to be loved, refused to be helped. It was saying the obvious, I reflect, that was so bewildering, so momentous. But the tide had me in its grip now. All my life you have seduced me then dismissed me, I said. It was not the words that surprised me, but the sound of my voice speaking them. You never let yourself be comforted, I told the woman standing before me, dressed in black. Her face was white. And now I have no comfort to give. I hate you, I told her, standing face to face in the cemetery, beside the family tomb, a great granite slab with the proud blazon of her family name. We were speaking Italian. It was her tomb, her language. And every time you turned me away I betrayed you, I told her. The words came out compulsively, as on a thousand previous occasions they had been spoken compulsively to myself, compulsively hidden from her. It was the confession I least expected to make, it occurs to me now, going over and over the scene in Andreotti's elegant reception room. Because the least appropriate, the most gratuitously cruel. I betrayed you, I said. Marco was forgotten again, I reflect, below his slab of granite, but at least you were telling your wife the truth. The cruel truth. After years and years of betrayal. At least he brought you to that. Your son Marco finally brought you to this showdown, I reflect, this terrible bloodletting. When he killed himself. Her face was a mask. Every time you rejected me I turned to another woman, I told my wife. Quite brutally. Suddenly the sense of distance was gone. I have had scores of other women, I told her. Suddenly I was catapulted right into the scene. I was face to face with my wife. One human being to another. I spoke directly and brutally to the white mask my wife's face had become. A death mask under the dazzling sun. It was the confession did it, brought me face to face with her. This woman I have lived with so long. The dead would not be disturbed by our quarrel. I hate you for doing that to me, I said. Her face has lost its charms. I hate you. Marco would no more be disturbed by us now than by the stony clutter all around him, the Madonnas and Christs and preposterous words. Yet something had moved. Something has shifted, I became aware, as I shouted out my hate. Some stone has slipped. I was looking directly into her eyes now. This entirely unexpected and gratuitous confession had given me an extraordinary sense of presence. Of being here. Of leverage. Myself and my wife face to face at last. Something shifting. I was seeing her again, at last. But you did it to everybody, I shouted. She looked at me. She was seeing me. You seduced everybody – I was furious – then dismissed them all. You lured us toward you, then turned your back. Suddenly it occurs to me that perhaps this was the burden of Gregory's letter. Perhaps this was what Marco read in Gregory's letter. A truth he recognised about his mother. She lured him and dismissed him. As she did with her husband, as she did with her lover. Inviting in a Jehovah's Witness, flirting with him, then suddenly dismissing the boy. As soon as she had sufficiently humiliated her husband. I hate you for making me live like that, I said, loving you and betraying you. With icy heat I said: I hate you for going ahead with this funeral without me. Once and for all – I spoke the words directly to my wife's face – once and for all it is over between us.

I turned. Behind me I sensed my wife had fallen back onto her chair. Where had she come by a chair in the cemetery? A café chair. It was a stunning blow I had dealt her. I knew that. You have struck your wife a terrible blow, I thought, precisely when she is least able to react. And sitting here in the reception room, beside a bust of Pious IX, in a gloom of velvet curtains and deep upholstery, the faint gleam of filtered light picking out the trophies on the low table – the silver cigar case, gift of the Nigerian ambassador, a huge iron key, symbol no doubt of some pathetic heraldic privilege – I am again aware – behind the bust is a papal portrait of preposterous self-importance – again aware of having destroyed everything. Everything that made me myself. You have destroyed the myth of your marriage, I reflect. Was it this Vanoli had been trying to warn me against? At last, I thought, stumbling among the tombs, at last you've done it. Destroyed it. Delivered the death blow. I experienced a strange delirium of power and of desolation. Vanoli wanted to give you pills because he was afraid you would destroy yourself and your wife by expressing your anger, I reflect. And by doing it what's more at the worst of all moments. Upon the death of your son. This was clearly the very worst of moments to talk to your wife about years of betrayal. The wall is full of photographs where Andreotti shakes hands with the greats of his era. It's as if you'd swept it all aside, I reflect. I sat on a tombstone under the blaze of heat and experienced an odd sense of power. I had conquered the *cimitero monumentale*. Got on top of it. The family tomb with its pompous stone. On it not under it. Something had shifted. It is as if you had brushed aside a whole life with a single gesture, I reflect. Your wife, your marriage. All your wife gave you. Italy, your career. I have the pages Andreotti gave me in my hand. The predictable responses no doubt. Do I need to read them? What else could a fallen leader say? A discredited Italian prime minister. And how long will the man let me sit here waiting for a photographer who never comes? It was as if every monument and memento that made our lives what they were had at last been swept away. The reception room swept away, the tombstones swept away. The myth of our marriage exploded in a moment. It takes years to come to believe in a thing, I reflect, to feel it is firm and immovable, decades even – to believe it is your destiny – and then in a moment it is swept away. Andreotti was simply swept from power. Clean sweep is a good expression. His party swept away after four decades of power. Finished. Clean forgotten is even better. Heaven and earth not so much moved as swept aside. A great slab swept away and not even a skeleton behind. Every relationship is a cosmos, I thought, and every self-respecting cosmos has its heaven and hell. Now there was neither. The skeletons scuttled off cackling and melted in the dazzle. The slab was gone and there was nothing behind it. Nothing.

Nothing left of Marco, I told myself. I looked at the tomb I was sitting on. Someone of remarkable achievements had gone to meet his Maker and share eternal bliss. A theatre director perhaps. I should go and sit in the shade. Or the author of some monumental book. I should go and sit under the portico. *Celebratissimo* no doubt. Nobody really believes in such sentiments, I thought. Nobody believes we go to share our Maker's bliss. Marco is dead. Such monuments pretend to gesture to a beyond, I reflect, but really they wall it up, they hide the dust. I too shall soon be dead. The fact that you've had your heparin, I thought, emptied your bowels, does not make you immortal. Monuments stiffen the veil they gesture beyond, the epiphanic veil. We mustn't see there is nothing behind. When you're dead they hide your corpse behind a monument. Suddenly that seemed obvious. Go deeper, I reflect, sitting in the deep upholstery of Andreotti's reception room, and there is nothing. Nothing behind my marriage, I said out loud sitting on a tombstone in the cemetery. Nothing behind the corpse on the pavement in Palermo. It would have been much better if we had cremated him. I stood up and sat down again. Much better if I had kept changing country, changing wife, reporting on this and that, filling my life with bric-a-brac, to gather it at the end in an elegant reception room. It was an elegant tomb I was sitting on with a fine marble bas-relief showing Christ on his throne. The more elegant the veil, the more easily one resigns oneself to not rending it, I thought. But vaguely. A crown was picked out in gold. It's important to buy an expensive coffin. My mind was wandering. Likewise a pretty little sceptre. To wall in the corpse beneath an elegant monument. Suddenly I felt tired. Gregory is much smarter than yourself, I reflect. Much cannier than yourself. I imagine a house full of mementoes. A new romance. In German. In Spanish. Gregory has a word or two of every language. He gets around. If people really went to heaven, it occurred to me, sitting wearily beside that tomb, there would be no need for monuments. No need for such extravagant craftsmanship. I felt exhausted. If people could really communicate there would be no need for institutions. A few words of a language is enough for a romance. More than enough. How wise Gregory is! Our marriage was mad, I thought. The decision to go deeper was mad. You should move to the shade. The doctors told you to drink and you have drunk nothing. You must get out of the sun.

I love you, she said.

A small, elderly woman has appeared in the room. I recognise her as the maid. A shrivelled, slightly stooped old woman. What's left of a glorious career, I'd been thinking, is a room full of bric-a-brac and an old woman to dust it. I still haven't managed to look at his answers to my questions. The photographer is very late, she tells me. Perhaps I could use a phone, I suggest. My mobile's broken. Unless he's here in the next few minutes it will be too late, she says. The president has another appointment. The title president, it occurs to me, when the man is no longer a president, is as ridiculous as an elegant monument on a corpse. An illusion. I ask: perhaps I could just speak to him for a moment, I can send the photographer another time. I climb to my feet. There is a sofa between us, its green upholstery topped with gilded wood. By the fireplace a furled flag. The tricolour. This was a written interview, she says. Her hands are folded on a black dress, as if already in mourning. The president's answers, she insists, are quite clear. Apparently she is more a secretary than a maid. How stupid of me. The devoted one who will not leave the sinking ship. His personal secretary. Her voice is soft.

The figure kneeling by the tomb. I have just one question I would like to ask him personally, I tell her. The president is ill, she says. It would be much better if he saw nobody. Just one question, I repeat. And then suddenly I am aware that she is making the reflection that I am ill too. Her voice is soft and sympathetic because she has seen that I too am ill. Very ill. I too am suffering like the man she is devoted to. My crumpled jacket, my unshavenness, my ghastly eyes. They all tell the same story no doubt. I too would do far better to forget this interview, to return immediately to hospital. The funeral, then immediately back to hospital, they insisted. Just one question, I repeat. There are all kinds of tests to be run. At least one glass of water an hour, they said. The ageing woman is looking at me from beyond the sofa. She is devoted to a man accused of all kinds of atrocities, a man who has ruthlessly and cynically wielded power for decades. Yet I find her devotion admirable. Andreotti inspired this devotion, I reflect, a calm and unquestioning devotion that I never found in my wife. It was admirable, outrageous. One question, I ask again.

A beetle scuttled across a blaze of stone. She was sitting beside me. Along the path a younger woman with flowers had noticed us, noticed that we were engaged in some kind of drama. My wife loves to play to people who have detected our drama, I thought. The beetle twitched its antennae. But she said nothing. There were no birds in the sky. The swallows desert the sky when the sun is highest. The air was empty. The beetle was safe. I too felt empty and exhausted. The granite glittered. I had destroyed everything. I'm sorry, I said. I'm sorry, I mean for speaking now. This was not the time to speak, I conceded. I'm sorry about that. The beetle scuttled across the stone and was gone. After a long pause my wife asked: Tell me. Tell me what they told you. I explained that Marco had somehow got hold of our Italian post. I had been offered a tax pardon but now it was too late. These are trivial details, I thought. I'd have to go to court, I said. There was a long letter from Gregory. Other trivia. A note saying how happy he was there at Villa Serena, how peaceful it was – the only thing in his own handwriting – how people didn't fight there, he wrote. It seems Paola and Giorgio were visiting him, I told her. The doctors didn't tell us for fear you would intervene. My wife sighed. Busi thought he was getting better. Then Sunday evening – after a day out – he stabs himself with a screwdriver. I began to weep. I didn't tell you, I said, as the tears unexpectedly began to flow, I didn't tell you for fear it would be too much for you.

For some minutes I wept. It is true. I sobbed. It was the exhaustion perhaps. And I have begun to weep again now in the reception room. Will Andreotti come to hear my question? My one question? We were sitting on the border round a seriously elegant tomb, some remarkable man who had gone to share his Maker's bliss. I can't believe he's dead, I wept. I bowed my face in my hands. I simply can't believe it. I couldn't tell you how. I couldn't. Poor Marco. Our Marco. I thought it would destroy you. He killed himself. I can't bear how you shut me out, how you grieve alone, how you rave against Paola. I can't bear it. You're mad, I said. Quite mad. It's over between us. I shall go and live with Paola. I stood up, struggling with tears. At least it's done that, I said. It's brought this farce to an end.

She said: Chris, I love you.

Andreotti's handwriting is smudged with tears. How am I to behave if he walks in now? How am I to present myself? It was ludicrous of me to come to this appointment. Ludicrous. To leave the cemetery, I realise now, and take a taxi directly to this appointment was madness. To get into a taxi and say: Piazza Santa Lucina. This was crazy. I'm mad. But where else should I go? Who am I? If not mad? And then the bric-a-brac of this room, it occurs to me, the silver mementoes and oval photographs, the busts and portraits, are so like the cemetery in so many ways. I came to a place so like the cemetery. To gather the final material for my monumental book. Though without the pitiless light, thank God. A book that would be a fitting monument to my career. Andreotti's reception room is without the glittering heat, spared the pitiless light of the cemetery. The post-war government was destined to deal with a difficult international climate, he has written, that to a great extent dictated our every course of action. What am I to say if he walks in now? This is not to say we did not make mistakes, he has written. I love you, she said. She spoke very quietly. My wife has a beautiful voice. I couldn't understand where you were, what had happened to you. There were long pauses between the things she said. Unusually she left a pause when somebody walked by. I was looking at the shale. It was madness of us not to move to the shade. For once your wife isn't playing to the pit, I thought. Madness to sit under a full and pitiless sun. I think a family grave is a gesture of love, she said. She spoke softly. I want us all to be together when we're dead. It's terrible, she said, that my father isn't there. It's a terrible thing his body was never found. And if I have started to weep again here in the reception room among the banners and bric-a-brac of Andreotti's extraordinary career, started to weep when I thought, climbing into that taxi, that I had set my jaw against all further weeping, it is because I have just remembered that this is why we read Foscolo together. This is why we read *I sepolcri*. She was still upset over the father she had never known, whose corpse was never recovered. There is nothing to help us remember him, she said. No grave to sit beside. My wife never really got over this. And I had forgotten that moment, forgotten that Marco was named after her father. He just disappeared, she said. Shot from the sky. I never knew him. And she insisted on reading Foscolo's poem, his great poem in praise of monuments and mementoes, in praise of that mad affection that reaches beyond the grave, believes beyond the grave, the madness that enchants itself with the notion of community beyond the great divide. We read Foscolo's hymn to the affection of stones. Now Marco has taken Marco's place. Now that name will appear in stone. For me it's an act of love, she said. Paola was morbidly close to him, she insisted. You didn't understand that. She always said to me: we're not flesh and blood, me and Marco. We're not brother and sister. Giorgio was jealous, my wife said. I was so happy they married so young, that they moved up north. I thought it would get her away from him. They were morbidly attached. But she was evil. We should never have let Marco study up north, she said. She started to sob. That's how they got back together. I shall never forgive you for insisting he be allowed to study up north. I shall never forgive you – my wife's voice was suffocated but sharp – never – she was sobbing – for being so stupid and so blind!

A policy can only be judged, Andreotti has written, in the light of the context in which it was formulated. But his words are smudged with tears. I must concentrate. In the same way a statement can only be evaluated in the context of the pressures under which it was made and the goal it strove to achieve. To what end am I sitting in the ex-prime-minister's reception room if he is to come in and find me trembling, in tears? During the present legal proceedings I have frequently been accused of prevaricating because I fail under questioning to recall this or that fact which then turns out to be well documented. But I do believe I recall the context, the drift, as it were, of everything I did. With this in mind, then, let us turn to your question on Moro. What was my question on Moro? Andreotti's handwriting is ferociously neat, as the mementoes in this reception room, it occurs to me, have been ordered and labelled with extraordinary neatness. The photos are arranged chronologically from left to right. And I can't even remember my question, let alone the answer I predicted, let alone the context in which we argued over Marco's departure for Milan. The graves likewise were neatly labelled. It was one of the very few battles I won. Tombs likewise invite a crude geometry. Milan, not Novara. Only what is dead is predictable. A question of escaping his mother's apron strings, I remarked to Vanoli. That's why I insisted. He must escape her apron strings. Petticoat strings, I almost thought. The woman couldn't have Gregory *and* our son. Perhaps there are beetles in the shadows here, in Andreotti's reception room. Help me, the boy wrote on the bathroom window. Had Giorgio already left then? That evening. Left the two of them alone. Marco and Paola alone in her flat. Taken out the children? We are not brother and sister, not flesh and blood. Why did he rub butter in her hair? What did it mean? Moro was in the hands of the Red Brigades, Andreotti predictably remarks, when he wrote those much-quoted accusations. Mud in his mother's. Can we really take seriously the words of a man writing from imprisonment with a pistol pointing at his head? Help me, Marco wrote.

My wife's voice had lost its urgency. She sat beside me. There was an unusual resignation about her. You too are overwhelmed, I thought, exhausted. You never understood, she said, how much Paola hated me for having another child. For having a son. She would have done anything to get back at me. But I had heard all this before. I don't want to hear anything against Paola, I told her. I shook my head. I cannot believe there was anything between them. I cannot believe he is dead. We were sitting together side by side on the low wall of the grave. Busi warned me, I said, he told me we all invent stories to explain these terrible things to ourselves. We invent the past. Where perhaps there is no explanation. I'm sure there was nothing between them, I said. My voice was conciliatory. Having told my wife I hated her, I was now conciliatory. The sunlight glittered on blind scales of quartz where an engraver had listed the deceased's considerable achievements. And it occurs to me now that the brighter the light, the more evident it is that revelation is denied. The more clearly one sees, I tell myself, the more inescapable enigma becomes. The horizon just above your head. Everything could be predictable and still the horizon of enigma would be just above your head. Whereas in a shady room where beetles perhaps hide in the corners, it is just possible to imagine that mysteries will one day be revealed. In a gloomy room, I reflect, carefully curtained against the bright Roman afternoon, against the squalor and bustle of the city, one is still ready to ask a question or two. Andreotti always surrounded himself with gloom and mystery. His answers are entirely predictable. Yet he eludes me. I recall nothing of the exact context in which certain decisions, perhaps fatal, were made. I was following Vanoli's prompting when I argued for our departure for England. It is curious, the psychiatrist said, that your wife would agree to sending your son to an English school if she was so averse to England and Englishness. It was to separate him from Paola, it now occurs. You didn't see that at the time. To separate him from the girl who wasn't his sister. Why did the Nigerian ambassador bring a cigar case when everybody knows Andreotti doesn't smoke? What lies behind that embrace between Andreotti and Podgorny? We too had our long cold war, I reflect. It is over now. People would be disappointed, the ex-prime-minister has written dismissively, to discover there was no mystery behind power. And yet I can assure you . . . All this was entirely predictable.

Mara, I said. I put my hand on hers. The skin is disturbingly cold, I thought. Mara. I repeated her name, my wife's name. You have spoken her name, I realised. It's over between us, I said. I have betrayed you in every possible way. You have made me hate you, Mara. We have lost our child, I said, lost our son, lost our daughter too, lost our grandchildren. There is nothing left for us. Mara. There is nothing left. All our lives we've done nothing but prepare an empty old age for ourselves. I've behaved terribly, I told her. I should have said all this ages ago. You have behaved terribly, Mara. This should have been said ages ago when there was still something to be gained from speaking. Instead we schemed, Mara. We fought. But without speaking. The note Marco left was all about how peaceful it was in Villa Serena. It was peace he wanted, peace he got. Our arguments can't disturb him now. And now because of your fight with Paola we can't even see our grandchildren. It's madness, Mara, for two old people to lose their grandchildren, to lose their place in life, their past. It's over between us, I told my wife.

I expected to leave, but found myself still sitting on the low marble ledge beside this pompous tomb, this man's remarkable achievements. The tension between us had gone, suddenly gone. You have used her name, I thought, your wife's beautiful name: Mara. You have told her quite straightforwardly, quite sensibly, that it is over between you, between Chris and Mara. Our life is over. I could feel the tension had quite gone from her cold hand and yet the light kept me cemented to this grave in the becalmed glitter of the cemetery. Only thirty years. She was silent. Mara, I repeated. It is strange to use her name. I said: Remember Foscolo. People seek out sadness with a lantern, I quoted. We moved heaven and earth, Mara, to make our lives as miserable as possible. Mara — it seemed important to keep repeating that name, a liberation — why didn't you want me to get on the flight? Why didn't you want me to come into the mortuary? Why do you always always always shut me out? Why did you always boast that Marco was absolutely different from myself? My opposite? And now you want me to believe you love me. Why? Why do you do it? Kill me, she said. My wife turned and tried to get me to look at her. She shook my arm. Kill me. You might as well. The tension had completely gone from her voice, from her icy hand. She shook me gently. Her charm and vanity have all gone. Punish me, she said. Please. Kill me, if I've hurt you so much. She said: I never meant to hurt you, Chris.

That isn't true! I stood up. That's a lie! You deliberately stopped me from seeing Paola every time we went north. And the children. My grandchildren. You deliberately humiliated me with Gregory. And I deliberately hurt you. I did. I did it deliberately. I hurt you. I deliberately humiliated you. I did it again at Courteney's party. This has got to end, I said. Mara. I stood up. It's got to stop! I've betrayed you in every possible way. In every possible way you've made life impossible for me. Mara, Mara! I was on my feet. We've lost everything. We couldn't have made each other unhappier. Then she was behind me and I was walking toward the arch and the flower stalls where the taxis tick over while the decrepit visit their dead, their plots, their family tombs.

Buona sera, he says. His shoulders are vulture-hunched, his face a spirit-owl. The man's a corpse, I reflect. Andreotti is finished. His hand when he offers it is a wet leaf in autumn. He gave you no more than three fingers. As if under water, his eyes are lost behind the thick lenses. He can't see you've been crying, I tell myself. How much can he see? I can't find his eyes behind their huge watery lenses. My own are stinging. The secretary has seen. The secretary knows I am ill. An old woman dressed in black, stooped. She has seen my eyes, the devoted servant. Our photographer, hasn't come, then? His voice is thin and wavering. But not without its hint of irony. Could he have understood? This interview is to be published in . . . *The Times*, I tell him. I lie. There is a silence. He has sat on a straight-backed chair. He sits bent forward over spidery crossed legs, a huge owlish face over a spidery body. His skin papery. Andreotti is finished, I reflect. His shoulders are hunched, predatory. Yet cordial. For he has begun to speak. About the bric-a-brac. His voice wavers after lost charm. The key a gift from the Vatican, he smiles. Did I know he had written a detective novel set in the Vatican? He is still trying to deploy his charm. Also a biography of Pious IX. He is still trying to satisfy his vanity. He gestures to the bust, the portrait. Where do you plan to be buried? I suddenly demand, and what do you expect will be written on your tomb? There is a knock on the door. The bodyguard is at the door. The secretary announces: Mr Burton, your wife is here. She says she needs to see you, urgently.

But Andreotti is already speaking. He is already answering your question. He doesn't seem to have noticed the interruption. My wife has found out where I am. Why has she come? It was ludicrous to imagine that a man of Andreotti's experience, a man used to answering every kind of cruel and provocative question under pressure would be even marginally unsettled by a brutal and contentious enquiry about his burial arrangements. He is smiling. If anything, I seem to have cheered him up. How ludicrous to imagine one could corner an old fox like Andreotti with a contentious enquiry about his tomb. He is rubbing his hands together. He does not seem to have heard his secretary's soft announcement. The old corpse is in action again. I have galvanised him.

One moment, I tell her. She has seen my eyes are smudged and bloodshot. She knows my wife and I are going through some kind of crisis. My wife is in action again, I reflect. She is moving heaven and earth after this afternoon's bloodletting. She is on the warpath. After Marco's death finally brought out the truth. Marco's suicide. What is she planning to do? Again I savour my voice pronouncing those words so long rehearsed. I hate you. Again I hear her name, Mara. I betrayed you in every possible way. Mara Mara Mara. She is here. Piazza Santa Lucina. But Andreotti is entirely engrossed in himself, engrossed in his tomb, his monument. You will be aware, Mr Burton – Andreotti hasn't noticed his secretary's intervention – that my first meeting with the great De Gasperi came in the Vatican library in '38. He purses his lips. The great Alcide De Gasperi! He hasn't noticed my bloodshot eyes, my obvious distraction. It was strange – he warms to his theme – I had no idea who he was, or how important, whereas he was already well aware of my modest activities in the Catholic youth movement. My wife has not accepted my decision, that much is clear. She has been making phone-calls, taking taxis. A woman, it occurs to me, who can get to a Heathrow flight-gate without a boarding card is also a woman who can talk her way into an ex-prime-minister's office. From that moment on, Andreotti is saying, from the moment the alliance with De Gasperi was formed – I feel tremendously excited, alarmed – from the moment we began to work together, he, myself and Moro, for the material and moral reconstruction of our country, first in the *Partito Popolare*, later *Democrazia Cristiana*, I knew that the die was cast, that this was to be my destiny: to help take a deeply divided Italy from the disaster and scission of a terrible war, a civil war at the end you must remember, toward a better future, both material and moral, using whatever resources God in His wisdom had given me.

My religious wife, it occurs to me, might even manage to burst into the room, make the sign of the cross, go down on her knees, or alternatively slap me across the face. When will Andreotti finish his answer? He is warming enormously to his answer. After refusing to see you, I reflect, he now doesn't wish to let you go. His secretary must be furious. After you asked a cruel and contentious question, he is now delighted to speak to you, he can think of no better way of spending the afternoon than making these otiose reflections on his career, his destiny, how it will appear on his tomb. Vanity and piety seem to call to each other, I reflect, to encourage each other. As those words material and moral won't leave each other alone. The material and moral reconstruction of my country, he is repeating. He is laughing, laughing at my presumption, my ingenuous assumption that an old fox like Giulio Andreotti could be unsettled by a brutal question about his tomb. A man of a thousand lives Craxi called him. Was it Craxi? Inspired by the great De Gasperi, this mission has been my unceasing labour, Andreotti expounds. He is determined to stress this aspect. And not without its fruits, he insists. A prosperous Italy, Mr Burton, at the heart of Nato, at the heart of Europe. A responsible, positive Italy. Such a thing would have seemed a miracle the day I met De Gasperi in the Vatican library, the day our alliance was formed. At the height of the Fascist aberration. Don't you think? I gave the old fox precisely the question he would most warm to, I realise. While my wife Mara is waiting for me in some corridor, some room that comes before the reception room. It must be obvious that she is distraught, harrowed, at the very limits of grief. Perhaps ready to plead. Perhaps to strike out. Or even seduce. Or kill herself. But whatever it is, she is waiting. That is unusual. No, it's unheard of. Unheard of for my wife to wait. Would she wait if she planned to strike? An armed bodyguard would be no impediment to my wife, I reflect, no obstacle to Mara if she chose to interrupt my interview with ex-prime-minister Andreotti. He is laughing. If my wife planned to humiliate me, I reflect, this would be her chance. She wouldn't miss it. Predictably he is using my brutal question to sing his own praises. It hasn't unsettled him at all. But this is a pluralistic society, Mr Burton, a democracy with an opposition. He has taken the trouble to remember my name and is determined to repeat it. The name of one of the thousands of journalists he has spoken to. I would not have it otherwise, he says, leaning forward over his spidery body. Andreotti was ever famous, I remember, for remembering everybody's name. As Blair for that matter. What a curious mixture he is, I reflect, of vulnerability and menace. At once a corpse and a vulture. A cadaverous gluttony. I would not have it any other way, he repeats. Certainly an enigma. But I must concentrate. The business of my wife's arriving has accelerated my mind again. My mind is working feverishly again. Too feverishly. All the thinking you have done, it suddenly occurs to me, is provoked one way or another by your wife, by Mara. Even if it wasn't the thinking you planned to do. But I must concentrate. Hence what I saw and see as my mission and my destiny, others have chosen, as you know, to represent in the worst possible light, possibly because this country was so deeply divided after the last war that a saint on one side could always be seen as a devil on the other. You are aware of that. And even more of a devil was anyone who chose, as I did, to heal those divisions, to bring about reconciliation, to seek the material and moral reconstruction of our nation. Through reconciliation. Through an insistence that the past must be laid to rest, however many the victims. Andreotti is smiling. As Vanoli likewise always smiles. There are even those, Mr Burton, who have managed to put together a persuasive account of my life which presents me as the mastermind of organised crime. Andreotti laughs. Sometimes I have even been half-persuaded myself. Andreotti is laughing. As Vanoli too was ever unshaken by your provocative questions. Italy's ex-prime-minister is laughing at you, I reflect, at the ludicrous presumption with which you tossed him this contentious question about his burial arrangements. Vanoli would do the same. Sometimes I have even wondered myself, he chuckles, whether I had not entirely misunderstood my destiny. He finds this extraordinarily funny. Why do I make people laugh? He hasn't enjoyed himself so much for months. What will be written on my tomb, Mr Burton? Suddenly he leans forward, plays the card of intimacy. At least my wife wept. Between ourselves, I expect my detractors' exaggerations will be their downfall and truth will out. That's what I hope. He sits back. Mara wept, is weeping now perhaps. But my reputation beyond the grave is a matter for others, Mr Burton. A simple man who served his country, that is what I would like the inscription to say, on our family grave, in the village where I was born. A simple man who strove to fulfil his destiny: the reconstruction of his country, the reconciliation of terrible wounds. That is what I would like my epitaph to say. But what matters of course is that I know in my heart that that is the truth. What matters is that I am serene in myself, despite anything others . . .

I have to go. I got to my feet. Finally I have surprised him. The words stop in his mouth. I have unsettled him. He used the word serene. Serene in myself. And it's true Andreotti is entirely serene, I thought. Obscenely serene. Madly serene. Villa Serena. This is a man whose lies to himself are entirely convincing, whose schizophrenia is perfectly stable, manageable, even useful, his master card in fact, no, his genius even. What is the point of talking to such a man? The serene are madder than those who torment themselves, I thought. There is no point in talking to a man whose sense of his own destiny is still serenely rock-solid, unthreatened, fixed as a tombstone, unmoving despite all evidence to the contrary. Vanoli never budged in his analysis. The viral origin. Perhaps rightly. Perhaps because still surrounded by his faithful servants, I wonder, his devoted servants who will write the most flattering words on his grave, kneel beside flattering scrolls of stone. Perhaps these other men are serene, Andreotti, Vanoli, because unchallenged by a disturbing presence like my wife, my Mara, a disturbing, provocative challenging presence, a woman who never never lets you settle. Mara never let you settle, it occurs to me, never let you sit back. She gave you Italy. Gave you your mind. Nobody has ever heard anything of Andreotti's wife. Never a whisper of scandal. Whereas life with Mara is exhausting. She gave you everything. Andreotti is surrounded, I am aware, getting suddenly to my feet, by servants who insist on the version that gives his life sense, gives their life sense, allows them to live in his shadow. Safe from the blaze of light I found in the cemetery. Andreotti has surrounded himself by a chorus of consent. Does his wife call him *presidente*? He orchestrates then accepts a chorus of acclaim. What is the point of talking to such a man? A man who is entirely obscenely admirably serene, despite a thousand terrible charges against him. I must see my wife. Why has she come? I must talk to Mara. One knows exactly what such a man will say. Any contentious question will prompt a chorus of self-acclaim. How foolish and presumptuous of me. But everything is predictable when seen with hindsight. There is no point in talking to people who don't doubt themselves, I thought, who have so easily and outrageously convinced themselves of their destiny. By getting up I had surprised him at last. Without planning to, or meaning it, I had finally shocked him. You shocked him. I must go, I said. I have to talk to my wife. For a second, perplexity animated the mask. The words stopped in his mouth. Has my wife begun to doubt herself? For a moment Italy's ex-prime-minister is groping, confused. I must go, I said. I have no further time for this conversation, Mr Andreotti. I have more important business to attend to. In the corridor the secretary told me: Your wife has left, Mr Burton, and she handed me a piece of paper.

X

Her face is equal to the light. She shines at the sun. Her dazzled dazzling eyes. Mara, demon tempter of the Buddha. For one–two–hundred–and–fiftieth of a second her eyes opened wide to challenge the sky. We laughed. Though that Mara was a man, a male demon. Whenever the gods saw a man was over-reaching himself, I told her – but that was years before – they sent a woman to distract him. The gleaming teeth, the wide and delicate mouth. To break the rhythm of his thought, I explained. You said that years and years before, at an embassy in Rome. The tall white neck. Or they sent another man to seduce the woman he loved. To distract him in jealousy. You said that when we met. In stumbling Italian. It was an embassy reception. She was dazzling in pink. To prevent Awakening, you expounded. What a serious young man! Your Italian was terrible then. I'm afraid you're going to be a serious distraction, the young man told the woman in pink. She wore bright-pink lipstick. The gods are terribly hard on ambition, you laughed in the small hours, first of many. The hair, if you look closely, is an explosion of dark ringlets, thick enough to arrest any comb – my impossible hair, she boasted – thick enough to arrest any caressing hand, any vocation for disentanglement. To push a hand into your hair, I whispered once – my crazy curls, she sighed – is to plunge it into happiness itself. Happiness, you murmured – but this was so long ago – your face buried in her hair as you spoke. Years later – fifteen, eighteen? – the smile is knowing, dazzling, triumphant. Over light and enlightenment. Made up. Behind is the Amalfi coast, a sun-drenched Naples. It was the boat from Capri. I focused the lens. On the contrary, she protested, Mara was the Baltic goddess of fertility. She cocked her head. Prize not punishment. We laughed. It was the French embassy, I recall. We didn't appreciate such things were not incompatible: punishments, prizes. Eighteen years later, I clicked the shutter. There is a terrible simultaneity to our marriage. The one-two-hundred-and-fiftieth of a second froze to a still, and through more years to come, still gazing, as I am gazing now, at that beautiful photograph, the best I ever took, at the face that will tilt and dazzle from the granite of her family tomb, a face you never got beyond I feel, never got beneath at all – though perhaps it is wrong to assume one can ever get beneath a face – through the years to come it would occur to me that the only relationship between the eye before the lens and the eye behind was the desire of the one to be recorded in the other, the desire of the other to possess the one. Two visions twined. The Nikon mediated an ancient haunting, our long protracted distraction. It's not true we were always unhappy, she wrote on that piece of paper. It's not true, Chris. Andreotti's secretary had read it of course. In English she wrote: I love you.

A voice calls mother. This is the house of ghosts. We had left the children with their grandmother. Actually, our only attempt at a holiday, I remember recounting to Vanoli, since Marco was born. I remember this now. Our only attempt to get away on our own, to turn a dangerous tide. We did know a dangerous tide was running. We left the kids with their grandmother in Rome, a woman I never got on with, a secretive old woman who in many ways, I felt – I was at the height of my career now – still resented our marriage, still resented the English who had killed her husband. Over Malta. I resented Sunday lunches invariably in her company. At the height of a career that still seemed strange to me. His body was never recovered. Marco called while we were making love. It is called the house of ghosts because for generations every single De Amicis died there. Without exception. Her father broke the tradition. The English broke the De Amicis family tradition. In the sky over Malta. It's a joke, *ciccio*, she coaxed. We were making love. It never occurred to her not to pick up the phone. No one's ever really seen a ghost, she reassured him. We were already entwined, entangled. There are no ghosts, she told our little boy over the phone. My hand was in her hair as she spoke. Her explosive hair. Certainly she never saw her father's. He too was called Marco. Her family had been dying in that house since the early seventeenth century. All of them. He was afraid of sleeping on his own, the boy said. In a room where people died. He called again. He's ten now, I objected. Why wouldn't she take the damn phone off the hook? For Christ's sake! There's his grandmother, his sister. We would never make love if she kept answering the phone. He can sleep with them, I said. I refused to put the suitcase in the car. Take the phone off the hook, I insisted. She phoned the station. You didn't hear him wailing, she said. He should never have had our hotel number, I told her, who gave him our number? What for? You don't give ten-year-olds your hotel phone number when you go away for a weekend. Mamma, calls the voice through the empty rooms, up the broken staircase. Mamma! The candlelight flickers on the photos, the family photos on the old credenza. He broke the staircase with a sledgehammer. It is typical of your wife, I tell myself, that she should make this sentimental gesture, this quasi-religious gesture of turning our old family photos into icons. She had locked herself in the bathroom. She fled when he rubbed mud in her hair. And now she lights candles before our photos. Am I gratified or appalled? Did she say a prayer before them? To bring me back? To bring him back? So much of what your wife does both gratifies you and appals you, I reflect. How can that be? The photo-faces are ghostly in the candlelight, in the house of ghosts. A moth flutters the dust, the shadows. Yet that was always the way. I was always gratified and appalled by her flamboyancy, her vanity, by the way she always sets out to move heaven and earth. Mamma, the voice calls. It's a child's voice, a boy's, carrying over stone floors. Other worlds are credible in candlelight, I reflect, but not under the brilliant sun that shone when Mara smiled that smile on the boat from Capri. One hears voices in candlelight. Not under the sun that sealed his grave. It is Marco's first night in his grave. Then you see things clearly. His body laid out under the great granite stone, his arms at his side. *All' apparir del vero* – Leopardi was the last poet we read together – *una tomba.* My eye moves across the credenza from her face to his. A young man in a sweatshirt. Eyes flicker. Perhaps a moth. In his grave. The chaos principle applies in candlelight, I reflect. I reassure myself. For at least fifteen minutes I have been staring at these photos. Perhaps longer. You can never predict how the shadows will shift in candlelight, especially when there are moths about. When the flame shifts, his features seem to move, the eyes seem to flicker. My son's eyes, Marco's lips. In his expensive coffin, beneath the granite. *All'apparir del vero* – at the dawning of the truth: a grave. Youthful promise unfulfilled. The voice is definitely coming from the stairs. Leopardi's theme. Youthful energy tossed away.

Definitely calling me to the broken stairs. The stairs to our room. People believe things in candlelight, I reflect. I'm haunted by voices. My son's. That's why they use candles in the *camera ardente*. Eros and Night were the daughters of Chaos. If I remember rightly. Isn't this the first sign of schizophrenia? Eros and Night. The two great unpredictables. She liked to make love by candlelight. At night, or with the shutters closed. She said sex was more liquid in candlelight. She had even brought some with her for the hotel room. They flickered on the furniture. Things will never be the same again, I shouted, if you insist on going back. She had snapped a switch. I was blinded. The candle-spell was broken. Her spell. The same as what, she sneered. These were the metalled ways of our arguments. Neither of us was surprised. I'm not driving you back, I said. Forget it. When the light snaps on, the candle loses all its power, I reflect, loses all its enchantment. We came here to be away from them, not to go running back, I said. The moths seem smaller. You always want to possess me entirely, she complained, you give me no space. I could turn the light on here too, here in the house of ghosts. I could kill the candles here too, I tell myself, on the old family credenza. Shrink the moths, the fluttering spirits. But as yet I haven't done that. His features seem to move when they flicker. Candle-life. You make no allowances, she said, for the fact that I'm a mother. Such was our customary back-and-forth. Neither of us was impressed. You're so cold and English, she said. She was dressing now. You're so fake and hysterical, I replied. Our script it seemed. I didn't need to add Italian. She said: Chris, there's something wrong, I sense danger, we must go. She blew out the candles. We must go back. It was the same day I took the photo. We had taken the boat to Capri. An enchanted day. Gorgeous light and white spray in her thick hair. The eyes wide open for one-250th of a second. There is a terrible simultaneity about the kaleidoscope of our marriage. He has his grandmother, I shouted, his sister. Let him sleep with them. For Christ's sake! A wearisome rearrangement of the same elements, round and round. You said yourself there are no ghosts. What can be wrong? I demanded. You spoil the boy. What on earth can happen that requires your presence? What is the point of a babysitter, if you go rushing back because a ten-year-old is afraid of ghosts? Because he gets on the phone and calls his mamma? I have a sixth sense for these things, she insisted. She blew out the candles. There is some kind of danger brewing, she said. It was an expensive hotel I had booked. A suite over the bay. The Bay of Naples. Gorgeous sunsets. There was a terrace bar. It was there, towards midnight, that I met Karen.

Karen! I phoned from the hospital. How shall I behave? I asked myself, walking up and down the long corridor of the hospital reading and re-reading my wife's note. Remember the good times, she had written. Remember them, Chris. Franco and Karen are out, a male voice was saying. Messages or facsimiles after the tone. Facsimiles! Just Chris here, I began, saying hello to Karen. I was standing in the hospital corridor. Outside *Urologia*. For more than an hour I had been walking up and down reading my wife's note. It isn't true we were always unhappy, she wrote. Remember the good times. Remember when we met! Your wife is moving heaven and earth to get you back, I thought, walking up and down the corridor of the *policlinico*. Perhaps you're right about the grandchildren, she wrote. Even Paola. But it isn't true we were always unhappy. Your third *policlinico* in as many days. All equally drab. Or rather, no, she wasn't moving heaven and earth. She was being delicate, she was making concessions. Perhaps you are right, she had written. I gazed at

227

a fire extinguisher. My wife was writing delicate notes, then making timely exits. It was unheard of. No comment on my betrayals, I noticed. There was a line of phone-booths. No unpleasant enquiries, no snide asides. This is a generous note, I thought. Your wife's behaviour on this occasion is exemplary, I conceded. She is making concessions. She is not attacking you. I left Piazza Santa Lucina, Andreotti's reception room, and went straight to the hospital, as ordered by the doctors. Straight to *Urologia*. I was obeying orders. How swiftly my wife changes, I thought, from the exquisite to the unbearable to the exquisite again. At the shake of a kaleidoscope, ever the same. The doctors had insisted I go to hospital at once. There is a terrible simultaneity, I thought, about the back-and-forth of our marriage. One has to respect the intuitions of trained professionals. Back and forth. Certainly I always respected Vanoli. If we went to England, it was because a trained professional felt our absence would be of benefit to the boy. Not because I wanted to have Mara to myself. Apex and nadir all in a day. Capri and Naples. I'm in Rome, Karen, I explained down the phone to a tape recorder, just for a few . . . Chris! Karen's voice cut in. It was Karen's voice after all these years. But why? Why was I phoning Karen? For more than an hour I had walked up and down the corridor at the hospital, and now all of a sudden I was calling Karen. I'll be at home, my wife had written. Please call. She meant the house of ghosts. A woman twenty years younger than myself. Please come, my wife had written. Instead I had got a girl on the phone. Why? You can come back tomorrow, the Roman urologist said. Tests at eight-thirty a.m. I was disappointed. I paced the corridor. Was it possible I didn't require hospitalisation? With all I'd been through! If you've passed water regularly today, I can see no point in keeping you, he said. A small ratty-looking man. Could I trust him? You've moved your bowels, he said.

A distinctly southern face. I have no reason to keep you. Chris! Karen cried, I don't believe it! I couldn't believe I didn't need treatment. You have the appropriate drugs now, he said. You'll be fine. And exactly as her voice cut through the recorded message, I thought: If I could understand why I was phoning Karen now, at this of all moments, of all crises, upon being denied hospitalisation by a ratty-looking southern urologist who had not even examined me, not even heard me out, then I would understand myself. Everything would be clear. Why was I phoning my ex-mistress – the number of beds we have is limited, the doctor insisted – when my wife was moving heaven and earth to get me back, to make one of her extraordinary changes from the unbearable to the exquisite? There's still so much life in us, Chris, she wrote. Temporary occlusion need not have further consequences, he reassured me. Mara has made you impossibly unhappy, I repeated to myself, walking back and forth along the corridor outside the urology ward. As the urologist sees it, I'm not even ill. You must leave her. I felt sure of that. What had my mind been telling me so insistently these last forty-eight hours, if not that? I must leave my wife. It was an imperative. It is finished, dead. Fleetingly, I remembered the Ferrantes, their extraordinary display of conjugal solidarity in grief. That was marriage. It's finished between us, I decided. How could my wife speak of there being life in our relationship? Just saying hello, I repeated. I heard you'd gone back to London, Karen said. In the background an infant was chattering. Our impossible alliance is over, I told myself. She chuckled. No, a little birdie told me, she explained. Does she keep tabs on me, I wondered? My ex-mistress. Five years of pleasure. She has a fruity voice. Then, amazingly, I was having a cordial conversation. I'm having a polite conversation, I thought.

With my ex-mistress. In the background a child was calling Mummy. She was working part-time. I was well, I said. I was having a polite conversation, in English, with the woman who once told me, Our lives are separate now. Still so much life, she wrote. It was when she said that that your heart dried up. No it was when she said that that you realised you would have to face your wife, your life, you realised you would have to breast the flood, this flood. Then you gave yourself up to reading, you spent every spare hour reading. Your son sought you out, but you were reading, preparing your monumental book. He was fifteen now, sixteen, seventeen. You were going deeper. So you told yourself. To hide from your wife, from the eye of the storm. We had long since moved into the house of ghosts. I was never happy there. Why do you give me your affection, Karen asked – she wept – if your life is elsewhere? You know it is. Five years it lasted. We chatted about my move to London. I didn't tell her I'd left Mara. You are not going to tell Karen that, I suddenly realised. I was saying how pleasant I found London after all these years in Rome. It is none of her business. You won't discuss it. Though the infant in the background might perfectly well not be hers. She was babysitting perhaps. Or with friends. It might be perfectly possible to renew this old relationship, I thought, with all the pleasure it gave. You never know. Karen is a beautiful woman. She knows how to give pleasure. You never even came close to leaving your wife, she once told me. Without bitterness. Not even close. Just over for an interview with Andreotti, I told her. The old fox! A book I was writing, I said. I always said you should write a book, she laughed. That was a banal and predictable remark, I thought. The woman is banal, I thought, and incredibly pleased with herself for some reason. I could sense it in her voice. You must have been determined indeed to punish your wife if you managed to fall in love with a woman as banal as Karen, I thought. Very beautiful, in a black kind of way, but irretrievably banal. She is flattered by your call, I realised. Predictably enough. You must have been furious indeed. I'd had some health problems, yes, I said. But the doctors tell me it's just a question of tension. Always the hypochondriac, Chris, she chuckled. Perhaps it's her Englishness I find banal, I reflected. Essentially, it was an erotic relationship. Her English turn of phrase. A little birdie told me! They've given me some pills, I said vaguely. Why had I called? Why had I sought another side-show? First the urologist, now an ex-mistress. My wife's note was in my hand. Her generous note. Your wife has written you a wonderful note, I told myself. Though hypochondriac was a bit rich, I thought, to a man who'd been through open-heart surgery. An enchanting note. You were always tense as a high wire, Karen laughed. Your ex-mistress seems extremely relaxed to find herself chatting to her ex-lover, I thought. And, in general, extremely pleased with herself. I wasn't annoyed. To be chattering to the man who once made eager love to her on a terrace in Naples. The night his mother-in-law died. How I adored that exotic black skin, together with the banal, the in-every-way-familiar and reassuring English voice. It was never a challenge. I've been quite tense myself, she laughed, since I had Carlo. Apparently the child was called Carlo. Clearly it was hers. This is a ridiculous conversation, I thought, a ridiculous and aimless conversation. We will never make love again. If I was annoyed with anyone it was myself. She is immensely pleased with herself, I thought, because this is her chance to show her ex-lover that she now has a proper man, a proper family. Not just a lover. Carlo, come and say hello to Uncle Chris, she was chuckling. It was fatuous. Come on! Carluccio! Plane and home, I told myself. Ciao, said an infant voice. Then began to whimper. Uncle Chris! Karen was on the line again.

You are not going to tell her about your son, I realised. It's no concern of hers. Fly via Turin, perhaps, to pick up the mobile charger, the suitcase. Back to England. You are not going to tell her about the crisis with your wife. These are things between yourself and Mara, I decided. I said goodbye. Mamma, the voice calls.

Mamma, Mamma! Was it all just a long distraction? Perhaps the truth is I never finally and definitively chose my wife. Could that be the case? This thought occurred to me in the taxi to the *policlinico*. Never finally chose Italy. Perhaps these things just happened to me, I told myself in another taxi, leaving the *policlinico*. My marriage, my change of country. I never really chose them. As I never chose this skin, this mind that will not stop working. What can it mean for a mind to work so hard? Myself. Will I be able to pay for four cabs a day when I have settled with the tax inspectors? Certainly you never felt at home in the house of ghosts. Via Livorno, I told the taxi-driver. The house of ghosts. What other address could I give? I'll be at home, she wrote. It is as if there were always some fatal distance between you and the life you lead, between who you are and what your life has been. Mamma! the voice calls, across the *salotto*, from the stairs. But I shall not turn on the light. A strange misunderstanding. I shall not kill the candles. A garment that was never quite me. But that made me more and more aware of me. Men and women do that to each other. To a point beyond all exasperation. Made me me by not being me. I often feel that when I speak Italian. Me not being me. My thoughts in the wrong clothes. I am exasperated with myself is the truth. This is grounds for annulment no doubt. You were attracted to your wife, I reflect now, gazing at her dazzling photo in mothy candlelight, the way somebody who is nothing and has nothing cannot help but be attracted to somebody who is something and has more, even if it wasn't quite the something or the more you had imagined. Even if it was dangerous.

Stop there, I told the driver. At the gate, the garden gate. My mind is full of voices. Why won't they call *my* name? An iron gate in a stone wall. A garden you never wished to tend. I paid off the cab. Of vines and shrubs. A foreign garden. Of oleanders and pittosporus. The De Amicis residence is a large and looming corner house, beyond the Parioli. The driver was impressed. I tip generously. Almost respectful. There is a St Anthony set in a niche. Who wrestled with demons. Like the Buddha. Who went into the desert. Was beset by demons. St Anthony. Your own family dissolved in your infancy, I reflect now, staring at these photos she has arranged in candlelight on the credenza. Italian is a language where the main piece of furniture is called a credenza, a 'belief'. I discussed that once somewhere. In some article. A language that believes in its furniture, in its household traditions, its saints in their niches. When was the last time you looked at photos of your mother and father? I ask myself, looking at my son's flickering face. Your own sense of place and home was tossed away in adolescence, I reflect. You never returned, never visit your parents' graves. You have no sense of place, of home. No furniture or beliefs. Outside the house the evening air was warm and mild. In his niche St Anthony holds a small electric light that burns in perpetuity. The English are tossing away their traditions, it seems. There is a photo of his grandmother too, who died that night. To spite me I sometimes thought. In perpetuity a bill arrives. Tossing away their religion. This was something I meant to discuss in my book. Wisely no doubt. Wisely tossing it away. What can it mean for a light to burn by an effigy? A candle by a photograph? As they wisely abandoned empire, as they have ceased to bury their dead in family tombs. The English are in retreat from their tombs, I had scribbled in a notebook somewhere. They toss their ashes into rivers and rose-beds. Their children must do sums in their heads with the rapidity of calculators. An Anglo-Saxon delirium of clarity. How could somebody who had rejected his own preposterous past not be attracted to Mara, to her family, her country, her credenza, her extraordinary sense of belonging. Here. In Rome. This city of tombs and monuments, moths and candlelight and balmy evenings. The lucid Anglo-Saxon is ever seduced by Latin enigma. As the west by the east. Man by woman. Was that distraction? And how not be disappointed to discover then that her prejudices were even more preposterous than those you had left behind? They're at mass together, Papà. Paola's voice. Or was it simply that she was not distracting enough? Italy was not distracting enough. Mara not tempting enough. How can I ever forgive my wife, I had thought, returning home from making love to Karen, for growing old? How can one forgive a temptress for ageing? For failing to distract. What would have become of St Anthony the day the devil ran out of tricks? Of interesting temptations. What reason for staying in the desert? Certainly she looked old that morning I drove back from Naples. The children were shocked. I was shocked myself. Their grandmother was laid out in her bedroom. For the first time my wife looked haggard, old. Her mother was dead. Marco was clinging to Paola. My wife's face had aged by a decade. While Karen's was so young. My mind was full of Karen's youth. I was fresh from fucking her after all. Another De Amicis had died in the night. In the house of ghosts. Sleeping beside the old woman, Marco had woken to find her cold. He had tried to phone but it was always busy. It was off the hook. I was fucking. My wife had been on the train. On her way back from her husband to her son. He had crept into his sister's bed. In a night and a morning my wife had aged a decade. Marco was shaken. He had slept wrapped round his sister's body. They weren't flesh and blood. While Karen was so young. And it comes to me now, staring at the photo I took of my wife on the boat from Capri, it occurs to me that its poignancy, its wonder, lies in its being taken exactly at the turning point. A dazzled, dazzling face, tilted upward to the sky, but the make-up is evident, the defiance is evident, the defiance of a beautiful woman beginning to age, flaunting her beauty at the sky. Defying the light, the sun. That night I would betray her. I kept the phone off the hook. While I fucked. She was right to choose this photo for her grave. My wife is a remarkable person, I reflect, a remarkable person, I thought, standing at the iron gate having paid off the cab, to have come back alone to the house of ghosts, alone on the very day she buried her son, on Marco's first night in his grave. To have come back, I tell myself now, and lit candles by the family photos, the icons, alone, the day her husband left her, the day her son was buried, that is a remarkable thing. It was midnight, unexplained hours had passed. My mind is full of voices, and one in particular calling Mamma, calling Mother, drifting through these dusty rooms, down the broken stairs. Despite having decided to leave her, I told myself, standing at the iron gate, you have returned. You have returned to the house of ghosts. Why? Why won't the voice call *my* name? I hear it, but it calls another.

It was when we moved to the house of ghosts that the schism was consolidated, I reflect, the split became obvious. I didn't press the bell, just stood by the gate peering into the garden. What constantly startles me, I tell myself, is how I can be so reasonable and so mad at the same time. You are making perfectly reasonable, even perspicacious reflections, I tell myself, and yet you are clearly mad, you are hearing a voice that cannot be there. It is the effect of the candlelight perhaps, the moths. Why haven't you turned the lights on? There are so many. A child's voice. At the funeral Marco went up to take mass with his mother, while Paola stayed back with her father. The schism was declared: the children one on each side, resenting each other, clinging to each other when we were not there. I phoned Karen afterwards to discuss the matter, to arrange another meeting. In Naples. I could never feel at home in the house of ghosts. We moved there at once. Immediately after my mother-in-law's death. It was roomier and better located. Certainly Marco clung to Paola after Gregory came along, after the BBC correspondent began to take up so much of his mother's time. I could imagine choosing my wife, it occurred to me climbing out of the cab in Via Livorno, and I could imagine choosing Rome, yes, when we were still in our rented apartment, but I could not imagine I had chosen this gloomy house with its coffin-inspired furniture and its photographs of the dead. Ageing, your wife is becoming like the dead, I thought, *her* dead, her ancestors who went before her. In the house of ghosts. Not your dead. Whose graves you never visit. She is still glamorous, I thought, still vain, I love her for that, she enchants me, but I could see their features in hers, and the same skull beneath them all. I could not feel I had chosen this. I could not forgive her for growing old.

Would you have fretted so much if it had been imposed on you? I stood by the gate of the house, but didn't ring the bell. Why am I here? What am I going to do? Would I have accepted it, enjoyed it – even the house of ghosts – if everything had been imposed by some authority I recognised? By family. By dynasty. Some ancient authority one would never question? The garden is choked and untended. Perhaps it is the notion of choice that has destroyed you, I thought, gazing through the gate at the untended garden. Did I make a mistake? Why have I come? I lived here nine years and more, I thought, staring into the shrubs and shadows, and never lifted a finger in that garden. At the height of my career that was. The garden is laid out in the style of her ancestors, a criss-cross of gravelly paths dividing arid flowerbeds overgrown with vines. I lived here ten years and never changed the furnishings, never moved the credenza. I was travelling constantly at the time. Later I began to read, constantly. I changed nothing. I ignored my son. I rattled the gate, but it was closed, locked. Don't ring the bell, I told myself. It was midnight. Don't wake her up. Am I planning to speak to her or not? Why have I come? There was a rustle among leaves in the garden and a wail. A cat. A voice wailing Mamma. I rattled the gate. This house always shut you out, I thought. More than anything else, it was the move to this house, its old photographs and gloomy furniture, that consolidated everything that was wrong between your wife and yourself and hence everything that was going wrong between yourselves and your children. I'm not a baby, I once remarked to Vanoli. I can see the obvious. If your wife shut you out before, she shut you out doubly in the house of ghosts, the place of her ancestors. It was a terrible mistake to come here. A soft moonlight slides on its roof. The evening air is warm. Again the vines rustle in the garden. What can one do when a voice is calling another's name, but hear and ignore? A voice calling another, a voice plaguing you on purpose by calling another. Not you. Though it is you who hears the voice. Can one die on purpose to return and haunt? Isn't that the echo of all the times you were shut out? A voice calling another. She shut you out. And now this gate is locked against the midnight. You are locked out of your own house, the house you hate. Yet you never objected to living here, I reflect. I am wandering through the rooms now. She has put candles everywhere. The house is ablaze with candles. I couldn't see them from outside with the shutters closed. You never actually refused to live here and you never changed the

237

furniture you hated in nine long years. Or ten. Your behaviour is absurdly contradictory, I reflected. I was scaling the gate, my fingers feeling among the broken bottle shards set in cement on the stone above. Madly inexplicable, to come here, to want to enter a house you hate, and at the same time not to go and ring the bell. If it's a place to sleep you're after, I thought, hauling myself up to the bottle shards, you could go to a hotel. Credit cards are welcome in hotels as they are not in taxis. I was breaking into my own home. A house I hated. Though you never actually refused to live here. It was such a convenient location. Even after the staircase was broken. Instead you used the alienation the place generated to feed your affair. Yes. That's it. You used unease to excuse betrayal. Never properly choosing your wife, but knowing you would choose no other. Imagining it imposed, but by an alien authority, an authority you couldn't and wouldn't recognise. A man should not exchange his own gods for his wife's perhaps. Perhaps that was your mistake. I've had dozens of affairs, you told your wife in the pitiless glare of the cemetery. I've betrayed you in every possible way. How can you go back to a woman after telling her that? After saying those words. However generous a note she writes. I hate you, you said. It was a liberation to say that. I hate you and hate you. An enormous pleasure. Yet, here you are, hopping to the ground, here you are breaking into your own house. Mara's house. I had torn my trousers. There are no good times to remember here. Ten long years and no good times. In the house of ghosts. It began with my mother-in-law's death. Yet I didn't actually object, I used that alienation to feed my affair. The trip to Naples was horribly ill-timed. We moved in immediately. We needed the space. Shut out, it was legitimate for me to indulge elsewhere. Mamma! calls the voice.

I'm in the long passageway between kitchen and *salotto*.

Stone flags. Presumably she's in her bed. She hasn't heard me. Paola too climbed the gate, the morning she found the dramatic scene she described so well in court. She described how she was shut out, how no one responded to the bell, how she climbed the gate, tore her dress, forced the *portafinestra* into the kitchen. The *portafinestra*. All your life your wife has seduced you and shut you out. It is pointless imagining it can change now. So why do you want to get in? You should go and live with Paola, I thought, walking round the house in the moonlight. To the kitchen side. The *portafinestra*. There were rustlings in the vines and a cat wailing. Yet how can I speak of being shut out and at the same time wonder if I ever really chose my wife, if I ever really said to myself, this is my woman, my destiny? Why do you give me so much affection, Karen asked, if your heart is elsewhere? You exploited a distance between what you are and what you do, I realise, stepping through candlelight in the house of ghosts, gazing up the staircase. The place is aflutter with moths. The light is liquid as thought, uncertain as memory. If there is inevitably a distance between what one is and what one's life has been, nevertheless you have exploited that, that existential conundrum. You deliberately make that gap wider, I tell myself. What would a monumental book be but another stone to roll aside? Another terrible weight. You sought out these situations, I realise, these distances, this foreignness, this alien tongue, these alien gods and customs. You have thrived on an energy of alienation. To excuse every sort of behaviour. For a second I fancy I hear a rustle, a voice calling from the top of the stairs. It is the voice that haunts the space between what I am and what I've done – I have behaved appallingly – the voice that chooses my head to call another's name.

The *portafinestra* had been repaired. Perhaps this was true of Andreotti too, I thought. He too exploited the distance between being and doing. Andreotti, a devout religious man, engaged in all kinds of shady activities. What was complicated about that? Doing a distraction from being. I pushed hard on the *portafinestra*, but it wouldn't give. The one an undertow of the other. What more need one say? Perhaps I myself had had it repaired. Perhaps language is the fizz between being and doing. I'm standing at the bottom of the stairs. The exploitation of that gap? Lying to yourself, in short. A mendacious fizz between opposing poles – essence, distraction – where patterns form and dissolve. Shadows shifted by moths in candlelight. You will never know the truth about Andreotti, I thought, pointlessly heaving my shoulder against a tall pane of glass. The *portafinestra*. It wouldn't budge. I didn't want to break it. I stood back and found my face reflected there, glossy black. It was a balmy, moonlit evening. No more distraught than usual. Apparently I wasn't in need of hospitalisation. I hadn't impressed the urologist. The light was soft on the glass, the air warm. A lover's evening, I remarked, and felt quite furious. You will never know what went on in Andreotti's mind, or even what happened in his governments, I told myself. You will never know what happened to your son, I thought. Or even between your wife and yourself, one warm spring evening outside the French embassy. I stopped for a moment to stare at the enigma of my face, as until a few minutes ago I stopped for so long to stare at the candlelit photographs on the credenza. All enigmatic. The eyes seemed no more distraught than usual, in the bright black slab of the window pane. His first night in the grave. There was a rich, perfumed smell in the untended garden. The air was very warm. I hesitate. This is definitely where the voice came from. The hall, the stairs. You set out to predict the future without even understanding the past, I tell myself now, thinking of the enigma of the photos, the bewilderment of the last forty-eight hours. What will I do at the top of the stairs? Mara's photo, Paola's, Marco's. We live between the inexplicable and the unpredictable, I announce out loud in the candlelight at the bottom of the stairs. I'm frightened. My wife always kept an endless supply of candles. A kitchen drawer full of candles. Can one ever speak to a voice that calls another's name? The dead house seems astir somehow. Mara, Paola and Marco are very ordinary names, in Italy. We were so unhappy here. It should be me in that grave, I thought, meeting my eyes in the glossy pane of the *portafinestra*. In the end I climbed in through the pantry window behind the wisteria. I tore away the wisteria, I who had done nothing in that garden in the nine years I lived here. In a sudden fury, remembering a balmy evening when we became lovers, I tore the big plant away, leaf and branch and bits of wire to bind. My wrists are scratched, my fingers are bleeding. I ripped it from the wall, guessing she might have risked leaving this window open to give the musty house some air. The dead house. But something is stirring. I sensed I heard a voice somewhere, a pleading, a whimper. Behind was a small window obscured by years of untended growth. It was open. One does guess some things right. I stripped the plant aside and tumbled in.

To do what? Why have I returned? I have left my wife now. Why did she light all these candles? was my first thought, on advancing from pantry to *salotto*. Why has she made icons of these family photographs? So like her. This room has the feel of a *camera ardente*! That was my first and immediate thought on entering the *salotto*, upon seeing the antique furniture I hated so much. The false life of candlelight flickering over faces. Photo faces. I never did anything to improve it, I left no mark. The house of ghosts was never my house, I told myself. But you have disentangled yourself now, I reflect. I'm standing at the bottom of the broken stairs. I'm about to go up. Having left my wife I'm about to climb the stairs to see her. There are paintings on the wall to the left. There are lacquer-black portraits and landscapes rising into the gloom. It was definitely from here the voice called. Why didn't I have them stacked away and replaced by something decent? Something modern. The moment we moved in. Something *mine*. She has put candles on every fourth or fifth stair. Why? Presumably it was her. Who else? Certainly it was here the voice was drawing me. Calling her. Found a place for them on the broken slabs. Her hair was so thick then, was my immediate thought on seeing her face in the photo. On the credenza. The first thing I did on entering the *salotto* was to walk to the photographs. Iconised as they were on the credenza. And my eye fastened on hers. A 250th of a second frozen at the turning point in dazzling light on the boat from Capri to Naples. Mara! Eyes equal to the glare. Her hair was so thick then – my impossible hair! – but now it has thinned, I tell myself. Now you are free. Her flesh has begun to sag. You have extricated yourself, I tell myself, standing at the bottom of the stairs. There's an umbrella stand. The banister is broken. No coats on the hooks. You are free of her spell. Her distraction. You should turn on the light, I tell myself. And go. Forget it. The house of ghosts was always a *camera ardente*. Always in thrall to the dead. A dead relationship. Turn on the light. This is unhealthy. It's unhealthy, I announce out loud, to imagine you're hearing voices. Go, I announce. Get out of here. It's finished. And again the voice calls from above. Mamma! Mamma! As when he came to our bed. As when he called the hotel in Naples. A dangerous tide was running. He was banging on the door screaming Mamma, Paola testified. He had a hammer in his hand. The same hammer he smashed the stairs with. Smashed the banister. And at last it occurs to me: *she too has killed herself.* Mara too has chosen to extinguish herself. My Mara. That's why the voice is calling. He is calling her to himself. Beyond the grave. Beyond the epiphanic veil. Beyond the stones and the monuments. *I sepolari*. I will fix her photograph to her tomb, the family tomb. She lit the candles, I realise, to prepare her own funeral chamber. Her *camera ardente*. I must go upstairs.

What was the power, then, that so disturbed the gods they must send men these distractions? I have often wondered that. Were they really threatened by a man's ambition, his monumental book on predictability, on racial destiny? Or was the story just a way of positing an imaginary and blissful space from which we humans are to be forever excluded? The gods distracting us precisely as our hand found the handle. Madness, like passion, was also sent by the gods, I remembered. Just a way of ennobling our illnesses perhaps, of enchanting ourselves with our catastrophes. I have often wished her dead, I told Paola, at the height of our alliance, our unspoken pact. How could I not remember these words as I began to climb the stairs? Very often imagined my wife dead. Suddenly I was sure something terrible had happened. Almost every day, I told my adolescent daughter. The girl was not my flesh and blood. Almost every day of late I have thought of the liberation of her death. The schism was plain to all by then. Only Paola spoke to me when I went on my travels. Only she stayed in to answer the phone. They're at mass together, she said. I was furious. But perhaps she was staying in to see Giorgio. Dear dull Giorgio. I am climbing the stairs, picking my way. The *portafinestra* was repaired, I reflect, against thieves and weather, but the broken stairs were not. The stone stairs to our bedroom were not repaired. I have often wished her dead, I told Gregory, the last time we met. That in itself would be cause for annulment, he said. But the BBC correspondent had lost his confidence by then. He couldn't understand why she wouldn't go to live with him. After all those letters in the style of Guinizelli. *Il dolce stil novo.* It was shocking to wish your partner dead, he said. You should leave her at once, he said. We could live together, Paola said. Just you and me, Papà. But they had both lost confidence by then. As Karen too lost confidence. Your life is elsewhere, she said.

Do I though? I stop to glance at the portrait of some ancestor. In shifting gloom above the candlelight. Is it the grandfather who killed himself? There's no hurry to climb the stairs. The voice has ceased to call. Thank God. My head is clearing. The adrenaline is clearing my head. Do I really wish her dead? Do I want to find my wife dead? At the top of these stairs. The similarity of De Amicis skulls down the generations is frightening. Minor aristocracy. I am frightened by what I might find in her room. Skin shrunk to a skull. Our room I rarely slept in. How could she write: All my life I have lived for you. How could she write such a lie? Women are a distraction, I told Gregory. I was seeking to comfort him. The last time we met. It is not unusual to find yourself seeking to comfort someone who has tried to hurt you. Sent by the gods to distract us, I tried to make him laugh. We were in the café at Stazione Termini. From what? he demanded. He was moving on. Why should the gods bother to distract us? Gregory grew quite angry with my little joke, my half-hearted attempt to comfort him. He had had enough. He thinks I'm exulting, I realised. He thinks I'm turning the knife. I had made a mistake. What would the gods ever be afraid of in people like us: our journalism? He was scathing. Now he has lost out, I noticed – we were in the café at Stazione Termini – he is no longer giving you your due. He is not being even-handed. From nothingness, perhaps, I thought afterwards. These passions distract us from nothingness. And climbing the stairs in the house of ghosts, it comes to me that if I lose Mara I will become ridiculous. I will become like the old theatre director, with his old man's vanity, his long swept-back white hair, his supposedly talented young Polish dancer, his dog Boccaccio. A ridiculous rootless nothing of a man who never saw his grandchildren, writing bad poetry to his opportunist mistress who didn't even share his bedroom. A sublime theatre director. It was the dog found him dead. I have no dog to lead the way up the stairs in the house of ghosts. I beg forgiveness if I have hurt you, she wrote. But I always loved you. How many women would write such a generous note, I wonder, even if it wasn't quite the truth, after everything I said to her over her son's fresh grave. I'll be at home, she wrote. Please call, Chris. Please come. And I didn't come. I didn't call. She has killed herself because you didn't come, I tell myself, climbing the stairs. You didn't come to her. To your wife, Mara. Now I don't know whether to rush or creep, to run or stop. My life will be empty and ridiculous.

At least the voice has fallen silent. I stand at the top of the stairs. There's an antique dresser of oak and marble. I always hated such things but never replaced them. A candle burns in the mirror. I stand quite still. Marco has fallen silent. That haunting voice. I listen to my breathing. My mind turning. A faint sizzle of wax. Or perhaps a moth's wings. Because she has already gone to him, I tell myself. She is already dead. Mara is dead. She has flown to him. He doesn't need to call her now. Her door is open. But there is no light in there. These panelled doors that squeak and sigh. Only the candle on the dresser outside, its flickering reflection diffused in the mirror, scribbling on the walls. Why don't I switch on the lights? Why don't I break this stupid spell that has gone on so long? Our destiny was to distract each other perhaps. In a world where you cannot go deeper, what else could destiny be but a long and fruitful distraction? We both resented it. I sensed that the very first night, at the French embassy. Outside in the garden. She sensed it. A garden I never tended. We both fought against loving each other. Against this passion. We fenced and fought against it. We both prayed the cup might pass. Scorched by passion. We both tried to seduce others, to be seduced by others. Even our children. We hurt others to avoid our love. Thus the rancour. But by the time you're praying a cup may pass you know it won't. You know it's the Father's will. It's the way meaning lies. Meaning lies the way of the bitter cup. Identity is in pain, I told myself on the night-train from Turin. I was in pain myself. Now my fingers are bleeding. Marco must have seen that when he turned the screwdriver in his veins. Seen that he'd been seduced to no end. That was where the rancour came from. If there is nothing when one goes deeper, what can one do but accept the destiny of a long distraction? Our long distracting marriage. Mara is such a remarkable person, I tell myself, standing in the doorway now, looking into the dark. Such a theatrical person. So fatally different from myself. I have lost her. I have destroyed her. Quite gratuitously, I told her things too painful for her to bear. I spent the afternoon interviewing politicians, consulting urologists, calling ex-girlfriends. Hours lost I know not where. As I step inside the bedroom a voice whispers: Marco.

Marco!

I stop, swaying. This is the room I so rarely slept in. I slept in the guest room on the floor above, next to Paola's. We would get on very well alone, she said. Papà.

Marco! It's a thread of a voice.

I'm on the threshold. There is no light inside. The shutters are closed. I must be a wavering silhouette against candle-shadows behind. I can't see. Only smell the staleness. The dust.

Marco! A wraith of a voice.

Mara!

The room is completely still and dark. Am I hearing voices again? Inside my head? In a sense, Vanoli once remarked, every voice we hear is generated inside our heads. Where can things happen but inside a head?

Mara! I repeat, almost shouting into the dark room. I was afraid I might not have spoken out loud at all. Afraid she was a ghost. She's dead. Mara, are you all right?

Chris. My wife's voice is suddenly quite normal. It's you, Chris.

Are you all right?

I was dreaming. I was dreaming of Marco.

I thought I heard his voice. I heard him calling you.

She says nothing. I can't see her. She sighs.

My hand moves to turn on the light. The switch clicks.

It's off she says. The power's off. I put candles everywhere. In case you came.

I can see shadows now, a whiteness in the bed. I move across to sit beside her.

Perhaps they always cut off tax evaders, she says.

How normal your wife's voice sounds! I tell myself. How sane! Even wry! Without being able to see them, her features are suddenly present to me. Mara's will always be a noble physiognomy, I tell myself, always a proud face, however scored by suffering.

How was the interview? she asks.

She isn't criticising you for going to the interview, I realise. Scandalous though that was.

I'm exhausted, I tell her. I stretch out beside her. It went okay.

I am lying beside my wife in the house of ghosts. It went okay, I tell her. Andreotti's such a predictable fraud. Then I tell her: that was a beautiful note you wrote.

Chris, she says. We're breathing together in the dark. Our hands are touching. My wife isn't dead. She hasn't killed herself. This is the bed her mother died in. The night Marco phoned and phoned. The night I fucked Karen. And then I begin to tell my wife we must leave this place. We must leave this house, Mara. We must find somewhere new to live. I can't live here. I was never alive here. It was a mistake to come here. Let's go now, I tell her.

Tomorrow, she says. We're both exhausted.

Now.

Tomorrow. I promise, she says. We can't go now. How can we go now? We're worn out. You've been ill.

Somewhere that can be mine and yours. Not here. Not London. Somewhere new.

You must get on with your work, she says.

My wife and I are planning the future.

I love you. All at once I am telling Mara I love her. I don't wish her dead at all. I never wished her dead. Did I? Have I chosen to come back? It seems that is what has happened. The enchantment isn't over. Our long distraction. I heard Marco's voice calling your name, I tell her. We're speaking Italian. In the hall. The *salotto*. I was so frightened you'd killed yourself. Or that I was going mad. Hearing voices. I was afraid I was going to see him. On the stairs.

I was dreaming of him, she says. Her voice is quiet. I dreamed he was calling me. He was well again. For a moment I was sure it was him at the door.

I love you, I repeat, with a kind of wonder that I can say such a thing.

I was thrilled, she said. Chris. I was terrified. This has exhausted us.

For hours now we have been lying in the dark, without speaking, without embracing. Marco is in his grave. I haven't heard his voice again. Tomorrow it seems we will move out of here. She means it, I'm sure. I can and will insist. We will move out of the house of ghosts. Tomorrow we can begin to mourn our son.